KNIT FAST, DIE YOUNG

KNIT FAST, DIE YOUNG

MARY KRUGER

WHEELER
CHIVERS

MT   MM

This Large Print edition is published by Wheeler Publishing, Waterville, Maine, USA and by BBC Audiobooks Ltd, Bath, England.
Wheeler Publishing is an imprint of The Gale Group.
Wheeler is a trademark and used herein under license.
Copyright © 2007 by Mary Kruger.
The moral right of the author has been asserted.

The text of this Large Print edition is unabridged.
Other aspects of the book may vary from the original edition.
Set in 16 pt. Plantin.

LIBRARY OF CONGRESS CATALOGING-IN-PUBLICATION DATA

Kruger, Mary.
  Knit fast, die young : a knitting mystery / by Mary Kruger.
    p. cm. — (Wheeler Publishing large print cozy mystery)
  ISBN-13: 978-1-59722-647-9 (softcover : alk. paper)
  ISBN-10: 1-59722-647-5 (softcover : alk. paper)
  1. Knitting — Fiction. 2. Knitters (Persons) — Fiction. 3. Women publishers — Fiction. 4. Massachusetts — Fiction. 5. Large type books.
  I. Title.
  PS3561.R775K58 2007
  813'.54—dc22   2007030016

BRITISH LIBRARY CATALOGUING-IN-PUBLICATION DATA AVAILABLE

Published in 2007 in the U.S. by arrangement with Pocket Books, a division of Simon & Schuster, Inc.
Published in 2008 in the U.K. by arrangement with Simon & Schuster, Inc.

U.K. Hardcover: 978 1 405 64302 3 (Chivers Large Print)
U.K. Softcover: 978 1 405 64303 0 (Camden Large Print)

Printed in the United States of America on permanent paper
10 9 8 7 6 5 4 3 2 1

In memory of my aunt Mae Manning,
who gifted us all with love,
laughter, and padded coat hangers.

CHAPTER 1

"Well, this is a bust." Diane Camacho rested her chin on her hands and looked glumly at the rain coming down in torrents outside the wide barn door. "I thought it was supposed to be nice today."

Ariadne Evans, sitting at the next table, didn't look up from her knitting needles. She was wearing a heavy parka, with a scarf made of fuzzy yarn tied around her neck. "April's rotten."

Diane looked over at her. "Not 'the cruelest month'?"

"Nope. Just rotten." Ariadne smiled briefly and then returned her attention to her knitting. This project wasn't the best choice, she admitted to herself. A shell of thin, silk-like ribbon yarn would be perfect for the summer to come, but it wasn't suited to today, especially not with aluminum needles. She needed warmth, wool, something substantial and weighty. An afghan, she thought, tossed over her knees as she made it. Why couldn't she have chosen to work on an afghan?

"No one's going to come out in this weather," Diane continued. "Anyway, I don't think we'd've had many customers. Not too many people are interested in wool festivals anymore."

"Well, not around here. The one in Rhinebeck draws in a lot of folks," she said, referring to the big festival held each fall in New York State.

"Well, we're not big."

"No." Ari glanced up and looked around the barn again. The Freeport Wool and Yarn Festival was an annual fixture in this area of coastal Massachusetts. Held on the Bristol-Rochester County fairgrounds, it attracted exhibitors from as far away as New York. What it didn't attract was customers. There were too many good yarn shops now, selling all manner of products, from pricy imports to homespuns. Ari had to admit that she was part of that trend; she was proud of the stock at her shop, Ariadne's Web. It didn't help that the area was becoming increasingly developed and urbanized. Interest in the old country crafts wasn't as high anymore.

Still, there were a good number of exhibitors, mostly women, and there were some interesting demonstrations going on, including knitting for beginners and the Sheep to Shawl competition. The festival was held in three of the fairgrounds' barns, unimaginatively named by letters. Barn A, the first one, was the most popular. Not only did it have a snack bar, it was the only one that was heated. Some lucky vendors had managed to rent space there. Barn D, at the far end of the row, had sheep pens, while Barn C, designed for smaller animals, wasn't used for this festival. The rain and mud meant that not many people had trooped to see sheep being displayed or sheared. Across a narrow lane from the barns was a large field. Originally sheep dog trials had been planned for the following day, but for now the field was simply a muddy parking lot.

Barn B, the largest of the barns, was the focus of the festival because it housed the majority of the vendors, including Ari and Diane. While it had ample display space, it was also cavernous and dark. There were few electrical outlets, which meant there were no space heaters to add an illusion of warmth. The dimness, combined with the pounding of rain on the steel roof, made it very dismal indeed. Today's rain, remnants of a storm that had swept up from the south, hadn't been expected.

"Good thing we live close enough to get warmer clothes," Ari commented.

"Yeah. Not like the woman from Buffalo."

"Buffalo? Who came that far?"

Diane had taken up her spinning again and was concentrating on making fine yarn. "Some designer. She's way down there." Diane pointed to her right. "Didn't you read the pamphlet?"

Ari leaned over her table, but the woman was tucked too far back in the corner for her to see. She did see a friend from the local area, Rosalia Sylvia, leaning over the woman's table. "I'll look at her things later. Maybe I'll buy myself a fleece from one of the bins while I'm at it."

"Are you taking up spinning?" Diane asked in surprise.

"No. I want to wrap it around myself to keep warm."

"Ha-ha. There's some good stuff over there, mostly Romney." She glanced over at the bins filled with unprocessed fleeces lining the wall opposite them. "I'm going to pick up some."

"Good idea. I can't keep up with the demand for your yarn."

"Yeah, having it used for a murder made it popular."

10

Ari shot her friend a quick glance, but Diane's face was impassive. Last fall, Diane's yarn had been used to strangle a local woman, something that had stunned both of them. "Well, I wish I had some right now, instead of this."

"Ribbon yarn?"

"Yes, and the needles are aluminum." She frowned at the shell she was making for summer. Instead of working from the bottom up, she was knitting the shell from the side. It added an interesting texture to the cool, slippery yarn, but the shaping, formed by increasing and decreasing, demanded concentration. "I'll probably go home later and get something else, though I think that if this works out it'll get noticed."

"If summer ever comes."

"Mm." Ari laid down her needles and stretched. In the last few minutes no one had approached her table to look at her designs. At this rate she wouldn't make back the money she'd spent renting the space. "I think I'll walk around for a little and then get some coffee."

"Get me one, too? Regular."

Ari nodded. "Cream, one sugar. I remember. I'll be back in a while. Watch my table for me," she said, and walked away.

Pulling her parka tight around her, Ari

stopped at a small enclosure formed by a short, portable fence in the center of the barn to watch the Sheep to Shawl competition. Each year two teams of people competed to complete shawls made from wool sheared from sheep early that morning. The team that finished first would win. Each person in a team had her own duties. Some had sheared the sheep, white for one team, black for the other. Others processed the fleece, separating and carding it, and removing any dirt and debris. From there the spinners, several to a team, took over, spinning the yarn into light, fine wool. Finally the weavers, each sitting at a huge loom, worked their shuttles and treadles quickly and industriously. It was too early in the competition to guess who would win, though the black shawl seemed to have a slight edge. Ari knew most of the women in the competition, and she wanted all of them to win.

After watching the competition for a while, Ari drifted away to explore other booths and other wares. The range and number of items offered were impressive. One woman sold yarn from her own flock of llamas, her pamphlet extolling its softness and warmth. Another displayed skeins of mohair yarns across her table, the price making Ari think twice about buying any. In the center of the floor across from the shawl competition, a man offered spinning wheels, both new and old, while a Peg-Board across from him displayed naturally dyed yarn, the colors subtle yet glowing. There was even knitting-themed jewelry. Charms depicting balls of yarn, spiderwebs to symbolize spinning, and snowflakes for Scandinavian sweaters hung from earring wires or heavy silver chains. Since the jewelry was made from real gold and silver the prices were a little high, but Ari couldn't resist. A few minutes later she continued wandering, a charm bracelet dangling from her wrist.

Eventually she found herself in the far corner of the barn, curious to find out why someone from Buffalo had traveled so far to attend a small festival. The sign on her table read simply Designs by Annie. The woman was working on what looked like a baby sweater, which she lowered as Ari looked over the various items spread out on the table. They were diverse, ranging from an Aran-inspired tunic to colorful socks. All were meticulously made, with distinctive touches such as cables crossed in unusual ways on the tunic or lace inserts in the socks.

There was something familiar about the woman, though Ari couldn't pin it down.

She was young, with fine, light hair and hazel eyes. Probably she was imagining it. "These are nice," Ari said.

Annie looked up, though she continued knitting. "Thank you. I'm selling the designs as well as the sweaters."

"You're Annie?"

" 'Designs by Annie,' " she said, with just a light tone of mockery in her voice.

"Well, you do nice work. Hope you do all right today." Ari smiled and was about to move on when Annie's voice stopped her.

"I remember you," Annie said.

Ari turned. "You do?"

"Yes. You came to a Knitting Guild meeting in New York once."

"Goodness, that was a long time ago! I used to belong to the Guild, but I haven't lived in New York for years."

"You'd just had that pattern published in *Vogue Knitting.*"

Ari frowned for a minute. "I don't remember — yes, I do! You were sitting in a corner." No wonder she'd looked familiar, though Ari wondered how old she could have been. She didn't look much older than her midtwenties now, while Ari was pushing thirty. *Thirty,* she thought glumly, distracted for a moment. "Aren't you from upstate New York?"

14

"I was living in Connecticut at the time, but I had friends in the city."

"You had to be in your teens then."

Annie shook her head. "Thank you, but I'm older than I look. I'd just started knitting then. You inspired me to try my hand at designing."

"I did?" Ari said, startled. She'd never thought to have any influence over people.

"Yes, and this is the result." Annie gestured at her work. "It took me a while to get anywhere near as good as I'd like, and I'm still not there yet."

"I like this." Ari fingered the Aran tunic, a complicated design of cables and knots in creamy white wool. "I have a friend who makes Aran sweaters for my shop."

"I'd like to see your shop. I've seen your designs online."

"How long will you be here?"

"I'm leaving tomorrow, after the sheep dog trials, if they're held after all this rain. I love dogs."

"Oh, too bad. The shop's open today, but then I don't open again until Tuesday."

"Oh. Maybe I'll make it back up sometime."

"Maybe." Ari smiled, and after exchanging business cards with Annie, she walked back to her own table.

15

Diane was spinning some bright, multicolored wool, similar to what Annie had used in her socks. "Where's my coffee?" she demanded.

"Darn it, I forgot." She looked through the door at the torrent of rain. "Don't make me go out there."

"You offered."

"I was nuts. When did you get that?" she asked, indicating the wool in Diane's lap.

"When I stopped at the snack bar before I came in. There are a few people selling rovings," she said, referring to wool that had already been processed and dyed. "Want to carry the yarn in the shop if I make it?"

Ari looked with disfavor at the wool. The roving combined bright, almost neon-toned colors in ways she didn't like. Red turned abruptly to bright yellow, which was followed by neon blue, all on the same strand. "Not with that."

"Aw, c'mon. You need to jazz things up a bit. Get some more color in there, besides beige."

"I don't have all beige," Ari protested, for if there was one thing she liked about her shop, it was the rainbow of colors in her yarn displays.

"No?" Diane looked pointedly at Ari's clothes. Her pants were of a heathered tan wool, paired with a cream-colored sweater. Over that she wore a parka in pale olive. The shades looked good on her and brought out the highlights in her pale golden brown hair, but they were undeniably drab. "I rest my case."

Ari made a face at her. "So speaks someone who wears mostly blue."

"I just think it's a good idea. Oh well, maybe I'll make some socks with it."

"For Joe? He should love those."

"Nah. They're for me, to wear with my clogs. Which will have felted uppers, of course, like everyone else's. I might as well fit in."

Ari shuddered. "Don't get too crunchy granola on me."

"*Moi?* Of course not. Did you see anything interesting?" Diane asked, changing the subject.

"Yes, there's some good stuff. Oh, I talked with the girl from Buffalo." Ari fished out the business card. "Annie Walker. Do you know we actually met once, when I lived in New York?"

"Small world, eh?" Diane glanced suddenly toward the entrance to the barn. "Jeez."

"What?" Ari asked, following her gaze.

"Look what just walked in."

"Wow." Ari stared at the woman who stood just inside the open barn door, eyeing the booths around her with a small frown. "Felicia Barr? What the heck is she doing here?" Ari asked.

"I didn't think she ever left Manhattan." Diane and Ari watched as Felicia began to make her way around the barn, her nose wrinkling as if she smelled something distasteful. She wasn't a tall woman, but she held herself so erect that she gave the impression of height. Unlike most of the others, she wore a fine-gauge turtleneck under a matching coat. From this distance, both appeared to be cashmere. Her tailored slacks looked equally expensive, and so did her high-heeled leather boots. Everything was black, as suited someone from Manhattan, except for the paisley shawl tossed gracefully about her shoulders.

"Are those designer boots?" Diane asked, sounding awed.

"You're asking me?"

"You're the former New Yorker."

"Yes, but I'm no fashionista. And I hate black. Wow, look at her," she added.

Felicia's presence had an impact all around the barn. Vendors had come to attention, with some scrambling to display their stock more attractively. It would probably be in vain, Ari thought. Felicia owned and edited a small knitting magazine, *Knit It Up!* which, like Felicia herself, had more influence than seemed warranted. If she liked someone's work, she said so, but if she didn't, the consequences could be disastrous. Her word carried a lot of weight.

"Brace yourself," Ari said. "She'll find something about your yarn to pick on."

Diane looked at Ari curiously. "You knew her, didn't you?"

"Years ago."

"I never heard you talk about her. Actually I've never heard you say much at all about New York."

"Oh, come on. I sent you emails all the time."

"Full of all the things you were doing there and sounding happy." Diane studied her. "I don't think you were."

Ari shrugged. Immersed as she was in her life here in Freeport, she rarely talked about the brief time she'd lived in the city after graduating from college. She'd been ambitious then, certain she'd make a huge splash in the design world. "I missed Freeport. I decided I could sell my designs just as easily from here. And of course I met Ted." That wasn't the whole story, but it would do for now.

"Oh yeah, Ted. He was a real catch." Diane's voice was sardonic, but her face, as she continued to study Ari, was thoughtful.

"Yes, Ted," Ari said firmly, hoping to close the subject. "It was a long time ago."

After a moment, Diane shrugged and returned to her spinning. "Did she ever criticize you?"

"Who, Felicia? Yes." Ari looked down at her project, wondering for a second what Felicia would say. It didn't matter, she told herself. She was as successful as she wanted to be; Ariadne's Web had turned a profit earlier than she had expected, and her designs, which she marketed herself, were popular. She had nothing to fear from Felicia. At least, she didn't think so.

"Who's that woman following her?" Diane asked.

"I think it's Debbie Patrino, her assistant. I've seen her picture in the magazine."

"The one who does all the work?"

"So people say. If she does, she's smart enough not to brag about it. Not like Beth Marley."

"Who?"

"Felicia's last assistant," Ari said. "It got her fired." Debbie trailed in Felicia's wake, and while her gaze was sharp, there was a half smile on her face. Like her employer she wore black, but there all resemblance ended. Debbie was tall, with flame-colored hair that spilled over her shoulders. She was also much younger. "I've heard Debbie doesn't take much from anyone."

"I wonder how Felicia handles that."

"Who knows? She seems to be spreading her usual joy," Ari added. Felicia was continuing her progress around the barn, leaving in her wake many angry and disgruntled vendors. "I wonder whose reputation she's going to slay this time."

"You think she will?" Diane asked. "This is a small festival."

"I don't think it will matter. Brace yourself."

Felicia was nearing Diane's table. Reaching down, she pulled out a skein of yarn Diane had spun, a rich teal blue, and frowned. "Chemical dyes," she said, as if that mattered.

"Yup," Diane answered cheerfully, like a typical New Englander. She never had been one to let people push her around. Besides, she had nothing to lose, Ari thought. Her yarn sold well in the area, and Felicia couldn't change that. "I find the natural ones too much work." Diane's gaze went to Felicia's expertly highlighted hair, styled in a French twist. "Chemicals can work miracles."

Ari let out a sound that was something between a snort and a laugh. It drew Felicia's attention to her. "What sort of work do you do?" she demanded.

Ari only smiled. In spite of her experiences in New York, she had never been intimidated by Felicia. "Hello, Felicia," she said.

Felicia looked at her more closely, and then recognition came into her eyes. "Ariadne Jorgensen, isn't it? I'd heard you live in the sticks now."

"Ayuh," Ari said, going Diane one better with her New England colloquialism. "I like it here."

"New York scared you," Felicia said flatly. "You ran away."

"Oh, give it a rest, Felicia," Ari said. In the past months she'd regained the confidence she'd lost during her divorce from Ted. Solving a murder tended to have that effect, she thought. "How have you been doing?"

Felicia looked vaguely surprised by this greeting. "Well enough. And you?"

"Happy. I like being my own boss. You should come by the shop. I think even *you'd* like it."

"I've seen some of your designs. They're not bad," she said grudgingly.

"High praise, Felicia," Ari said.

"Humph." In spite of her apparent annoyance, a smile lurked in Felicia's eyes. "It's more than can be said of most of the stuff here."

"Oh, come on. That's not true."

"There's not an original design in the bunch."

"Then why did you come?" Diane asked.

Felicia looked Diane up and down, frostiness in her manner again. "Do I know you?"

"No," Diane said, still cheerful.

That seemed to put Felicia off-balance, if only temporarily. After giving Diane another look, she turned back to Ari. "I understand you live near here?"

"Yes," Ari said.

"We're staying at a dreadful motel. Not at all homey."

"Maybe you should find a bed-and-breakfast," Diane said.

"I can help you find one if you want," Ari said.

"Thank you." Felicia looked anything but grateful. "I suppose I must inspect the rest of the place."

"Are you doing an article on the festival?"

"Maybe," Felicia said vaguely, and with a brief wave, she walked away.

"Whew!" Diane said. "What a bitch. Do

you think she was trying to get you to invite her to stay at your house?"

"I'm not sure. Maybe." Ari looked after Felicia, now stopped at the table covered with yarn from llamas. "She's really not that bad, you know."

"Could have fooled me."

"No, really. You have to stand up to her. When you do, she backs off. You saw that. Most people let her boss them around."

"How to lose friends and influence enemies," Diane muttered.

"Maybe — oh my God."

"What?"

"At the door." She indicated the woman who had just entered the barn. "It's Beth Marley."

"Felicia's former assistant?"

"Yes. This should be interesting."

"You've got to be kidding me. *She* worked for Felicia?"

"I know." Ari studied Beth, who could not have been more of a contrast to the elegant Felicia. Small and plump, she had evidently tried to emulate her former boss, but without much success. Her driving coat was well cut, but even from here the cloth didn't look as fine as Felicia's, and the length was not flattering to her figure. She also wore boots, but under jeans rather than expensive slacks. The entire effect was undercut by the pink crocheted beret pulled down on her head instead of at a jaunty angle. "Hard to believe, isn't it?"

"I can see why Felicia fired her," Diane said dryly.

"Mm. I'm sure her appearance didn't help matters." Ari sat back. "Beth's never been able to get a job with a decent magazine since."

Diane looked at Ari. "Where's she working?"

"For *Knit Knacks*. In New Jersey, no less."

"I'll bet that's where she got the pattern for the hat."

"Probably," Ari said. *Knit Knacks* was not known for original, or particularly stylish, designs.

"She must hate Felicia's guts."

"Probably. Uh-oh." She leaned forward, riveted by the scene unfolding in front of her. Across the length of the barn, Felicia and Beth had spotted each other.

Diane followed her gaze. "Trouble?"

"I think so."

"Jeez," Diane said as the two women slowly, warily approached each other. "High noon."

"Or a duel. Needles at ten paces."

"Well." Felicia's voice, as high and com-

25

manding as ever, echoed through the barn. If people hadn't noticed the coming confrontation before, they had now. "Look what the cat dragged in."

"Not particularly original, Felicia." Beth stood her ground, not appearing the least cowed, and her voice was unexpectedly deep for someone her size. "I suppose that's to be expected," she said, stopping a few feet away from Felicia.

"You should talk." Felicia looked Beth up and down. "Where did you get that appalling hat? Oh, let me guess. You made it."

"I did." Beth seemed to stand a little taller. Whatever else she was, she wasn't a coward.

"And proud of it? Dear, dear." There was a slight smile on Felicia's face. "How the mighty have fallen."

"Not yet."

"What is that supposed to mean?"

"Your day will come, Felicia. When you fall you'll have a long way to go." Her smile was almost evil. "I can't wait."

"Oh my God," Ari, watching in fascination, gasped.

"Was that a threat?" Diane whispered.

"I don't know."

"Wow. I never thought a wool festival could be so exciting."

"Talk about falling," Felicia was saying. *"Contributing* editor. Your reputation precedes you."

"I do a lot for that magazine," Beth said defensively, because her current position was lower than her previous one.

Again Felicia looked at her hat. "It shows."

"At least we don't steal people's designs," Beth shot back.

Felicia gave her a hard look. "Let's go, Debbie. I don't care for the odor in here," she said, and, to everyone's surprise, stalked out into the rain, Debbie scurrying behind her.

"Wow," Diane said.

Ari nodded. She was watching Beth, who was staring in openmouthed surprise toward the door. "I'm amazed they didn't beat each other up."

"Is what Beth said true?"

"I doubt it," Ari said. "Felicia can be harsh, but I've never heard of her stealing anything. She seems to have some integrity."

"I thought she praised people if they bought advertising, and criticized them if they didn't."

"I don't know. She was complimentary to me, and I never advertised with her. I'm not sure she deserved that." Beth was now strutting around the barn. Ari thought much of her attitude was bravado. "Her articles about advertisers are a little more tactful, though, even if she doesn't like their work."

"Well, that woke everyone up." The atmosphere in the barn was almost back to normal, though the buzz of conversation was louder than it had been. "Speaking of which, I could really go for that coffee now."

"Go, then."

"Out in the rain? I don't think so."

"Oh, all right." Ari stretched and rose. "I could stand to get out of here for a little while. What size coffee?"

"As large as possible."

"Okay. See you in a minute." Ari walked across the barn, tugging up the hood of her parka as she went. The rain, windswept and strong, hit her full in the face as she stepped out. She could just make out the shape of Barn A, even though it was only a few yards away, and the parking lot to her left was a blur. Her wool slacks were immediately soaked from the water running down off her parka, and the mud pulled at her feet. Thank goodness she'd had the foresight to wear low boots, although even they were beginning to feel a little damp.

It was a relief to reach Barn A, its blast of warmth welcome indeed. She looked around with interest at the demonstrators and vendors who were crowded into the small space. The wares here tended to be notions such as hand-turned wooden knitting needles or brightly colored rovings. Reluctant to go back out, Ari browsed among the tables, stopping here and there to talk to people. She'd half expected to see Felicia here in the warmth, but there was no sign of her. *She probably left,* Ari thought, moving over to the snack bar at last. *But how had she managed in the mud on her high heels?*

Finally, with two coffee cups firmly wedged into a cardboard holder, Ari walked out of the barn and stopped under the eaves in dismay. In the short time she'd been inside the rain had intensified, and it showed no signs of letting up. She waited for a few minutes, but when water started splashing down on her from the gutters, she gave up. She was already soaked. Better to get it over with.

Head down against the weather, Ari moved toward Barn B as quickly as she could, without spilling the coffee. She scolded herself as she hurried. No one else was stupid enough to be outside. At least, she couldn't see anyone, though with her head down against the rain there could be a huge flock of sheep twenty feet in front of her and she wouldn't know. Maybe that was why she stepped into a puddle so deep that the water sloshed over her ankles into her boots, making her curse. That did it. She was going home.

At first, looking down as she was, all she saw were boots approaching. It took her a moment to identify them as expensive Italian boots, a second more to realize that they could belong to only one person. Ari looked up to see that she wasn't alone in the rain after all. Felicia was coming toward her, her gait uneven. The black wool slacks that had been so pristine were now soaked; her boots were mud bespattered. And she wasn't wearing her coat. "Felicia?" Ari said, startled.

"Mud," Felicia gasped, and stumbled. Instinctively Ari put out a hand to steady her, going off-balance herself when Felicia grasped her arm.

The coffee flew everywhere, splashing Ari's parka and hands. "Ouch!" she exclaimed, and let go. Without Ari's support, Felicia lurched forward, and before Ari could move, Felicia collapsed against her.

"Felicia," Ari said, startled. "What in the world?"

"I — tried to get — the mud —"

"What?"

"Help," Felicia said, and sagged. Ari grabbed at her arms, too late. Felicia slipped away and crumpled to the ground, pulling Ari off-balance again. This time she dropped the coffee, but that wasn't what made her stumble back. There was, Ari realized with horror, a knitting needle sticking out of Felicia's back.

CHAPTER 2

"Felicia!" Ari exclaimed, and, heedless of her own comfort, fell to her knees on the ground. *Where was Felicia's coat?* she wondered. It would have afforded her some protection against the needle, which, Ari now saw, was in deeper than she'd realized. *Unless it's a ten-inch needle,* she thought. Because if it were a long one . . .

"No, no, not again," she gasped. She didn't dare turn Felicia over, not with that needle in her back, but she could at least get her face out of the mud. She tipped Felicia's head to the side, but, to her horror, blood trickled from Felicia's mouth. She felt frantically at Felicia's throat for a pulse. It was there, weak, barely perceptible, and then it was gone. "Oh God! Help!" she screamed.

The wind and the rain took her words and blew them away, but she kept yelling. Someone finally heard her. The sucking sound of someone struggling through the mud reached her. A woman dropped to her knees beside Ari. "I'm a nurse," she said briefly as she reached to steady Felicia's head. Across from her, a man Ari vaguely recognized as a vendor had started performing CPR on Felicia. Someone else had a cell phone in hand. It was all a blur to Ari, who knelt back, as far out of the way as she could get. It seemed an eternity before an ambulance came screaming onto the fairgrounds; a brief moment before the EMTs, taking charge, gave each other quick, grave looks. It confirmed what Ari already knew. Felicia was dead.

Joshua Pierce, a detective with the Freeport police, looked down at Felicia's body. She lay as she had when the EMTs had finally given up all attempts at resuscitation; partly on her side, with the knitting needle visible. Not quite an hour had passed since the initial 911 call had come in. "How do you get yourself into these things, Ari?" he asked.

"Do you think I do it on purpose?" Ari said crossly. She was huddled against the barn, about twenty feet away, and was swallowed up by the long black slicker a patrolman had given her. Even so, she looked like a drowned kitten, with her hair plastered to her head and her pants thoroughly soaked. A wet, rather annoyed, and thoroughly miserable kitten.

"This takes it all." Josh looked away, past the yellow police tape that cordoned off the area, toward another cluster of barns. "Fifty more feet," he said softly. Fifty more feet, and this would have happened on the Acushnet side of the fairgrounds. It would be Acushnet's problem, not his.

In fairness to Ari, he knew that she didn't want to be involved with this any more than he did. He'd become used to the sight of violent crime as a detective in Boston, but this was different somehow. The victim's clothes had been expensive, he noted, and yet that didn't matter. In death she looked as small and vulnerable as any body he'd ever seen.

Charlie Mason, the chief of police, ambled up beside Josh. He, too, wore a long black slicker covering his burly form and balding pate. "I'm calling in the state police," he said, drawing Josh aside.

"Why?" Josh said, startled.

"This is a county fairgrounds, remember? It straddles two towns."

"Yeah, I know," he said, gazing toward those distant barns again.

"Can't be just us involved. Besides, look

34

at this place." The wave of his hand encompassed the entire fairgrounds. "There've got to be a hundred people here, at least. We can't question them all ourselves."

Josh nodded in reluctant agreement. It would take days for Freeport's small force to talk to everyone, and they didn't have that long. Too many of the participants were from out of town, with plans to leave tomorrow. Beyond that, the state police had resources that Freeport didn't, including skilled technicians to process the crime scene. "What about Ari?"

Charlie glanced toward her. "Damn. She doesn't have to be out in this mess. What were you thinking?"

Josh drew himself up. "That she's a witness."

"Not much of a crime scene. Eileen'll kill me," he added.

In spite of the situation, Josh almost smiled. It was no secret that Charlie was interested in Ari's mother, Eileen, who so far was running shy. "She did see what happened."

"Yeah, well, not much to see now." He looked morosely at Felicia's body. "Someone from the ME's office is on the way, so we can't move her yet. We won't find any evidence in this mud," he added.

Josh nodded. Any physical evidence that might have helped them figure out what had happened had likely been washed away, or trampled into the mud. There was a chance they'd find something, but it was small. This wasn't television, after all. "Okay, I'll tell Ari to go in," he said.

He walked over to her. "There's nothing more for you to do here."

Ari looked up. "Then I can go?"

He shook his head. "Yes, back in the barn."

"But I'm soaked," she protested. "I want to go home and get dry clothes."

He noticed that she carefully avoided looking at the crumpled figure on the ground. "You know better than that. Has it occurred to you that someone here is probably a murderer?"

That stopped her. "Not me."

"No, I know."

"She fell against me. That's all."

"I know. Still, you might have seen something —"

"I told you when you first got here that I didn't."

"— without realizing it," he finished.

"I told you, no. It happened too fast. Could I at least have someone bring me something dry to wear?"

36

"Yeah, I don't see why not. Just let me know who'll be coming, so we can tell them at the gate."

"Thank you. I'll call my mother."

That made him smile again, thinking of Charlie's reaction. "Okay, no problem. We can't let her in, but she can drop off your things at the gate. But, Ari," he said, touching her arm.

She turned. "What?"

"Be careful. Don't tell anyone what you saw."

Ari frowned. "They'll know already."

"Yeah, but we don't need to let out all the details."

Ari sighed. "I won't say a word," she said, and went inside, leaving him gazing thoughtfully after her. There was another reason he wanted to keep her here. She probably hadn't seen what happened, but the murderer might not know that. If everyone stayed put, the police could keep track of them easier. He could keep his eye on her. There was a murderer on the loose, and again Ari was involved. He couldn't shake the feeling that she knew more about what had happened than she realized.

Diane jumped all over Ari as soon as she came into the barn. "Ari! Is it true? Are you okay? Oh, look at you! You're soaked."

I'm fine." Ari dropped onto the chair behind her table, feeling anything but fine. She was upset, shaken, and suddenly tired. She wanted nothing so much as to go home, put on her fleece robe, and curl up with a cup of tea.

"You've got to get out of those clothes." Diane was taking off her jacket. "Take your parka off and put this on."

"Thank you." Ari snuggled gratefully into Diane's warm coat, though her sodden slacks and shoes still made her shiver.

"Here, put this over you, too." Someone tossed an afghan made of soft wool in jewel colors over her. Ari looked up to see a woman she didn't recognize.

"I can't use this," Ari protested. "You're selling it."

"Not today. I'll wash it when I get home."

"Thank you. It's nice of you."

"We're done for today," Diane said gloomily. "Not that we were doing very well before."

"What happened out there?" someone asked. "Is it true Felicia's dead?"

Ari nodded. "Yes."

"Was there really a needle through her throat?" someone else asked.

Ari remembered Josh's admonition just in

38

time. "There was a needle," she said cautiously.

"Oh my God." The words were repeated in a murmur of agreement that filled the barn. There were more people there than there had been, Ari noticed, as well as two patrolmen at the door. People from the other barns must have been escorted here, though she hadn't noticed that when she was outside. But then, other, more important things had held her attention.

She shivered again, this time not from the cold. For the first time the enormity of what had happened hit her. Whoever had killed Felicia couldn't be a stranger, not at a place where so many people had a common interest. In all likelihood, the killer was in this very building.

"You won't get warm if you keep those wet pants on," Diane said, mistaking the reason for Ari's reaction. "Why don't you take them off?"

Ari stared at her. "What?"

"I'll hold up the afghan."

"For God's sake. No."

"I'll hold up the afghan," she repeated. "Come on, Ari. No one will see."

"Oh, all right." Ari struggled out of her wet wool slacks behind the screen the afghan provided, and then wrapped the afghan around her again. "Oh, this is better."

"This'll help, too." The woman who raised llamas handed Ari a thermos. "It's coffee."

"Thank you." Ari drank deeply, and almost choked when she realized it was laced liberally with brandy. "My God!"

The woman smiled at her. "It's the only way to keep warm today."

"I guess!" The warmth of the drink spread through her. "Thank you. Thank you, everyone, for being so kind."

"Why can't you go home to change instead of staying here?" Diane asked.

Ari shook her head. Josh was right. She did know better. After a murder, until the police sorted out who had been where, and when, no one would be allowed to leave. "I'll call my mother to bring me something."

"Your mother?" Diane's eyes danced. "She'll give Chief Mason holy hell."

Ari smiled for the first time since Felicia's death and dug into her bag for her cell phone. "Yeah, I think she will."

"Well, nothing's going to happen for a while." Diane pulled her chair over to her spinning wheel, picked up the wool, and began to spin it into yarn. As if that were a signal, the other people dispersed to their own tables or booths or, to Ari's surprise, to the Sheep to Shawl enclosure. Those who

40

had been herded here from other barns milled around aimlessly, looking lost, until gradually they found places to sit.

Ari picked up her project and then quickly dropped it. If the rayon yarn and the aluminum needles had felt cool to her before, now they were icy. "Why didn't I bring a shawl to work on instead of this?" she complained.

"Maybe your mother will bring something."

"I doubt it."

She wronged her mother, though. A little while later a patrolman, his long black slicker dripping, crossed the barn, two large plastic bags in his hands. "The chief told me to give this to you," he said, and left.

"Oh, bless her," Ari said. She looked in one of the bags to see what her mother had sent and started to laugh. "Oh, Diane, look at this!" She held up a pair of wooden needles and a ball of rug yarn. "She wants me to make coat hangers."

Diane grinned. Padded coat hangers, originally made by Ari's aunt Laura, were something of a joke among Ari's friends and family. Everyone Ari knew had a more than ample supply of them. "Where are you going to change?"

Ari emerged from under the afghan, where

41

she'd struggled back into her damp slacks. No need to get the jeans her mother had sent wet before she had to. "I guess in the bathroom in the other barn," she said, rising. "If they'll let me."

The patrolman standing guard at the door nodded when Ari made her request. Josh had apparently cleared the way for her. She slogged her way through the mud and the rain toward Barn A, thinking inevitably of Felicia. Why had she been killed in this particular place, at this particular time? She had made enemies, certainly, but since she rarely left New York, wouldn't she have been a better target there? It didn't make sense. But then, nothing about murder made sense.

Walking into Barn A was like walking into an interrogation room, Ari thought. Josh and Paul Bouchard, another detective, were sitting at the small luncheonette tables in the snack bar area. Across from them was one of the vendors, looking bewildered. Both of the detectives broke off as Ari came in and looked at her.

"I'm only going to change my clothes," she said, holding up her bag.

"Yeah. I saw your mother," Josh said.

"She let the chief have it," Paul said, grinning. He glanced at Mason, who was talking on his cell phone. "Hey, you planning to make a habit of finding murder victims, Ari?"

"That's enough." Charlie's voice was sharp as he flipped his phone closed, and his face was red. Since his color was usually high, Ari couldn't tell if he was embarrassed or not. Her mother, usually quiet, could be vociferous in defense of those she loved. "We've got things to do."

Paul winked at Ari as she headed toward the ladies' room, and then turned back to the vendor, who looked more confused than before. Ari felt for him. Soon they'd all come under the same scrutiny. Since there were so few police there, she suspected it would take a long time.

The restroom was small but adequate. Ari shivered as she stripped off her wet clothes. Bless her mother, she thought again as she looked in the bag and found not only clothes more suited to winter than to a supposed spring day, but a thick towel and her low hiking boots. There was even, luxury of luxuries, a hair dryer. Briefly she used it to blow hot air over her body, and then set to work on her hair. Without a round brush to smooth it, it dried into somewhat frizzy curls and waves. Finally, dressed in flannel-lined jeans, a cotton turtleneck, and a heavy

Scandinavian sweater made by her grand-mother, she walked out of the restroom, blessedly, deliciously warm.

Barn A had emptied while Ari was changing. Only Josh remained, sitting at a table with a brown cardboard cup of coffee before him. "Want one?" he asked.

"All right," she said, welcoming the delay in going out into the storm again. She plopped her elbows onto the worn green finish of the Formica-topped table, rocking slightly on the uneven chrome chair, and watched Josh. Behind the counter he did something with filters and small aluminum packets, and soon the enticing scent of fresh coffee filled the air.

"How'd you know how to do that?" she asked as he set another cardboard cup in front of her, his fingers just brushing hers as she reached for it.

He sat down again. "I worked as a short-order cook one summer."

"Oh. So that's where you learned to cook." The coffee was too hot to drink just yet, but she held the cup anyway, for its warmth.

"No, but it got me started."

"Where is everyone?"

"Outside. Someone from the ME's office is here."

"That was fast."

"Apparently he was in the area already."

"So you'll be releasing the crime scene?"

He shook his head. "Not yet."

"So this isn't my official interview?"

"We'll get to it." He looked at her searchingly. "How are you?"

She kept her head down, avoiding his gaze. "I'm okay."

"Yeah?"

"Yes."

"I'm sorry for what I said before," he said.

"About what?"

"About getting involved in these things, like it's your fault."

"Why does it happen to me, Josh?" she said, almost plaintively. "This is the second time. Except." She closed her eyes. "Except this time she practically died right on me."

"I know." His hand covered hers for a moment, and then pulled back. That was the story of their relationship, she thought, from last fall to now. Sometimes they'd go out, for dinner or to a movie, and thoroughly enjoy themselves. They'd be laughing, talking, finishing each other's sentences, and then, just as Ari was beginning to feel close to him, he'd pull back. Or she would. She liked Josh, and she knew he liked her. Of course, she still felt a little raw from her divorce. Maybe that was why they hadn't progressed beyond friendship, at least on her part. She wasn't sure of Josh's reasons.

"I don't understand it any more than you do." He rubbed his hands over his forehead, as if he had a headache. He looked tired, Ari thought, and this investigation had hardly begun. "I didn't expect anything like this when I left Boston. Two murders in a small town."

"It's usually so quiet and peaceful here. But, anyway." Ari straightened. "I suppose you want to know about Felicia."

Josh had taken out a steno notepad and a pencil. He was all business now, and she put aside the thought of anything more personal between them. Again. "Yeah. Everything. It's all new to me again." The wave of his hand encompassed the barn, and by extension, the entire festival.

"Well." She folded her hands and sat silent for a moment, thinking. "I never could quite figure her out. She could be a b- . . . witch — but if you stood up to her she'd back off. I always got the feeling she was softer inside than she let on."

"Why?"

"I don't know. Maybe something in her eyes. I don't know."

"Did you stand up to her?"

"No, not really, but I never let her bother me, either. She actually acted human with me. Of course, I had nothing to lose with her."

Josh looked up. "What do you mean?"

"How much do you know about her?"

"Not much."

"She owned a knitting magazine called *Knit It Up!* It's nothing like *Vogue Knitting,* but somehow she made it influential. She knew everyone, I think."

"Meaning who?"

"Anyone who had anything to do with knitting or yarn. She knew who was designing what for which clothing company, she knew who was putting out a new book, she knew everyone at every magazine and every manufacturer. It gave her a lot of influence."

"I'll bet."

"If she didn't like something about someone's design, that person was in trouble. If she did like it, then that designer's career would go far."

"How many people did she actually praise?"

"What makes you think there weren't many?" she said in surprise.

"People like that enjoy their power, maybe too much sometimes."

Ari nodded. "True, usually she was critical. But, you know, she was generally right."

"Did she criticize you?"

"No, but she didn't exactly gush over me, either."

"Sounds like she might've made some enemies."

"Oh, a lot," she said, nodding in agreement. "A lot of people were terrified of her."

"So there won't be many who're sorry she's dead."

"No."

"Are you sorry, Ari?"

Ari opened her mouth to answer, but at that moment her cell phone rang. Saved by the bell, she thought, giving Josh a falsely apologetic smile as she flipped it open. He was only doing his job, she reminded herself. "Hello?"

"Ari, what the hell have you gotten yourself into this time?" a voice roared at her.

Ari winced and held the phone away from her ear. "And hello to you, too, Ted," she said. "I can't talk right now."

"Why not?" Ted demanded.

She glanced at Josh, who had hooked his arm over the cracked red vinyl back of the chair. The two men were not exactly friends. "Detective Pierce is here."

"Don't tell him anything. I'm going to get you a lawyer."

"I don't need one, Ted."

"Then I'll come over myself. Don't say anything until I do."

"Ted, you can't," she protested. "What about Megan?"

"I'll leave her with your mother."

"Ted, no. How did you find out about what's going on?"

"Your mother called," he said after a minute.

She'd deal with her mother later, Ari thought. "And of course she suggested babysitting. No. Megan went through enough last time. I want to keep her out of it as long as I can."

"Damn it, Ari," Ted said, his voice softer. "You're in trouble. What am I supposed to do?"

"The best thing you can do for me now is take care of Megan. Please. She looks forward to her weekends with you."

"Ah, hell. All right. You're right. But you call me if you need me, you hear me? And don't say anything to that cop."

"Thank you, Ted," she said, and pressed the Off button on her phone. "Whew."

"Is he coming?" Josh asked.

"That would be all I need. No, he's going to stay with Megan instead."

"I'll bet he told you not to talk to me."

49

"Yes.

"He might be right, you know."

Ari raised her eyes to him in surprise. "Why? I didn't do anything wrong."

"I know, but I think you should be careful anyway."

"Why?"

He leaned closer to her. "We're not going to have control of the investigation much longer. The Freeport police, I mean."

"What? Why not?"

"The chief's called in the state police for help."

Ari's eyes went wide. "Really?"

"Yeah. We need help on this, and, Ari, they don't know you."

Ari nodded, remembering that last fall Josh hadn't known or trusted her, either. "You and the chief can vouch for me."

"Yeah, but this is the second time you've been involved in something like this, Ari. Of course they're going to suspect you, especially since no one saw you after you left this barn. No one did, did they?" he added.

"Not so far as I know, but the rain was coming down so hard that I didn't even see Felicia until she was almost on top of me."

"Mm." He looked down at his notebook. "What else do you know about the victim? Family? Friends?"

"She's married. Her husband's older than she is."

"How old was she, by the way?"

"I don't know. Midfifties, I'd guess, wouldn't you?"

"I wouldn't know."

"Oh. No, of course not. She has no children. And friends?" She shrugged. "She didn't let anyone get close enough."

That made him look up. "Is that something you know for a fact?"

"No, just an impression. Josh, when you asked about enemies, I think you should know . . ."

"What?" he asked when she didn't go on.

"There aren't many people who knew her well, so far as I know. Only Debbie Patrino and Beth Marley."

"And they are?"

"Beth used to be Felicia's assistant. Debbie is her current assistant."

"Did Beth quit?"

"Well . . ." Ari hesitated and then plunged in. "You'll hear about this anyway, so you might as well hear my version. There was a fight," she began, and went on to relate all that had happened today between Beth and Felicia, and the reasons for the confrontation. When she was finished, Josh sat back, looking thoughtful.

"Where was Beth before Mrs. Barr was killed?"

"I don't know. Josh, this is a big place and people could be anywhere."

"Yeah, but the weather would keep them inside. What about Debbie Patrino?"

"I don't know. I haven't heard anything against her, Josh."

"Does she get control of the magazine now that Felicia's dead?"

"I don't know. I imagine Felicia's husband has some say in it."

Josh capped his pen and rose. "Yeah, we're going to talk to him. He's on his way here."

"Is he?" Ari said, getting up as well. "Oh, poor Winston."

Josh turned from the door, which he'd been about to open. "You know him personally?"

"I met him once. He's a dear. Very old world, very charming. And he doted on Felicia," she said in some surprise. "I don't think I realized that before."

"Where did you meet him?"

"At a party Felicia gave for the magazine's fifth anniversary. At their apartment. What a place, Josh."

"Yeah?"

"It's in one of the old buildings on Central Park West, with a doorman and Art Deco decorations everywhere. It actually has two floors, with a spiral staircase."

"That sounds like money."

"Serious money. I think most of it is Winston's." She looked up at Josh. "I don't think Felicia was all bad, Josh."

"Most people aren't." He opened the door for her, and then paused. "Look, Ari."

"What?"

"I want you to be careful."

"Yes, I know," she said impatiently. "You've already told me."

"I know you, Ari. You'll want to be involved in this."

"Oh, no, not this time. I'll leave it to the police."

"Ha. Don't forget there's a murderer loose."

"Josh, no one's going to go after me."

"Well, just make sure you're never alone."

Considering how many people were there, Ari thought she could reassure him on that point. "I won't be."

"I don't want anything happening to you."

That made her look at him. "Nothing will, Josh."

"Good," he said, and again briefly touched her hand. "You'd better go."

"Yes," she said, and turned, flinching as

wind blew needle-sharp rain into her face. Had Josh just spoken to her as a cop, or as someone personally concerned about her? She couldn't tell. Anyway, she thought as she hurried back to the main barn, she really did have no intention of getting involved in this investigation. Once was enough.

The scene in Barn B was less chaotic than it had been when Ari left. Vendors, back at their tables or wandering around the barn, chatted with each other, examining yarn or spinning wheels or other equipment. One woman was showing a customer, who'd had the bad luck to be present when Felicia died, how to carry one color of yarn behind another for Fair Isle knitting. The spinning wheels of the women in the shawl competition spun so fast that their spokes were a blur. The loom treadles made a continuous thumping sound. It was almost as if nothing had happened, Ari thought as she sat beside Diane again.

"You were gone awhile," Diane commented.

"I was talking to Josh."

"Anything new?"

Ari, mindful of Josh's warning, shook her head. "They're calling in the staties to help out. They've got to question everyone," she said.

"Well, duh. I knew that. That knitting needle didn't get stuck in Felicia's back by itself."

Ari started to answer, to correct her, and then stopped herself. Diane was her oldest friend, and Ari could trust her, but someone else could overhear. "Mm."

Diane looked at her suspiciously. "Ari, is there something you're not telling me?"

"No, of course not — oh, look. Chief Mason's here."

Chief Mason had stepped in beside the patrolman and now stood there, his hand raised. "Folks," he called, his voice booming through the cavernous barn. "Can I have your attention, please?"

"Now what?" Diane muttered as people around them shushed each other.

"Settle down, okay? Okay. Now." He stood with his legs slightly apart and his face stern, not at all the genial man Ari knew, but very much someone in charge. "You've all heard what's happened here," he said. "You all know that someone has died. Now, wait." He held up his hand again and the buzzing caused by his words subsided. "If it was natural causes, there'd be no problem, but it's a suspicious death. We gotta question all of you about it."

Again the voices buzzed, and this time Charlie had to raise his voice to be heard. "People! Can we have silence, please? Good. Now. I know you all want to get out of here, and I don't blame you, but we have to keep you here until we've had a chance to talk to you."

"How long will that be?" a vendor down the row from Ari asked.

"As long as it takes." Charlie seemed unperturbed, even with everyone talking at once. "The state police will be here soon and they'll help, but there's a lot of you. Until we've had a chance to question everyone you have to stay."

"But only for today, right?"

He glanced around. "Maybe."

That brought an uproar, and out of it that same speaker's voice came. By craning her neck, Ari saw that it was the woman who raised llamas. "I can't stay! I have work on Monday."

"I only have a room booked for one night," someone else protested.

"I don't have one at all," a third person chimed in.

"It's my understanding that the festival runs for two days," Charlie said.

"Yes, but I'm planning on going home

tonight."

"That might not be possible."

"But —"

"You can't think someone here had anything to do with Felicia's death," the llama breeder said.

"That's exactly what I do believe." The chief, arms crossed, looked around the barn again. "Someone at this festival is a murderer."

CHAPTER 3

"Well, that'll do it," Diane muttered to Ari under the protests of horror and denial that met Chief Mason's statement. "It'll take forever to question everyone."

Ari shook her head. "The state police will do some of the questioning. My bet is they'll eliminate nearly everyone right away. After all, most of the people were here, or in the sheep barn or snack bar, where people could see them. The Sheep to Shawl people certainly don't have anything to worry about."

"That's true." A frown puckered Diane's forehead. "Are you a suspect?"

"Probably."

"Jeez, Ari. You gotta admit, two murders within a year is a little strange."

"I know." Ari sank her chin onto her fist. "God knows what the staties will think."

"Yeah." Diane watched the door, where one of the vendors was being escorted out by a patrolman. "Where are they doing the questioning?"

"Barn A. At least it's warm in there."

"It'll be my turn soon, I bet."

Ari looked at her. "Why? You were here."

"Well, no."

"What?" Ari stared at her. "Then where were you?"

"I went out for a smoke," Diane admitted, if a bit defiantly.

"Oh, Di, and after all you went through to quit. When did you start up again?"

"A while ago." She hesitated. "Last fall."

"That long ago?" Ari said, surprised. She'd never smelled smoke on Diane's clothes, or, for that matter, her yarn. But then, she could understand why Diane had picked up cigarettes again. Last fall, first Diane and then her husband, Joe, had been prime suspects in the murder of Edith Perry, whom Ari had found dead in her shop. The incident had taken its toll on all of them. "Well, you were just outside the barn, weren't you?"

"Well, no," Diane said again. "I was around the side so I could get under the eaves. I don't know if anyone saw me."

"Oh, Di."

"I came out when I saw the ambulance."

"So you'll be a suspect, too."

"Yeah." Diane glanced at her. "We're partners in crime again."

"It's not funny, Di."

Diane's lips set. "No, it won't be when that detective of yours finds out about it."

"He's not going to suspect you," Ari protested. "And he's not my detective."

"Good thing."

Ari let that pass. After last fall's events, Diane had good reason to dislike Josh. "What reason would you have to kill Felicia? You didn't even know her."

"I'll still be a suspect. I was out at the wrong time." She glanced around the barn. "Do you really think the murderer is here?"

"It has to be one of us. Who else could it be?"

"Don't you think whoever stabbed her could have left?"

Ari frowned. "Maybe. I didn't see anyone driving out, but I don't think I would have noticed anything right then. I was too concerned about Felicia."

"I wonder if the police are thinking it?"

"Maybe." Josh hadn't indicated anything about it to her, but then, he wasn't under any obligation to give her information. "I don't know, Diane. I think the person could still be here. It would be the best way of avoiding suspicion, wouldn't it?"

"I'd want to get as far away as possible."

"Maybe whoever it is couldn't. Anyway, there are enough people here who had grudges against her."

"Like Beth Marley."

Ari nodded. "She's the most likely person. Hm."

"What?"

"I was just thinking. Felicia wasn't tall."

"So?"

"Neither is Beth. I wonder just how the needle went in."

Diane shuddered. "Ari —"

"Well, I do. The height of whoever did it would affect the angle. I'll bet they'll figure that out at the autopsy."

"You don't have to be so ghoulish."

"Seriously, Di. Whatever the angle is, it'll give them some indication of how tall the murderer is."

"What I want to know is, how did a knitting needle get through all her clothes? Needles just aren't that sharp. And how did the murderer know where to stab her?"

Something flitted into Ari's mind, and then was gone. Something to do with Felicia. A needle was an unlikely choice of weapon, she thought. "Just luck, I think."

"Luck!"

"Bad luck. You know, Di, whoever did it

61

probably didn't mean to."

"You mean someone just saw her chance?" Diane asked.

"Maybe. Or maybe she was just trying to hurt Felicia." She glanced around the barn. "Where's Beth Marley?"

"I don't know." Diane scanned the area, too. "I haven't seen her since she went storming out, now that I think of it. Do you think she's with the police?"

"I didn't see her outside, either." Ari paused. "I did tell Josh about her."

That made Diane look up. "You just handed her to him?"

"That's not fair," Ari protested. "If I didn't tell him about the fight, someone else would have. She's got to be the prime suspect."

"What about Debbie Patrino?" Diane craned her head to look around the barn. "I don't see her, either."

"She hasn't been in here for a while."

"No, that's right. She was trailing Felicia like a shadow." Diane looked down at her spinning wheel, and then set it in motion. "Where was she, I wonder?"

Ari opened her mouth to answer, but at that moment there was a commotion at the door. "I'm attending this thing, damn it," a voice said irritably. "Let me in."

"Speak of the devil," Diane muttered. Debbie stood just outside the door, her way in blocked by a patrolman.

"She doesn't look very wet," Ari answered.

"Of course I want to come in here," Debbie said, apparently in answer to something the patrolman had said. "Anyway, what are you doing here? Guarding the sheep?"

"Let her in," Josh said from behind them.

Debbie turned toward him. "Who are you?" she asked.

"Detective Joshua Pierce. And you are?"

"Detective?" She stared at him. "What's happened?"

"There's been an incident. Your name?"

"Debbie Patrino. What kind of incident?"

"A murder."

"Murder!" She stared at him. "Who?"

"Felicia Barr. I'm sorry."

"Felicia?" Debbie's gaze was blank, and then she took a deep breath. "Well! I was afraid that would happen."

The barn was suddenly silent. "Excuse me?" Josh said.

"She really did it?" Debbie said "She went and got herself killed?"

"Yes." So this was the assistant, he thought, looking down at his notebook. At least, the current one. He had yet to meet

Beth Marley. "You don't seem surprised."

"I'm not. Oh, just let me in," she snapped at the patrolman. "I'm getting my ass rained off here."

The patrolman blinked and looked at Josh, who nodded slightly. "We need to talk, Miss Patrino."

"So talk," Debbie said as she furled her umbrella.

"Not here. Would you come with me, please?"

"What, out in that rain again? Why can't we talk right here?"

"Miss Patrino, I don't think you quite realize what's happened."

"Oh, call me Debbie. Of course I do. It's only what I've been saying for months now."

"Ms. Patrino." Josh stepped closer and pitched his voice low; there were too many people listening for his comfort. "You can come to the other barn with me on your own, or I can have Officer Santos here escort you."

That made her look at him. "You're kidding."

"No. Well? It's your choice."

Debbie's mouth quirked in annoyance. "Oh, all right, I'll come." She snapped her umbrella open again and stalked out, somehow retaining her air of insulted dignity.

Josh couldn't quite figure her out. He'd seen people react to violent death in many ways, but this cavalier attitude was new to him. Her boss was dead, she herself could be a suspect, and yet she seemed more annoyed than anything else. Maybe it just hadn't sunk in yet.

Charlie was sitting at a table in Barn A when Josh walked in, leaning forward and listening intently to the woman sitting across from him. He acknowledged Josh with a nod, but went on with his questions. The woman clearly had nothing to do with the murder, Josh thought, listening to her answers. Few people here would. Questioning everyone to winnow out those few, though, would take forever. Josh wondered when the state police would show up to help, with their mobile crime-scene van and additional manpower.

Josh seated Debbie at a table as far from Charlie's as he could, and then went to the coffee urn. A few minutes later he set two cups down on the table, and then sat across from Debbie, taking her measure. She was sitting still, and her eyes had an inward quality, as if she were seeing something far, far away. He wondered if she realized yet how damning her reaction was.

At last Charlie rose, sending the woman

he'd questioned on her way. With a jerk of his head he gestured Josh over. "What's the story?"

"Barr's assistant. She's acting damn weird," Josh said, and quickly filled him in on Debbie's behavior.

When he was finished, Charlie was frowning. "Never saw anything like that before," he said.

"Me either."

"You think she could be the one?"

"Maybe. She wasn't around when it happened."

"Hm. You're right. Damned odd. Well, let's get it over with." He moved over to the table. "Miss Patrino? I'm Chief Mason. I'm sorry for your loss."

"Ms. Patrino," she said absently, as if it were something she'd done many times before.

"Okay, Ms." Charlie nodded, though there was a slight frown on his face. Debbie's reactions still were odd, off. "I understand you were the victim's assistant."

At that, Debbie came to herself. "Victim," she said thoughtfully.

"Yes, Miss Patrino. You realize we have to ask you some questions."

"Why?" She looked up at him. "I didn't have anything to do with it."

"We're talking to everyone." He reached across the table and pushed a button on a small tape recorder. "Mind if I record this?"

"No."

"Good," he said, though it didn't matter whether she did or not. They would be recording the statements of everyone involved in this case, no matter how peripherally.

After speaking his name, the date, and Debbie's name into the recorder, Charlie turned toward her. "Now, Ms. Patrino." He leaned back, apparently at ease. "What did you mean by what you said before?"

"I don't know. What did I say?"

"You said you knew Felicia would be murdered."

"Someday," she said. "I said 'someday.' "

"Meaning?"

"She made enemies." Debbie's gaze was straight and level. Whatever her inner absorption had been, it was gone. "I used to tell her someone would stab her in the back if she kept it up."

"Really." Charlie sat back. "Why that particular way?"

She shrugged. "I guess because people said a lot behind her back, but never to her face. I can't think that anyone she hurt would do it, though."

"Why not?"

"Well, they never had the guts to stand up to her, did they? By the way, how did she die?"

"She was stabbed in the back with a knitting needle," Josh said.

Debbie stared at him. "You're kidding me."

Josh and Charlie exchanged quick looks. "No. Mind telling us where you were?"

"When?"

"When Felicia was killed."

"Wait, wait, wait." Debbie put up her hand. "You don't think I did it?"

"Where were you, Ms. Patrino?"

"In my car. Well, it was cold," she said defensively. "I ran the heater to warm up."

"Then why didn't you see the police cars and the ambulances?"

"I guess I fell asleep."

"You guess?"

"Yes! I fell asleep. Is that a crime?"

"It's mighty convenient."

She stared at him and then slapped her hand on the table. "I didn't kill her."

"We hear she was hard to work for," Josh said. "She fired someone before you. Was she going to fire you, too?"

"No! Beth Marley dug her own grave."

"What do you mean?"

Something shifted in Debbie's eyes. "She talked too much, bragged she was the real power at the magazine. I was smart enough to keep quiet and keep my head down. Where is Beth, anyway? She's the one you should be looking for."

"Why is that?"

"Because she had a knock-down, drag-out fight with Felicia."

"Oh?"

"In a manner of speaking. You must have heard about it. Everyone saw it."

"We'll be talking to her as well. Ms. Patrino, did anyone see you in your car?"

"I don't know. I was asleep."

"Did anyone know you were going there?"

"No. I didn't say anything because I knew how Felicia would be. She likes — liked having me right there. Oh God. Is she really dead?"

It was the first crack in her façade, and the first normal reaction they'd seen from her. "Yes, Ms. Patrino. She's really dead."

"What do I do?" she said, almost to herself. "What do I do now?"

"For now you stay at the festival."

She looked up. "Are you arresting me?"

"Not yet." Charlie stood up. "We'll look at your car. In the meantime, Detective Pierce will take you back to the other barn."

"Okay." Debbie, subdued now, rose and allowed Josh to lead her to the door. Josh sent Charlie a quizzical look over his shoulder, though. Debbie was their best suspect so far. It didn't make sense to send her away just yet.

As he reached for the handle, the door blew open, bringing with it gusty rain and a very large man. If the room had been cool before, now it was chilly, and not just because of the wind. The man's glacially blue eyes took in the barn and its occupants, and not one trace of emotion showed on his set face to give a clue to his thoughts. Debbie shrank back against Josh. Not an unreasonable reaction, he thought. There was something sinister about the man as he stood there in his black leather trench coat and gray fedora — something forbidding — until he suddenly smiled.

"Hey, Charlie," he said. The door slammed shut behind him as he walked into the room.

"Bill." Charlie advanced with his hand outstretched, and the two men shook hands with easy familiarity. "So you're in on this?"

"Yes." Bill looked around again as he removed his fedora. "What've we got?"

"Tell you in a minute. This is Josh Pierce, one of my detectives. Josh, Detective Briggs, state police. He and I've worked together before."

"Detective." Josh shook his hand. "Good to meet you."

Briggs nodded, his gaze trained on Debbie. "Who is this?"

"Debbie Patrino, one of our witnesses," Josh said. For some reason he suddenly felt protective of her. "I was just bringing her back to the other barn."

Briggs took out a walkie-talkie. "I'll get one of the troopers to do that. We three need to talk."

"Sure." Josh stood near the door with Debbie while Briggs, after taking off his trench coat and placing it carefully over the back of a chair, sat at the table with Charlie. He was grateful when the trooper Briggs had summoned came in. "Trooper" — he paused to glance at the man's name tag — "Lopes will bring you back instead."

"Okay." Debbie, her head held high, started out, the trooper following her.

"No, wait a minute," Charlie called. "Lopes."

The trooper turned. "Yes, sir?"

Charlie looked at Briggs. "You bring the mobile command unit?"

Briggs nodded. "It's right outside."

"We need help questioning people."

"How many?"

"About sixty or seventy, give or take a few. It'll go quicker if we have others doing the questioning," Charlie said.

"Yeah." He spoke into his walkie-talkie for a minute. "All right. I've got two teams in the unit ready to go. Lopes."

"Sir?" the trooper said.

"After you leave Ms. Patrino in the other barn, start bringing the others to the command unit."

"Yes sir," Lopes said, and he and Debbie left the barn.

"All right, so what do we have?" Briggs asked. For the next few minutes Josh, with help from Charlie, filled in the details about the murder.

"So that's where we are," he finished. "We've got one, maybe two, people who look good for this."

"Three," Briggs said. "The assistant, the former assistant, who's MIA, and Mrs. Evans."

"I doubt Ari has anything to do with this."

"The woman's been involved in two murders now."

"Yes, Bill, but she didn't kill Edith Perry," Charlie put in.

"It looks damned suspicious to me. How many people get into something like this?

Regular people," he amended. "I'm not talking about gangs or lowlifes."

"She didn't do it." Josh's tone was flat. "She didn't kill Perry and she didn't kill this woman."

"Let's make no assumptions." Briggs leaned forward, looking at them thoughtfully. "You folks need another eye on this. You're too close. Until she's cleared she's a suspect."

"Cleared how? No one saw her with Felicia until she called for help."

"That's the kind of thing we can find out. I realize you can't help being biased, but I'm not." He looked at them coolly. "If you were coming to this cold, what would you think, given the circumstances?"

Charlie's mouth quirked, and then he nodded. "Okay, I see that," he admitted. "But I'm betting that when we get it all sorted out, she'll be out of it."

"You just proved my point."

Silence descended on the room. He was right, Josh thought. They couldn't start an investigation of this magnitude with any assumptions. That didn't mean he had to like it. That didn't mean he couldn't resent Briggs or his suspicions, if he wanted to.

The door opened with another dramatic bang, and the wind riffled the papers on the tables. A state trooper, in a long black slicker and the high peaked hat of his uniform, stood there, holding a woman by her elbow. She was small and dumpy, and she wore a black coat and a pink angora beret, along with a strong air of indignation. "Detective, I thought you'd want to talk to this lady," the trooper said.

"Stop manhandling me," the woman snapped, pulling her arm free.

Briggs twisted his gold Cross pen closed and sat back, still ramrod straight. "What's the story?"

"She was driving into the fairgrounds, sir."

The woman glared at them, hands on her hips. "Why shouldn't I?" Briggs glanced at the list of festival participants. "Do you have a booth?"

"No. I'm attending this festival. Is that a crime?"

It was an interesting choice of words, Josh thought. "We'll explain in a minute. For now, can you tell us your name?"

The woman glanced around the room, and then back at them.

"Elizabeth Marley. Who are you?"

"Detective Briggs, Massachusetts State Police," Briggs said gravely, and Josh glanced at Charlie. Beth Marley, he thought.

Felicia's former assistant and a very current suspect in her murder.

CHAPTER 4

Diane let out a prodigious yawn. "Debbie's been gone a long time, hasn't she?"

"She was missing a long time," Ari said. "They're going to have a lot of questions for her."

"Mm. When do you think they'll let us go?"

"I don't know. There are still a lot of people here who haven't gone out for questioning yet." Ari continued knitting as she glanced around, her fingers moving automatically. She'd put aside the ribbon shell in favor of the rug yarn and large needles needed for padded coat hangers. The design was so simple she could do it in her sleep.

She wasn't the only one keeping busy, or at least trying to. Across from her, one woman worked industriously at her spinning wheel, though Ari noted that her eyes darted about from time to time. Several people stood together near the booth displaying hand-dyed yarn, discussing the merits of natural versus chemical dyes. Oddly enough, few people had left their own tables or booths. In such a big barn, with a tragedy to unite them, everyone was staying separate.

Diane had given up any pretense of work and sat back with her arms crossed. "You did a yarn over."

"What?" Ari glanced down at the long knitted strip and saw the mistake she'd made several rows back. Without realizing it, she had brought the yarn forward over the needle, thus adding another stitch but also making a hole in the fabric. Clicking her tongue in annoyance, she pulled the piece off the needles and unraveled it past the mistake. "I hate these things."

Diane was looking at the work with her lips pursed. "You know, Ari, if you used different yarn you could make lace hangers."

"Be real."

"No, really. Use DK or fingering yarn and make a lace design. They'd be a hell of a lot nicer than that."

"Hm." Now Ari frowned thoughtfully. DK, double-knit yarn, and fingering yarn were both thin and light. "That's a thought. Luxury coat hangers. I could use silk ribbon, or something plain and line it with satin."

"Yeah, that's a good idea, too."

Ari scrabbled in her knitting bag for the pad she always kept there in case an idea came to her. She began to sketch out a small design. Yarn overs to make lacy holes, stitches knitted together to form the pattern. "I can't wait to get home to try this out."

"If they ever let us go," Diane said.

Ari set down her needles and plunked her elbows onto her table. "They'll let you go, but not me."

"They can't keep you here."

"Of course they can," she said crossly. "I found the body. Again."

"They're sure taking their time questioning people," Diane pointed out.

"I don't think they have any other place to do interviews except the snack bar."

"Which reminds me. When are we going to get something to eat?"

"Good question. I — oh."

"What?" Diane said, and then looked toward the door, where Debbie Patrino had just entered the barn, escorted by a state trooper. "She's b-a-a-ck."

"They didn't arrest her."

"Wonder why not. She's a good suspect."

Ari frowned. Debbie was now wandering aimlessly around the barn, looking at people's wares, oblivious to everyone staring at her. It was odd. "I don't know about that. What reason would she have?"

"The magazine," Diane said. "Working under Felicia had to be tough." She glanced at Ari. "Did you ever hear anything about them fighting?"

"No, but I'm not too plugged into the gossip anymore."

"Was there anything in the online group you're on?"

Ari shook her head. She had gone from being computer illiterate to being a computer addict. Once she had discovered that there were Internet groups for knitters, she had joined as many as she could. "I told you, she was keeping a low profile."

"Yeah, but there could be stuff we don't know about her. I mean, look how she was following Felicia around before, like Felicia was the queen and she had to stay ten steps back."

"What are you talking about?"

"Like Debbie was Felicia's servant."

"Oh, okay. I get it." Ari rested her chin on her fist. "Still, I get the feeling that Debbie did that on her own. I told you, she's smart."

"Maybe, but no one seems to want to have

anything to do with her."

Ari leaned past Diane to see what she meant. At the end of the barn to their left, Debbie had stopped at a booth selling mohair yarn. Though Debbie seemed to be admiring the yarn, the vendor wasn't looking at her. "You know, this is only going to get worse."

"How?"

"Once the police question everyone, then we'll all be stuck here. All of us suspects."

"You think they'll keep us here in the barn?" Diane asked, surprised.

"I don't know, but they'll want to keep an eye on us."

"What about the out-of-towners?"

Ari began to answer, but at that moment Diane's cell phone rang. While Diane talked to her husband, Joe, Ari turned away to give her some privacy. She was just starting to knit again when she became aware of someone standing near the table. She looked up to see Debbie looming above her.

"Hi," Debbie said brightly. "How's business?"

It was such an odd thing to say that Ari raised her eyebrows. "Slow. What do you think?"

Debbie shrugged. "It's something to talk about. There doesn't seem to be much else."

"For goodness' sake, Debbie."

"Well, is there?" Debbie said challengingly, and suddenly Ari understood. No one was going to talk to Debbie about Felicia.

"Maybe." Ari pulled the other folding chair out from the table. "Here, sit down. You look tired."

Debbie shrugged again and sat down. "Who's that hunky cop?"

"Who do you mean?"

"That detective. He's good-looking."

"Josh?" Ari glanced away. Josh was attractive, with his autumn-colored hair and his deep brown eyes. She'd noticed that about him immediately last fall, though at the time she'd been a murder suspect. "Yes, he is."

"You know him?"

"It's a small town."

"Oh, yes, I'd forgotten. I'd be interested if he didn't think I killed my boss."

"Well, did you?"

The two women stared at each other, and then Debbie grinned. "Don't you know? I thought you were the one who found her."

"She stumbled into me," Ari said, shuddering at the memory. "For what it's worth, I didn't see you around."

"I did a good job of disappearing, didn't I?"

Ari frowned at her. "If you keep talking

like this, they'll really think you did it."

"Oh, la-di-da. How the hell did I pull that off? Knitting needles aren't that sharp."

"I don't know," Ari said. "Apparently with enough force it can happen."

"It has to be someone strong, then," Debbie said, pulling back her sleeve. "Hm. What do you know. Muscles."

Debbie's arm was indeed solid and strong-looking. "Debbie, this isn't the time to be talking like that."

"It's how I talk. Anyway, if I lie they'll trip me up later."

"I'm not talking about lying," Ari said, surprised that Debbie was thinking that far ahead. Most people in her predicament would be scrambling for a way out. "You should probably just keep some of your thoughts to yourself."

"I can't. Never could. I'm not going to change now."

"That must have made working with Felicia hard." Diane said. She had just put her phone away and was leaning forward to look at Debbie.

"Felicia was cool with it."

"Cool with it?" Ari said. "Felicia?"

"Yeah, she was okay."

Ari and Diane exchanged glances. "How was she to work for?"

"She was okay," Debbie repeated, and set her lips. The silence that descended upon them was so uncomfortable that Ari wished she'd never asked Debbie to sit down. She wasn't going to learn anything about the murder this way, she thought.

Sighing, she picked up her needles again. Debbie watched her for a moment and then reached for the design Ari had sketched earlier. "What's this?"

"Just an idea for a coat hanger."

"A lace coat hanger. Are you going to line it?"

Ari glanced at the sketch. "Yes, I think so, or the wood will show through."

"It's an interesting idea."

"Thanks."

"Have you ever thought of writing a book?"

"A book? No. I've got enough to do." Ari worked quietly for a moment. "A book about what?"

"Design. Ideas, and how to work them into something. Turning something ordinary into something unusual. Hell, I don't know. Write about solving knitting murders."

"That's enough." Ari laid down her needles, feeling as if she were talking to her daughter, Megan, rather than to a grown woman. "It's one thing to spout out whatever's on your mind, Debbie, but that's going too far."

"It would sell."

"Oh, for God's sake! I'm sorry I asked you to sit down."

Silence fell again, tense and awkward. "What happens to the magazine now?" Ari asked after a little while.

"Oh, that depends on Felicia's will, and what Winston thinks. Her husband, you know. No." A muscle in her cheek twitched. "Her widower." She jumped up from the chair. "I can't just sit here anymore. How can you two just sit there?"

"What else is there to do?"

"Move around, get some exercise."

Ari watched her go. Debbie's steps were uneven, jittery, and she seemed filled with manic energy as she flitted around the empty Sheep to Shawl pen. Something was wrong, Ari thought.

"Someone didn't take her lithium this morning," Diane muttered.

"Just what I was thinking. She's acting weird."

"Do you think she's bi-polar?"

Ari watched as Debbie, apparently finished examining one of the looms, walked back toward them. "Something's wrong."

"Her boss was killed."

84

"No, beyond that."

"You know, I probably will take over the magazine," Debbie said without preamble as she returned. "I've always wanted to be the boss."

Ari stared at her. Debbie had just confessed to a motive. "I heard you actually run it."

Debbie laughed. "You've been listening to Marley too much. Where is she, anyway?"

"I don't know."

"It doesn't matter. She's a jerk. Felicia had control of that magazine. You'd better believe that."

"Did she really give bad reviews to people who didn't buy ads?" Diane asked.

"No, that's a myth. She was more professional than that. She could be hard on people she didn't like, though."

"That seemed to be everyone," Ari said.

"No. I told you, she wasn't as bad as she seemed. Me, I'm different. I'm an equal opportunity offender. I'm going to insult everyone."

Ari stared at her. "For God's sake, why? You'll make as many enemies as Felicia did."

"I don't think so. I'm funnier than she was."

"If you make fun of people, that won't matter."

"You've got to go by context," Debbie said, suddenly serious. "If I say things in a mean way, of course, I hurt people. But if I praise their work and speak well of them, it won't be so bad. People will be lining up to be insulted by me."

Ari doubted that very much, but it was useless to protest.

Ari's attention was caught by movement near the door. A man wearing a slicker over the unmistakable gray and slate blue uniform of the Massachusetts State Police had come in, and was talking to one of the vendors near the door. *Good. The interviews will go faster now,* she thought.

"So there are the staties," Diane said.

Ari watched as the vendor spoke to the trooper and then pointed across the barn. The trooper nodded, touched the brim of his hat, and began walking across the barn. He was, Ari realized with surprise, coming for her.

Some minutes earlier, the door to Barn A had closed behind Debbie Patrino and the state trooper escorted her to Barn B. Left behind was a short and very angry woman facing the three policemen. "What is this?" she demanded before anyone could speak.

"Mrs. Marley?" Briggs, who with the others had risen, left the table. "I'm Detective Briggs, Massachusetts State Police."

"Yeah? What are you doing here?"

"Well, Mrs. Marley, we thought you'd know about it by now," Charlie said.

"About what?"

"About Felicia Barr's death."

The color leeched from Beth's face, and with it her anger. "What are you talking about? Nothing's happened to Felicia."

Josh moved forward. He didn't know how this woman would react to bad news, but he didn't like her pallor, or the suddenly hunted look on her face. "Mrs. Marley, I'm sorry, but Felicia's dead."

Her eyes, slightly magnified by the thick lenses of her glasses, stared unblinkingly at him. "Dead? You're sure?"

"Yes ma'am."

"She can't be. She can't."

"Here, Mrs. Marley." Josh caught her elbow. Her face was chalky and her hands were shaking. "Sit down. Can I get you some coffee?"

"My God." Beth sank into the fourth chair at the table, staring blindly ahead. "She can't be dead. She's too tough a broad." She looked up. "What was it? Heart attack? Stroke?"

"I'm sorry to tell you this, but she was killed."

"Killed? Felicia? I don't believe it. This is coffee," she said, looking down at the cardboard cup Josh had set before her. "I want tea."

"I'll see if there's any," Josh said, and went back to the snack bar. Of all the people they'd interviewed so far, Beth Marley was the only one showing what he would consider a normal reaction. Yet, by all accounts, she had disliked Felicia intensely.

"I'm sorry, Mrs. Marley." Briggs's voice was surprisingly gentle. "She was stabbed to death."

"Stabbed!" She recoiled. "Are you sure?"

"Yes. With a knitting needle."

"A what?"

"A knitting needle."

"Oh, really! That's plain silly. A needle's not sharp enough for that."

The same thought had occurred to Josh. It was an odd choice of weapon, dull pointed and too thin to have much strength behind it. Yet someone had succeeded.

"But how could it possibly have happened? Felicia wouldn't have let anyone attack her like that," Beth added.

"She was stabbed in the back."

"Was she? Hm."

"You don't sound surprised," Charlie said.

"Oh, I am," she assured them. "Of course, I could have predicted she'd come to a bad end. She wasn't a very nice person, you know."

"We've heard that you had trouble with Mrs. Barr," Josh put in.

Beth had crossed her arms across her chest, ignoring the cup of tea Josh had set before her. "That's something I don't care to talk about."

"We hear you fought with her this morning."

Beth audibly sniffed. "I shouldn't have lowered myself in such a way."

Briggs had sat back and was studying her through narrowed eyes. "Care to tell us about it?"

"No."

"We've heard details from other people," Josh said. "It might help if we heard your side."

"Humph." She glared at them. "I'd rather not talk about that woman ever again."

The three policemen cast each other quick looks. If they hadn't realized it earlier, Beth's posture told them how reluctant, and difficult, a witness she would be. So did her mouth, clamped together in a tight, petulant pout. Maybe, Josh thought, it's time for a different approach.

"Ma'am, we need to know where you were," Briggs said, as if he had read Josh's mind. "Why did you leave the fairgrounds?"

She wrinkled her nose at her tea. "I was not about to eat here."

"Then you went to find someplace else for lunch?" Josh said.

"Of course." She fixed him with that glare again. "Does this strike you as a particularly pleasant place to eat? The atmosphere is horrible, of course, and all they had were greasy hamburgers. I wouldn't be caught dead in a place like this."

No one said a thing. The silence hung heavily, and yet Beth seemed unaware of what she had just said. "Where did you go?" Josh asked.

"A seafood restaurant. The Freeport Chowder House, I believe it's called. I had a lobster salad roll and a passable cup of chowder."

"Passable?" Josh said, diverted in spite of himself. The Freeport Chowder House arguably had the best seafood chowder in the area, and had won awards at various cook-offs.

"It didn't have tomatoes and the broth was too thick. Far too much dill, and far too much cream. Not at all what I'm used to."

Before Josh could protest that New England chowder, rather than the Manhattan style, was the real thing, Charlie pointed out, "We can check that easy enough."

"What time did you leave here?" Briggs asked.

"I don't know. I wasn't watching the time. Perhaps around eleven."

"And you went directly to the restaurant."

Beth hesitated. "I heard there's a good yarn shop in town. I stopped to see it first."

"Ariadne's Web?" Josh asked.

"Yes, that's it."

"Now, why would you want to see more yarn, Mrs. Marley, after being here?" Charlie said.

Beth stared at him. "Surely you're not serious."

"It doesn't make sense, ma'am, for you to leave one place with yarn to go to another," Briggs put in.

"It's a yarn shop," she said, sounding exasperated.

"There's yarn here."

"Yes. Lamb's wool, sheep's wool, llama. Hand spun, hand dyed, spun by the last mule-spinning factory in America."

"Excuse me?"

"In Maine," she said, as if that explained everything. "This is a *wool* festival. There's

91

no silk here, no cotton, no imports. Nothing interesting. I visit yarn shops wherever I go. Ariadne's Web looked attractive." Her voice was grudging. "Very bright inside, though I wonder if all those windows fade the yarn. All in all, a very nice shop for a town this size."

"I see," Briggs said, though by the look on his face he didn't. Josh understood, though. Through Ari he'd learned about knitters' passion for yarn. Of course Beth would want to visit a yarn shop. He suspected other participants at the festival did, too. "Did you go in?"

"Oh no. I will have to, though, before I write my article."

"What article?" Josh asked. For a few minutes he'd forgotten that Beth worked for a knitting magazine.

"Our readers like hearing of new yarn shops." She made a face. "My editor wants an article about small wool festivals."

That explained why Beth was here, though the fact that her former boss had also been in attendance was awfully coincidental. "Why didn't you go into the shop?"

"It's raining, in case you haven't noticed, and there wasn't an open parking space. I'll try again this afternoon, when it's less crowded."

Briggs frowned. "Mrs. Marley, I don't think you understand the seriousness of what's happened here."

"Of course I do," she said scornfully. "But I was gone, so surely you can see I had nothing to do with it."

"Did anyone see you outside the yarn shop?"

"I doubt it."

Briggs sat back, his face impassive. Josh suspected he didn't want to come out with any accusation just yet. "What time was it when you got to the restaurant?" he asked.

"Eleven forty-five," she said promptly. "I saw a clock in the lobby."

Since it was now around one, that sounded right, allowing time for Beth to eat and then return to the festival. "Did you come right back here?"

"Yes." Beth frowned around at them. "Who's in charge here?"

"I am," Briggs said. "Why?"

"Then, for God's sake, *you* ask me the questions and stop tag-teaming me!"

"We're questioning everyone, Mrs. Marley. We have to find out what happened to Mrs. Barr. What did you fight about with her this morning?"

"If someone else told you about it, then you know already."

93

"We don't know all of it. Wouldn't you like to tell your side?" Charlie asked, deceptively genial.

Beth's lips were so tightly set that her skin showed white around them. "I want a lawyer. Are there any good ones in this hick town?"

Damn it, Josh thought. "We'll get you a phone book."

"Ha. An ambulance chaser? No, I'm going to call my own lawyer." She stood up. "Can I go now?"

Briggs and Charlie exchanged looks, and then rose. "For the moment," Briggs said. "Trooper Lopes will bring you back to Barn B."

"I can get there myself, thank you."

"Regardless, he'll go with you. Lopes? Take Mrs. Marley to the other barn."

Lopes stepped forward. "Yes sir," he said, and looked down at Beth. "Ma'am?"

"Oh, all right," she snapped, and flounced out of the building, completely ignoring the trooper. The door slammed shut, and she was gone.

Josh wasn't the only one of the men to let out a harsh, exasperated sigh. "That ends that," he said.

"For now." Briggs sat down. "Have you constructed a time line yet?"

Charlie shook his head. "Only a preliminary one. There's been too much to handle."

"I'll get someone started on it." Briggs tapped his pen against his lips. "The main person we need to talk to is Ms. Evans."

"Yeah," Josh said after a moment. He knew full well that Ari hadn't killed Felicia, and yet he had to admit that the circumstances were suspicious. Of course she would have to be questioned, if only to shed more light on the morning's events. "I'll get her."

Briggs had just finished using his walkietalkie. "They've handled ten people so far in the mobile unit," he said.

"Anything?"

"No. All vouched for."

"Still a lot left," Charlie said.

Briggs looked at the clock. "Did anyone order food for the others?" he asked.

"One of my officers did, a while ago." Charlie looked at Josh. "Are you going?"

"Yeah," Josh said, and, putting on his jacket, went out. Ari, he thought, was in for it.

CHAPTER 5

One by one, the Sheep to Shawl participants had left the barn in the company of a state trooper to be questioned. One by one, they returned and began packing up their belongings under the envious stares of those still left. "And then there were none," Ari murmured.

"What?" Diane said.

"Nothing. Just that we're being picked off one by one."

"Strange way to put it." Diane picked up a sub sandwich from its nest of white paper and took a bite. "It's about time they fed us," she said, with her mouth full.

"I know. Marty's must be doing a huge business because of us," Ari said, referring to the town's deli/convenience store from which the police had ordered the sandwiches.

"Because of the food or the gossip?"

"Both," Ari said. The news of what had

happened at the festival had to be common knowledge by now. Marty's was a prime gathering place in Freeport, and a prime location to spread gossip.

"I wish I had a bowl of kale soup instead. Can you imagine it? Not Marty's, but my mother's. Big pieces of linguica, kidney beans, chunks of potatoes —"

"Stop it," Ari said, looking now with disfavor at her cold-cut sub. She glanced over at Beth Marley. Since coming into the barn Beth had sat in the far corner near the fleeces, as far away from anyone as possible. She looked extremely disgruntled. "I'd like to know where she's been all this time."

"Who, Beth?" Diane looked toward her, too. "One thing's for certain. She's not going anywhere soon."

"No, and we aren't, either."

"They haven't questioned me yet."

Ari looked toward the door, where a state trooper stood guard. "No, but they will."

"At least you've got someone on your side — that policeman of yours."

"I wish you wouldn't talk about him in that way, Di."

"Why shouldn't I? He treated Joe and me rotten last year."

"I know." Ari sighed. She could understand Diane's attitude, but it made her life

97

difficult. If she ever developed a relationship with Josh, and that was a big *if,* she would be caught between him and her best friend.

"What's going on between you and him, anyway?" Diane asked, as if she'd read Ari's mind.

"Not much." Ari rested her chin on her fist. "We haven't gone out together in a long time."

"Why not?"

Ari shrugged, though it was something she didn't fully understand, either. "I don't know. Things get in the way. Either he has to work, or I have Megan, or something comes up."

"There are ways around stuff like that. Do you like him?"

"Of course I do. He's a nice guy."

"C'mon, Ari, you know what I mean. Do you *like* him?"

"I think I do," Ari said after a moment. "I'm not sure that matters, though."

"What do you mean?"

"I don't know how he really feels about me. To tell you the truth, I'm not sure about myself. I'm kind of enjoying not having to answer to anyone anymore." She rested her chin on her fist. "Being married to Ted was difficult. You know that."

"I know." Diane was quiet for a minute. "He was always working."

Ari shook her head. "No, that was only part of it. All that anger." She looked at Diane. "I know that's how he expresses his emotions, but it's hard to live with. I had to get out, for Megan's sake, if not my own. I don't think I'm ready for anything serious just yet."

"Who said it has to be serious?" Diane asked

Ari turned to look at her. "If you don't like him, Di, why are you pushing this?"

Diane picked at the unspun wool on her table with a fingernail. "Just because I don't like him doesn't mean he's not a decent guy."

"He thought he had a good reason to arrest Joe," Ari said, bringing up a dangerous subject.

"Ha."

"He did. He *is* a decent man, Di. I wish you could like him."

Diane shrugged. "Well, all I know is you deserve someone good, after Ted."

"Mm." She frowned. "You know, Di, there's something holding Josh back. It's not just me, you know."

"Well, give him a kick in the butt, then."

"Di, honestly."

"You know what I mean." Diane's face was serious again. "Maybe all he needs is a push."

"I don't know. I think I'll just let things run their course."

"Then nothing'll ever happen. Ha! Here's your chance."

"What?" Ari asked, and then saw Josh coming into the barn. "Oh."

"He's coming over," Diane said. "Go to it, girl."

Ari wanted to kick her, and yet when she looked up at Josh she was smiling more brightly than usual. The thought flickered through her mind that Diane was right. She'd better make a move if she wanted any kind of a relationship with Josh. It didn't look like he'd be the one to make the first move. "Hi. Thanks for sending us lunch."

Josh blinked. "Uh, yeah. You had to eat."

"Diane wanted kale soup," she went on, still smiling.

"Yeah. It's a good day for soup." His eyes flicked toward Ari, and in them she thought she saw concern. "Ari, can I have a word with you?"

"Of course."

"Not here. In Barn A."

"Oh." Ari's happiness faded. Josh wasn't here to see her, at least not personally. He was investigating a murder. She shouldn't have forgotten that. "Of course."

"More questions, Detective?" Diane said.

"We're talking to everyone."

"I thought you talked to Ari already."

"Oh, please," Ari said, before she could become an excuse for a full-blown quarrel. "I told you the police would want to talk to me again." She shrugged into her parka. "I'll see you in a few minutes, Di."

"I hope so."

Ari huffed out her breath as she walked away with Josh. "I have told you everything I know, though," she said.

"Detective Briggs wants to talk to you," he said.

"Who?"

"State cop," he said as they walked out into the storm. By the time they reached Barn A, Ari's hair was damp again and the hems of her jeans were soaked through. And all because of Felicia Barr, whom she suddenly resented with an irrational intensity.

"Ari," Chief Mason said, rising from one of the tables near the snack bar. "Come and sit down. Wet out there, eh?"

"Hi, Chief. A little." Ari unzipped her parka and sat down. "How's it going?"

"Okay. Ari, this is Detective William Briggs, of the state police. He's helping us with the investigation."

"Detective." Ari shook the man's hand, taking him in with a swift, comprehensive glance. A good, if conservative suit, military bearing, ice blue eyes. He was not a man to take lightly.

"Ms. Evans." He sat across from her, his gaze never leaving her face. "I want to go over a few things with you."

"Of course." She sat back, hoping she presented a picture of relaxation. "What do you want to know?"

He seemed to want to know everything, she thought a few minutes later, reeling from the barrage of questions. What time did she leave the main barn to go to the snack bar? Did she see anyone on the way? Did she talk to anyone in the barn? Who? And what time was that? Did she have to wait for the coffee? What time was it when she went back out? Did she see anyone? When did she realize Felicia had been hurt?

"When she collapsed on me," Ari snapped. "You know all this."

"Ms. Evans, we need to —"

"Ask me these questions. I know. Been there, done that."

"I was going to say that we need to understand what happened," Briggs said. "You're in a position to help us."

"Oh." Though there was no reproach in Briggs's face or manner, Ari felt chastened by his very calmness. "I'm sorry. This isn't easy."

Briggs didn't acknowledge her apology, but continued, "You didn't see the knitting needle when she was walking toward you."

"It was in her back, and she was walking toward me. I couldn't."

"You're sure there was no one else around? Think about it," he said before she could answer. "Think about what you were doing. Try to see it again."

"I can't help but see it," she said frankly. "It's not something I'm likely to forget."

"You've just left the snack bar. You have two cups of coffee. How did you open the door to get out?"

"Someone opened it for me."

"From the inside or outside?"

"Outside," she said, surprised she hadn't remembered that detail before. So someone could corroborate where she'd been in the minutes before Felicia's death. "A man. I don't know who he was."

"Can you describe him?"

She frowned. "I only saw him for a second. Middle-aged, I'd say not fat, wearing a green parka. I think he might have been a vendor in here."

"Would you know him again?"

"Yes."

"Now, why would a vendor from Barn A be outside?" Briggs said reflectively. "He wouldn't have had to go out for coffee or to use the bathroom."

"I don't know. Maybe he went to his car? I don't know."

"Did you see which direction he came from?"

"He opened the door as I was going out, Detective. How would I know that?"

He nodded again. "Okay. You come out of this barn. The main door or the side?"

"The main door."

"Why? The side door is closer to Barn B."

"I don't know." She gave a little smile. "I think I wanted to look at everything again."

Briggs nodded and jotted something down in his notebook. "What did you see when you went out?"

"Rain."

"Think about your answer, Ms. Evans."

"I am," she protested. "It was pouring, and I put my head down right away."

"You were facing toward the parking lot."

"Yes, but I didn't really look at it."

"So you didn't see anyone near any cars?"

"No. All I wanted to do was get back to the other barn."

"Okay." He shifted in his chair. "Let's try something. Close your eyes."

"All right," she said.

"Now, go back to this morning. You've just come out of this building. What do you see? Don't answer right away. Try to really see it."

"I'm looking at the field across the road," she said after a minute. "The grass is already green. And farther back are all the cars and trucks."

"Anyone stand out?"

"No. No, wait. I did see someone getting into a car." She opened her eyes, frowning. "There was a car just pulling in, too. A green minivan. Wow." She looked at him. "I didn't know I saw so much."

"So now, you've turned left and you're heading toward Barn B. What do you see?"

"Mud," she said promptly. "I was looking down."

"Before that?"

"Well, I saw the barn, of course, and the other buildings beyond it, but that was all."

"You didn't see Mrs. Barr?"

"No." She frowned again. "That's odd. Where did she come from? Even if I had my head down, I should have seen her."

"Could she have come from between the two buildings?" Charlie asked.

Ari thought about that. "I don't know. I was headed straight for Barn B — no." She frowned. "Barn B is set farther back from the lane than this building, so I was actually going at an angle. I thought Felicia was heading right at me, but she wasn't. She was directly in front of the barn. She had to have come from somewhere else."

"Where do you think she came from?"

"I don't know."

"Where were you in relation to the buildings? Closer to Barn A or Barn B?"

"I think I'd just reached the corner of Barn B." She looked up. "She couldn't have come from in between. We were in front of Barn B."

"And yet no one saw her," Briggs said, more to himself than to the others.

"No," Ari agreed. "She didn't come from a car, either, because then she would have been to my right. Oh, I don't know."

"It's okay, Ari," Charlie said. "You're doing fine."

Briggs nodded shortly. "What happened when you did see her?"

"I noticed she was stumbling. I think I said her name, and then she was on me. That was when I saw the needle. Aluminum, orchid color, size nine, and not a new one, either."

That got the others' attention. "Why do you say that?"

"The button at the end of it was made of steel."

"So?"

"That's the old-fashioned style. Round and flat — flattened, I should say — with the size on the end. The newer ones have plastic buttons that are squarish, and the sizes are on the side."

"An older needle," Briggs said musingly. "Where would someone find one of those?"

"Oh, they're not unusual, Detective. People don't get rid of their needles. Well, no, that's not necessarily true."

"Why not?"

"A few years ago there wasn't much choice in needles, at least around here. There was aluminum or plastic, even in yarn catalogs. But now you can get wooden ones again, or bamboo, or even handmade ones with blown-glass caps. I carry those. They're lovely, one of a kind, and they sell well."

"Didn't some of the vendors here sell needles?" Charlie asked.

"Yes, a few of them."

"Apart from the needle, what else did you notice?" Briggs asked.

"She said something about mud." She

frowned, trying to think. "She said, 'I tried to get the mud.' "

"She tried to get the mud?"

"Yes."

"What does that mean?"

"I don't know. I remember thinking earlier that she must have had trouble walking with those boots."

"And that was all she said?"

"Yes."

Briggs sat back. "Is there anything else you can tell us?"

Ari sat, head down. It had all happened so fast, and had been such a shock, that she'd lost awareness of all else. Yet, she realized now, shock had also implanted odd details on her mind. She didn't remember noticing Felicia's perfume, but now she could almost smell it. Chanel No 5. She hadn't remembered the fine gold chain Felicia wore, or the large mole on her neck. She felt again the softness of Felicia's sweater, saw the fine gauge of the knit, and was struck by a sudden realization.

"Did you find her coat?" she asked, opening her eyes.

Briggs glanced quickly at the other men. "Was she wearing a coat?"

"Earlier she was. Black cashmere."

"First I've heard of it," Charlie said.

"The first you've heard?" Briggs glared at him. "How's that?"

"The EMTs were working on her when we got here," Josh said.

"And no one noticed that she didn't have a coat on, in this weather?" Briggs pulled out his walkie-talkie, barked some orders into it, and then put it away. His face was thunderous. "Anything else?" he said to Ari.

Ari was almost sorry she'd mentioned the coat. Before the atmosphere had been if not relaxed, at least comfortable. But now there was tension between the men in the room. Of course, not looking for Felicia's coat, or even realizing it was missing, was a big blunder. It probably had set the investigation back. "Yes," she said, almost meekly, because there was one other detail she'd just remembered. "There was a piece of yarn on her shoulder."

"Yarn?" Briggs turned again to the other men. "Was there yarn on her?" he demanded.

Josh shook his head. "Not when I saw her. It probably fell off her into the mud somewhere."

Briggs nodded. "We'll look for it. What kind of yarn, Ms. Evans?"

Ari visualized the strand, bright against the black of Felicia's sweater. "Light blue

DK," she said.

"Excuse me?"

"Oh, I'm sorry. DK means 'double-knit.' It's a sport-weight yarn . . . Relatively thin," she added at their mystified looks. "It has a little fuzz on it, but not much. It may have been wool. I'm not sure."

"Would you know it if you saw it again?"

"Of course," she said, surprised.

"Hm. Anyone here selling yarn like that?"

"I don't know. A lot of people here were spinning or knitting. I have two projects with me."

"We'll look for it," Briggs said, dismissing the half-formed plan in Ari's mind to search for the yarn herself. She wasn't part of the police team. She wouldn't be part of the investigation. Briggs wouldn't allow it.

At that moment she met Josh's eyes. He looked steadily back at her, and she thought she understood what he was trying to communicate. Who better than she to find the yarn, after all? Certainly the police would look, but she'd recognize it immediately.

Ari gave a tiny nod, and then looked away. "Are you done with me?"

"Not yet." Briggs regarded her coolly. "You knew Mrs. Barr before this, didn't you?"

"Yes, but not well. I've already told Detective Pierce about it."

"I've heard she wasn't a friendly woman."

"She wasn't, but I had no reason to dislike her personally. I hadn't seen her in years before today."

"When did you last see her?"

"When I lived in New York, before I was married."

"You've had no contact with her since?"

"No."

"No ads in her magazine?"

"No."

"No articles?"

"No, nothing." Ari crossed her arms. "Detective, are you accusing me of something?"

Briggs shrugged, and then rose. "I think we're done for now."

"For now?"

"We might need to talk to you again."

Ari sighed. She knew what that meant. In Briggs's eyes, she was still a suspect. "What happens now, then?"

"I'll bring you back to the barn," Josh said. He stood beside her, holding her parka.

"Thank you," Ari said, and went out the door with Josh, both drained and relieved.

While Josh, along with Charlie Mason and Detective Briggs, questioned Ari, other interrogations were taking place in the crime van. About the size of a motor home, the van was painted blue and slate gray — the colors of the Massachusetts State Police — and was large enough to accommodate multiple witness interviews simultaneously. Paul Bouchard, Josh's colleague and fellow detective, was in charge of this phase of the investigation.

As Paul supervised one interview after another, he realized most of the festival participants had nothing to do with Felicia's death. They could prove where they were when she died, they hadn't seen Felicia before her death, they hadn't seen anyone approach her, and they certainly hadn't seen her killed. Many of the participants had never even heard of Felicia until learning of her murder, and so one by one they were allowed to leave until there were only a few suspects left.

Nancy Moniz and Rosalia Sylvia, both local residents, remained suspects because neither could prove their whereabouts at the time of Felicia's murder. Nancy claimed she'd been in her car at the time of Felicia's death, calling her son on her cell phone. Though the call records on her cell phone proved that the phone had been used at that time, the police couldn't prove she'd actually talked with anyone. Unlikely a suspect as she was, Nancy still couldn't be ruled out.

Rosalia told the police she had been between buildings at the time of the murder. That in itself was suspicious since she should have seen Felicia if she was outside, but she claimed she hadn't seen anything in the pouring rain. Though she had no known connection to Felicia, Paul still considered Rosalia a suspect and asked her to return to Barn B along with Nancy Moniz.

Paul's attempt to question Beth Marley further proved fruitless, too. Beth still refused to say anything without first talking with her lawyer in New Jersey, but she couldn't seem to reach him on the phone. Instead she sat across from Paul with her arms folded and a scowl on her face. His repeated attempts to question her were met with silence. Annoying as this was, there was nothing the police could do about it but continue to hold her with the other suspects. They couldn't force her to talk if she didn't want to.

Lauren Dubrowski was another matter. From the start of her interview, she told Paul that she had nothing to hide and freely admitted that she'd disliked Felicia, who had been critical of her work. Lauren had managed to secure a good job in spite of that criticism, though, and she claimed to have no motive. Paul had seen people killed for less reason and remained skeptical about Lauren's protested innocence. Lauren still had to be considered a suspect, he decided, and he sent her back to Barn B.

During his interview with Annie Walker, Paul realized she was the first person he'd spoken with who had anything good to say about Felicia. Annie admitted her designs were to be featured in an upcoming issue of *Knit It Up!* and that she believed Felicia had liked them. At least, she amended, Felicia had accepted them. Now she wasn't sure what would happen or if the magazine would even still be published. For Annie, Felicia's death was a blow, but Paul decided she should still be detained since her business relationship with the victim ought to be explored further.

Finally there was Diane. Though Paul took his duties seriously and questioned her at length, he had known Diane for too many years to consider her a true suspect. She explained that she'd sneaked out of the barn for a forbidden cigarette and didn't have any personal connection to Felicia, but since nobody had seen her or could vouch for her whereabouts at the time of the murder, Paul was forced to keep her in the suspect pool.

When the last festival participant left the van, Paul stared down at the notes he'd taken, pinching tiredly at the bridge of his nose. He would make a verbal report to the chief, who would decide whether the detained suspects should be questioned further. Paul reminded himself that people tended to hold back information, though not always deliberately, and that sometimes one little fact that was considered unimportant could prove crucial to solving a case.

His cell phone buzzed, and he flipped it open. "Bouchard. Yes. What did you find? Where?" he asked, and picked up his pencil. "Okay. Yeah, I'll tell the chief," he said, and ended the call. He immediately dialed the chief's number. This, he thought as he looked at the note he'd scribbled, was the kind of information he liked. They had something concrete to work with at last.

Outside the rain had let up a bit, so that Ari and Josh didn't have to dash to the barn.

"Look, don't worry," Josh said. "We know you didn't do anything. I think Briggs does, too."

"He didn't sound like it. He's lucky Ted's not here."

Josh chuckled, and then grew serious.

115

"Yeah. But we screwed up."

She turned, though the hood of her parka blocked her view. "The coat?"

"The coat," he agreed. "That was stupid. We should have realized she had one."

They walked in silence for a moment, their feet squelching in the mud. "Is it important?"

"Of course it is. Why wasn't she wearing it, in this weather? When we find it, it might tell us where she was attacked."

"There'll be clues, then."

"Evidence. Yes, I hope so."

"What about the other needle?"

"We're looking for it, but no luck yet."

"It could be hidden in plain sight."

"What do you mean?"

"Well, think. How many people here are knitters? It'd be easy to hide one needle among many."

"Not if it doesn't have a match. Here we are."

They had reached the entrance to Barn B. Ari, looking in, saw that it was much emptier than it had been. Of those who were left, a number were packing their belongings. "So many people are gone," she said.

Josh, hands in pockets, nodded. "There wasn't any reason to hold most of them."

"What are the reasons, Josh?"

"If they can't account for their time, and if they had any contact with Mrs. Barr."

"Such as?"

"Acquaintance, ads in the magazine, articles, anything."

"I wouldn't think too many people here would fit."

He shrugged. "Maybe. Listen, Ari."

"What?"

"About that yarn."

"Josh, I'd recognize it if I saw it."

"I know. I don't want you to go looking for it, but . . ."

"But if I see it, I'll tell you."

"Yeah. Be careful, though. I don't want you to be another victim."

"Of course I'll be careful. Detective Briggs doesn't want me involved, does he?"

Josh shook his head. "No, I — excuse me," he said as his cell phone rang. He flipped it open and turned away from her. "Detective Pierce," he said. "Yes. What? Where?"

The urgency in Josh's voice made Ari stop walking. He was standing tense, alert, frowning as he listened to the caller on the phone. Dread filled Ari. Had someone else been hurt?

At that moment Josh snapped his phone shut. "I have to go."

"What is it? Is someone hurt?"

117

"No." He pulled up his hood, hesitated, and then turned to her. "You might as well know. They found the coat."

CHAPTER 6

Ari watched Josh walk out the door of Barn B after he had told her about Felicia's coat feeling oddly abandoned. Before her the barn stretched cavernous, with most of the vendors gone, and the Sheep to Shawl pen empty. Except for Annie Walker, still tucked into her corner, the few people left were clustered in the middle of the barn near a vendor's table. Diane was nowhere in sight. Sighing, Ari began to walk to her table. Halfway there, though, she changed direction. The last thing she wanted right now was to be alone.

"Mind if I join you?" she said, pulling a chair over to the group of women. She wasn't surprised to see Debbie Patrino there, or a disgruntled Beth Marley, sitting a bit apart from the others.

"Sure." Debbie moved to make room for her. "Have they been rough on you?"

Ari shook her head. She wasn't about to

tell them what her real role in the investigation was. "No, not bad. Nancy, what are you doing here?" she asked the young woman sitting beyond Debbie. "You weren't in here before. And Rosalia? You don't have anything to do with this, do you?"

Nancy Moniz, a local spinner who had come to the festival to sell fleeces, grimaced. "They want to ask us both some more questions."

"What? But neither of you knew Felicia, did you?"

"I didn't, but I can't prove where I was when she was killed."

"Where were you?"

"Out in my van calling my son. I couldn't hear a thing in here, with the rain on the roof."

"And I was a customer," Rosalia Sylvia said, looking up from the sock she was knitting. Like Nancy, she was a local. Ari didn't know her very well, but she couldn't imagine that Rosalia had killed Felicia. But then, she couldn't imagine that anyone here was a murderer.

"Yes, I remember seeing you at my table," Ari said. "Why are you still here?"

"I was between buildings when everything happened," she said. "Of course no one noticed me."

"So we're both stuck," Nancy said.

Ari looked at her. "They can check your cell phone records for the call, can't they?"

"Yes, for what that's worth. I didn't reach him, so he can't back me up. The little brat. He was supposed to stay home today and study. He flunked his last history test, can you imagine? I could kill him." She stopped abruptly. "I didn't mean that."

"Of course not," Ari said. "Everyone says things like that at one time or another."

Nancy sighed. "True. Anyway, I decided to bring in more fleeces. Then I heard the sirens and saw the ambulance, so I decided to leave them there."

Ari sighed. The fleeces would have given Nancy an alibi of sorts, since it would be hard to kill someone with arms filled with unprocessed wool. Without them, she had no proof of where she had been. "They would have made you noticeable."

"With everything that was happening? I don't think so. Anyway, it's just as well I didn't bring them in." She glanced toward the bins. "I'm not going to sell any now."

"None of us will sell anything now," a voice behind Ari said.

Ari turned to see the woman who had lent her the afghan earlier. "I'm sorry," she said. "I don't remember your name."

"It's okay. There was a lot going on this morning. I'm Lauren Dubrowski."

Ari took the hand Lauren held out. "Nice to meet you. Let me guess. You can't account for your time, either."

"No. I had to go to the bathroom. The man behind me watched the table for me."

"I've never seen a place where so many people left the tables where they're selling things," Ari said. Especially at the time when Felicia had been killed, she added to herself.

"Why don't you bring your stuff over and sit with us?" Debbie asked her. "We're calling ourselves the Suspects Club."

"Humph." This was from Beth, but other than that she made no sound.

"All right. I'll go get my knitting. I might as well keep busy," Ari said, and got up.

Ari put her printed designs into a folder and packed her samples into sweater bags. She'd have liked to bring the samples to her car, but the police weren't letting anyone out.

Ari glanced at the far corner, where Annie still sat alone. Putting her things down, Ari walked over to her. "Hi, Annie. How are you doing?"

"How do you think?" Annie said, not looking up.

"This is hard on everyone. Have you been interviewed yet?"

"Yes."

"Oh. Let me guess. You can't prove where you were, right?"

"I was here." Annie's glare was fierce. "Not that anyone noticed me. They put me in a crappy spot back here. People couldn't see me because the spinners were in the way."

"Oh," Ari said, a bit taken aback. Annie had been much friendlier this morning. "A lot of people have to stay for similar reasons."

"Yeah." Annie threw the yarn over her needle without first picking up a stitch. Ari frowned. It would create a hole in the work. Looking closer, though, Ari saw that the yarn over was deliberate, a part of a lacy design. "That's pretty. What are you using?"

"An angora and wool blend." Annie worked in silence for a moment, as if Ari wasn't even there, and then stopped to count her stitches. She was using a circular needle, Ari noted, probably because the shawl was too big to fit onto two regular needles.

"Is it a shawl?"

"Yes." Annie turned her work, began knitting the next row, and then, somewhat

123

reluctantly, held it up. It *was* pretty, Ari thought. The center of the triangular design was made up of lacy shells with a scalloped border.

"That's really nice," Ari said. "Did you design it?"

"Designs by Annie," she said as she had this morning, but with a hint of a smile.

"Oh, how stupid of me," Ari said with just a bit of sarcasm.

That brought a full-blown smile from Annie, who finally looked up. "Sorry." She laid the shawl down in her lap. "But this whole thing sucks. My only contact with Felicia was positive. I don't want to stay here."

"None of us do. Why don't you join us? At least you'll have company."

"Maybe."

"Come on. We're all part of the Suspects Club."

Annie glared at her. "That's not funny!"

"Sometimes if you don't laugh, you cry," Ari said after a moment, regretting the invitation. Annie's prickly character wouldn't cheer anyone up. "Well, all right, then. Maybe we'll talk later."

"Wait!" Annie called as Ari began to walk away.

Ari turned. "What is it?"

Annie bit her lip, and then began stuffing

her work into a tapestry bag. "I'll come with you."

"Okay," Ari said, wondering why Annie had refused in the first place.

"I'm sorry. I didn't mean to be rude," Annie said as she reached Ari. "This has me upset."

"We're all upset," Ari said, more gently than she had planned. But then, something about Annie drew that out of her. Somehow she looked fragile. "Why don't you go over, and I'll be there in a minute."

Annie looked uncertainly toward the group. "Do you think they'll mind?"

Ari blinked in surprise. "Why would they mind?"

"I don't know."

"They're nice people. Mostly," she added. "Go on. I'll be right there."

"All right," Annie said, and Ari headed back to her own table. She felt infinitely older than Annie, though she knew the woman couldn't be that much younger than her.

Ari had just bent down for her knitting bag when Diane showed up. "Where have you been?" Ari asked, straightening.

"In the state police van, being questioned."

"How did it go?"

"I don't have a connection with Felicia, so that helps. But, boy, did they grill me about where I was and what I saw." She grimaced. "Pretty expensive cigarette."

"I told you to quit smoking."

"Yeah, yeah, little Miss Perfect. Joe's gonna freak when he hears I was questioned."

Ari stared at her. "Haven't you told him?"

"No, not yet. I don't want him to worry until he absolutely has to."

"You're innocent, Di."

"So? That doesn't always mean anything. I swear, Ari, if that cop of yours had questioned me —"

"Well, he didn't. I'm on the hot spot, too, you know. So are they." She gestured toward the other women. "Debbie's calling us the Suspects Club."

"She would. What's wrong with her, Ari? She's acting weird."

"I know. So is Beth."

"I mean, the police'll suspect her just on her actions."

"I know, but I don't know her, Di. She might be like this all the time."

"Yeah." As Ari had done earlier, Diane glanced around the barn. "Is this all that's left of everyone?"

"Yes."

"They're a motley crew, aren't they?"

Ari nodded, though she really hadn't given the others a good look until now. There was short, plump Beth Marley in her expensive but dowdy-looking black coat. There was Debbie, tall and thin with red hair spilling over her shoulders, who was once again pacing back and forth with manic energy and gesturing as she talked. Nancy Moniz sat near the others on a folding chair in front of a spinning wheel, but she was ignoring the wheel as she gazed down at her complicated-looking digital camera, apparently viewing pictures she had taken that day.

"You know Nancy," Ari said to Diane, gesturing at the woman with the camera. She'd noticed that Nancy had recently dyed her hair ash blond, to cover the gray hair that was coming in even though she was only around Ari's age. "She was out getting more fleeces when Felicia was killed."

"I wish I had room for as many sheep as she does," Diane commented. "But jeez, what about Rosalia? Why is she here?" Rosalia wore a heavy Icelandic sweater, Ari noticed, with her dark hair pulled back in a ponytail. She sat at the front of the table.

"She was a customer, caught in the wrong place at the wrong time," Ari said. "She doesn't have any connection to Felicia that I know of. And that's Annie Walker sitting next to her. She's the dealer from Buffalo."

"So that's everyone?"

"Except for you and me. The Suspects Club."

"Oh, come on, Ari. We didn't kill Felicia."

"As I said, the Suspects Club."

Diane stared at her. "You're kidding."

"No."

"You think one of them —"

"Killed Felicia? Yes."

"Ari, the murderer could be gone already."

"I'm sure the police checked to see if a car left at the right time."

"If they can't figure out where we were, how would they know that?"

Ari shrugged. It was true. How many people would have paid attention to a car leaving the fairgrounds after Felicia's death? "If someone did leave, it meant leaving her things behind."

"Unless the killer's a customer."

Ari shuddered at the thought of what that would mean to the investigation, and to them. "Don't even think it. No, Di, I think the murderer is here in this barn."

Barn C, not used for the festival, was small, set back from the lane and nestled between

Barn B and Barn D, where the sheep pens were. What little light there was came from a small cobwebbed window in the back wall and the open front door. It gave faint illumination to a gloomy, grimy interior, a small central space surrounded by low railings. Another door, this one closed, was set in the side wall. A faint, earthy aroma hinting at the barn's former occupants permeated everything. Except for the white-suited crime-scene technicians searching each pen and dusting for fingerprints, the barn was empty. And while it was bare of any equipment, there was one item that had caught everyone's attention. Hanging on the back wall was a black cashmere coat.

"The main door was locked," Briggs said. He stood just inside the door, along with Charlie and Josh, watching the technicians work. "Apparently the wool festival people didn't need this barn. Not surprising it got overlooked."

"Any thoughts why Felicia left her coat here?" Charlie asked.

Briggs nodded. "There's dried mud near the hem. From all reports Mrs. Barr was neat and well dressed. I can't imagine she'd want her coat to be dirty."

"So she took it off to clean it, and she hung it there to make it easier," Josh said, and frowned. "Why here, though, and how did she get in if the door was locked?"

Briggs shook his head. "The trooper who found it asked the manager for a key to get in. As to why here? Maybe she was lured here."

Josh studied the barn again. In the dim light, he couldn't see any signs of a struggle. The barn floor was made of hard-packed earth, embedded with ancient wisps of straw that looked as if they hadn't been disturbed since the barn was built. This building hadn't been used for a while. "Why wasn't this barn used for the festival?"

"They didn't need it. The three barns were enough. Also it was too small for shearing sheep."

"I wonder if anyone else asked for the key."

Charlie looked at him. "You're thinking this is where the stabbing took place?"

"Maybe," Josh said. "Look at the location. It's just on the other side of Barn B and it's set back, but it's also not far from where Felicia collapsed. I'd say this is it."

"I agree," Briggs said, and Charlie nodded. "I doubt we'll get any evidence, though, except for the coat."

"There's no blue yarn," Josh said, shaking his head. "Either the murderer picked up any stray pieces or she didn't know there was a strand on Felicia's sweater."

"Probably the latter."

"Probably." Josh looked closer at the coat, careful not to touch it. Close up, he could see several strands of light hair on it, as well as the bits of lint that a black coat would attract. He crouched down to study the dried mud, glancing first at the floor and frowning. There were signs, if faint, that something had disturbed the dirt of the floor near the coat. It was very slightly lighter in color, and smoother, as if something had been brushed across it. The hem of the coat maybe? Looking up, he saw that there was, indeed, a slight coating of dust at the bottom of the coat. He filed that observation away for future study, and turned his attention to the patch of dried mud on the coat. It was small, but if Felicia had been as meticulous as everyone said, she certainly would have wanted to clean it off. This barn might have seemed as good a place as any to her, except for one thing. How had she gotten in?

Still crouching, Josh glanced down the aisle formed by the low railings toward the side door and frowned. From this angle he could see any disturbances that had been made in the dirt floor. There were marks from the troopers' boots, but, more important, he could see tiny indentations as well.

"Detective Briggs," he said, and rose. "Come here a minute."

"What is it?" Briggs came to stand by his side.

"Those marks in the dirt." Josh pointed. "Couldn't they have been made by a heel? Mrs. Barr was wearing high-heeled boots."

Briggs crouched down as Josh had, first hitching up his pant legs to preserve their crease. He studied the marks for a moment and then looked at the side door. "Is that door locked?" he demanded of the trooper who stood guard there.

"Yes, sir," the trooper said. "We couldn't open it."

"From outside or in here?"

"In here, sir."

"Damn it," Briggs said, and Josh had a very good idea of what he was thinking. The troopers could very well have destroyed important evidence. "Go out and try it from there."

"Yes, sir," the trooper said, and went out.

"If those are heel marks, that explains where they came in," Briggs said, more to himself than anything.

"There are other marks, too," Josh said. "Someone else was here."

That made the others look at him, but before they could speak, there was a rattling at the door. The doorknob turned ineffectually. "Locked," Briggs said, just as the door was suddenly wrenched open.

"Stuck," Charlie answered, without any inflection.

"Did you try that door yourself? Don't come in," he added as the trooper began to move.

"Yes sir. I did try it. It wouldn't budge. Where the front door was locked we thought —"

"Never mind." Briggs turned sharply away. "Take a look at those marks over there," he said to one of the technicians.

"Yes sir." The technician approached the marks carefully, squatting down to study them. "About three quarters of an inch square," he said after a moment, "with one side rounded. Less than a quarter of an inch deep. I'd have to measure." He angled his head. "The farthest the marks go is about two feet from the door. See how the dirt's built up over here?" He looked up at Briggs, indicating the floor in back of him. "It's lower here, and it looks softer."

"What do you think the marks are?"

"Can't say for sure, but I'd say they're from heels of a woman's shoes."

"Anything else?"

The technician studied the floor again, his lips pursed. "There's some lines that look like they came from the sole of a shoe."

"Size?" Briggs demanded.

"Hard to tell without measuring, but they're pretty big. I'd say a large woman or a small man."

"Do they look fresh?"

"There's still some wetness around the heel, so I'd say yes, fairly fresh."

"Humph. OK. Mark off the area and get casts of the prints." Briggs turned away, his lips set. "Damn it."

"She came in with her attacker," Charlie said.

"It looks that way," Briggs agreed. "When we have a suspect we'll take casts of her shoe, but there probably won't be any dirt left on them."

"Even if there is, it'll be mixed with the mud outside."

Briggs nodded. "So they came in that way," he said, nodding toward the side door. "Mrs. Barr wanted to get the mud off her coat. She could have gone to the main barn, but maybe this was closer."

"To what?"

"At this point it's only a guess, but I think the killer lured her in here for some reason.

Mrs. Barr hung up her coat, but didn't brush off the mud."

" 'I tried to get the mud,' " Josh said, more to himself than to the others.

"What?"

"That's what she meant. She tried to get the mud off her coat." He looked up. "I think she was trying to tell Ari what happened."

"And she died before she could."

"Yes. She didn't get the mud off, either."

"Maybe she didn't have time," Charlie said.

Briggs nodded. "The attack probably happened too fast. It happened there." They turned to look at the marked-off space against the back wall, where Felicia's coat still hung. "The killer attacked Mrs. Barr and she fell there."

"Too bad there's no way to prove that," Josh said.

"Yeah. The rain must have washed away any dirt from here off her clothes."

"Our killer got out of here damn fast," Charlie said. "Ari didn't see anyone."

"That only means the killer was out of sight. She could have stayed in here, hiding."

"Especially since no one paid attention to this barn," Briggs put in.

"If she was in here, she was out of sight. Hell, she could have been one of the people who came out to help when Mrs. Barr collapsed."

"I don't think so." Briggs shook his head. "The killer was out first."

"How do you figure that?"

"If Mrs. Barr fell, I don't think the killer would have let her up again. No. The killer attacked her, left her for dead, then left the barn. But Mrs. Barr wasn't dead. She got up, went out the door there, and then died outside."

"It works," Charlie said after a minute. "It gives the killer a chance to get undercover and explains why Mrs. Barr was outside. Yeah." He nodded. "It narrows the time frame."

"Maybe," Josh said. He had been quiet for a while, puzzling out the sequence of events. "We're assuming the killer came prepared to kill Mrs. Barr. But a knitting needle's a chancy weapon, isn't it?"

Charlie looked at him. "What do you think happened?"

"The killer lured her in here for another reason. I don't know what, and I don't know why she had her knitting with her, except . . ."

"Her knitting?" Briggs interrupted. "What

136

are you talking about?"

"There was yarn on Mrs. Barr's back."

There was silence for a moment. "It could have come from the killer's clothes."

"It could've, but I don't think so," Josh said. "You don't know these people, Detective. Knitters, I mean. I think she was showing her knitting to Mrs. Barr."

Briggs frowned. "Why?"

"Maybe to get it written about in the magazine. Look. If the killer had only a knitting needle with her, don't you think it would have looked suspicious?"

"You yourself said it's a strange weapon."

"Yeah, and that's why I don't think she intended to kill anyone."

"Are you saying it was an accident?"

"No, it was murder all right, but in the heat of passion. I think they were here awhile, and then Mrs. Barr did something to make the killer angry. Barr bent over to get the mud off her coat, and that's when the killer struck. I don't think she meant to kill," he went on. "But if she was angry enough she probably used more force than she intended."

"Wait a minute," Briggs said. "We don't know the killer was a woman."

"There's a good chance of it. More women knit than men. And there are more women attending the festival than men."

"No assumptions, remember?"

"Yeah," Josh said after a minute, though he thought he was right. "I think the killer had something on one of the needles, made of light blue yarn. Maybe the strand was on the killer, but I think it could have come from whatever the project is. Knitters always have scraps of yarn around."

They were silent for a moment. "We can't expect to find the knitting," Briggs said finally. "If we do, we find the matching needle. Whoever the killer is, she must have gotten rid of both."

Josh almost smiled. No assumptions, Briggs had said, and yet he seemed to think the killer was a woman, too. "The needle, maybe, but not the project," he said. "Knitters value their projects too much to just throw them away."

"Maybe," Briggs said, but he looked skeptical. But then, he didn't know knitters as Josh was coming to. "We'll keep the knowledge of the yarn to ourselves for now."

"Is that how you think it happened, Josh?" Charlie asked.

He nodded. "I think so. It explains why the killer had knitting needles with her. Old ones, that is. She didn't buy those here. It explains the yarn, too. They had to talk long enough for the killer to show Mrs. Barr her project."

"We'll go with your theory for now," Charlie said, turning to Josh. "Mrs. Barr had her enemies, but I think you're right. Whoever it was didn't come prepared to commit murder."

CHAPTER 7

"Oh, no," Diane said firmly, after Ari had made her pronouncement. "You're not getting me into that again."

Ari looked at her. "What are you talking about?"

"Investigating. Last time was really dangerous."

"I'm not investigating," Ari protested. "It's just that we're involved again."

"Uh-huh." Diane's voice was skeptical. "You forget that I know you, Ari."

"There are more police here this time."

"Yeah, and if they can't figure it out?"

"Can you see me outdoing Detective Briggs?" Ari demanded.

"Well, no," Diane admitted. "He's scary, isn't he?"

"How did your questioning go?"

Diane shrugged. "About what you'd expect. Paul asked where I was, I told him, and then he sent me back."

"Mm-hm." Ari suspected he'd been a little more thorough than that, but Diane obviously didn't want to talk about it. "Come on, get your spinning wheel and let's go join the others."

"Yeah, all right. Spinners and knitters and murderers, oh my."

Ari laughed and made her way back to the Suspects Club. "What were *you* laughing at?" Beth said sourly as Ari sat down with them.

"Oh, Diane and I are old friends."

"You were looking right at me."

Ari turned to her, startled. "No, we weren't, Beth. I was telling Diane to join us."

"You were looking right at me," Beth repeated.

"I'm sorry," Ari said, though she didn't feel the least contrite. "We didn't mean to offend you."

"Humph." Beth crossed her arms across her chest and glowered at Diane, who'd just put her spinning wheel down. Diane looked from her to Ari.

"I have to get a chair," she said, and walked away.

"Is everybody happy?" Debbie chirped.

"Oh my God," someone muttered. Ari didn't know who it was, but she agreed with the sentiment. This was surreal.

Nancy leaned forward. "Ari, what's going on? Do you know?"

Ari spread her hands. "Not much more than you do."

"Well, tell us. Ari has an in with the local cops," she explained to the others.

"I do not, Nancy."

"No? Aren't you dating Josh Pierce?"

"Are you?" Lauren asked.

"Not really. We're friends, sort of."

"He's cute." Lauren's eyes sparkled. "If he didn't suspect me of murder I think I'd go for him."

Ari rubbed her eyes with the heels of her hands. "Everyone's nuts," she muttered.

"So, tell all," Debbie said, leaning forward. "What's he like when he's not a cop?"

"Honestly, Debbie."

Diane had set up her spinning wheel and was digging in her bag for the multicolored roving. "Ari's too modest to admit it, but she helped the detective solve a murder last year."

"I'd heard that." Debbie's eyes were bright with interest. "Tell us. Inquiring minds want to know."

Ari glared at Diane. "Someone was killed in my yarn shop," she said. "I gave the police some help, that's all."

"I heard you solved it single-handedly."

"No. The FBI and postal inspectors were involved, as well as the police."

"So are you playing Nancy Drew now?" Beth said.

"I'm as much of a suspect as you are. Maybe more."

"Your cop friend will get you out of it."

Ari stared at Beth a moment, and then turned to look at Nancy, who, like Diane, was spinning. "What are you working on?" She changed the subject.

"Nothing, really." Nancy deftly fed in the natural-colored, unspun wool through the orifice of the wheel. "I might dye this later. What are you making?"

"Coat hangers." Ari held one up, making Nancy laugh. "My mother's idea."

"That would be a good pattern for *Knit Knacks*," Debbie commented to Beth.

"Humph."

Debbie turned back, rolling her eyes. "You don't mind if I don't ask you to submit the pattern to *Knit It Up!,* do you, Ari? It doesn't suit our style."

"I taught everyone in the Knitting Guild in New York how to make them," Ari said coolly. "It was a hit."

"Oh." For once Debbie seemed at a loss

for words. "I must have missed that meeting."

"In fact, I plan on updating the idea and selling it on my website."

Debbie leaned forward. "I've checked out your site, you know. I meant what I said this morning. You really should write a book."

"Who would be interested?" Ari asked.

"I think a lot of people might. I know a few people at Leisure Works," she said, mentioning a large publisher of craft books. "They might be interested in doing a booklet with you."

"I'm not sure I have the time."

"Sure you do," Diane said. "You've got pictures of everything, and the patterns are already printed."

"I took the pictures for the site," Nancy put in. "And for the patterns she sells, too."

"People always like reading about how designers work," Debbie went on. "Why don't you submit an article to *Knit It Up!*? Maybe that's what your book should be about. How to design a sweater."

"That sounds like a big project."

"You could do it."

"In between solving murders," Diane said.

"I'll think about it," Ari said, still doubtful. "Thank you for offering."

"I'm glad to help," Debbie said.

"That's a switch," Lauren said from behind them. "Someone from *Knit It Up!* actually helping someone's career instead of ruining it."

"What, did Felicia screw you over, too?" Beth said.

"You know she really didn't," Debbie said.

"How would you know?" Lauren demanded. "Were you there?"

"Yes, I'd just started, and to tell you the truth, Lauren, she was right. You weren't up to that job."

"What happened?" Ari put in, before the tension between the two erupted into something more serious.

"I was up for a job at Echo Fashions, designing knitwear," Lauren said, still glaring at Debbie. "I was *this* close to getting it, and then Felicia slammed my work in the magazine. She said it was uninspired and amateurish. Of course I didn't get hired."

"Was Felicia that powerful?"

"Humph." This from Beth, again.

"She did you a favor," Debbie said.

Lauren looked down, and then nodded. "I suppose she did."

"Why?" Ari asked.

"I heard afterward that Echo is a terrible place to work. The head designer takes credit for other people's work."

"I never heard that."

"Didn't you ever wonder how he could design something avant garde one season and then a classic cardigan the next? Never mind. It all worked out."

"How?"

"I got another job, at Weston Knitwear." She glanced at Debbie. "It doesn't pay as well, but I'm happy."

Ari nodded noncommittally. Lauren might sound content, but the police wouldn't see things the same way. "Did you tell the police?"

Lauren looked up from her knitting. "No, why should I? I can't prove she had anything to do with my losing the job."

"What did you do to offend her?" Beth asked.

"I don't think I did anything. I knew my work was going to be featured in her column, but I didn't expect her to do what she did."

"Lauren, maybe Felicia wasn't responsible for what happened to you," Debbie said.

"Then who was?" Lauren demanded. "I'd had my second interview. There was only one other person up for the job."

"Believe it or not, Felicia didn't go around telling people who to hire."

"People read her magazine. I've heard of companies scouting designers in it. I'll bet it works the other way, too."

Debbie opened her mouth to speak, and then sighed. "I've heard you're doing well at Weston, though."

"Yes." Lauren smiled. "I love it there."

"What do you do?" Ari asked.

"I'm assistant to the chief designer. I'm a glorified secretary, but one of my designs is going to be in the fall line."

"That's wonderful!"

"I know, isn't it? I'm really learning a lot, and my boss is making sure everyone in the company knows about my work."

"So in the long run, Felicia helped you," Debbie said.

"I guess." Lauren concentrated on her knitting. "But it hurt at the time."

"Things happen," Ari said after a minute. "Sometimes they turn out for the best."

"Like you and Ted," Diane said, grinning.

"Yes, didn't you have a career starting in New York?" Lauren asked. "You were freelancing."

Ari gave Diane a look. Ted wasn't a subject she wanted to discuss just now. "But then I got married and moved here. As I said, things happen."

"I can't imagine ever leaving New York."

"I'm happy here. I have my family and my shop."

"I drove by it," Beth said unexpectedly.

"Really? When."

"This morning. It's cute."

"Thanks," Ari said, all the while thinking furiously. If Beth had left the fairgrounds, she couldn't account for her time. That made her a strong suspect. She had motive and, perhaps, opportunity. But where had that piece of blue yarn come from? She glanced speculatively at people's workbags. Maybe if she asked everyone what they were working on, she'd find the answer.

"How long are they going to keep us here, Ari?" Rosalia asked, interrupting Ari's musings.

"I don't know. I know they have to interview everyone."

"They must have finished by now," Debbie said. "No one else is here except us."

"What about you?" Nancy leaned forward to look at Annie. "Why are you here?"

Annie looked up. "I was in the wrong place at the wrong time like the rest of you. I have a long drive home. I don't want to stay here."

"I don't blame you," Beth muttered.

"Oh, stow it, Beth!" Debbie glared at her. "*Nobody* wants to be here." She frowned at

148

Annie. "Your name sounds awfully familiar. Oh, I know! Your work is supposed to be featured in *Knit It Up!* next month, right?"

Annie nodded.

"It is?" Ari asked, surprised that Annie hadn't told her that fact sooner. "Did Felicia like your work?"

"Oh yes," Debbie said, but there was something odd in her voice that made Ari look at her. Debbie's smile was falsely bright. Annie, concentrating on her work, didn't appear to notice. "That's a nice shawl," Debbie added.

"Thank you," Annie said.

"The sweater you were working on this morning is pretty, too," Rosalia put in.

And yet Annie hadn't bragged of a favorable mention in Felicia's magazine, Ari thought. Was she just being modest? "What time is it?" Ari asked aloud.

Diane looked at her watch. "Close to four. I should probably call Joe again."

"How long will they keep us?" Debbie asked. "This is really getting old."

"I don't know, but I think you'll be here overnight," Ari said.

"Here? At the fairgrounds? You're kidding me."

"No, probably not right here, but at a hotel."

"I don't have reservations anywhere."

"Were you and Felicia really going to drive back to New York tonight?"

"Yes."

"Oh." It seemed strange that Debbie and Felicia would take such a long drive just to attend a small, regional yarn festival, even if they planned an article for the magazine. "I'm sure the police will find someplace for you to stay."

"We're locals," Nancy said. "They'll let us go, won't they?"

"I don't know what they'll do," Ari said, exasperated. "They don't tell me what they're thinking. I'm a suspect, remember?"

"Well, I hope they let us know soon." Diane had stopped spinning and was sitting stretched out, her arms behind her head.

"So do I," Ari began, and then stopped as a man appeared in the doorway, his figure shadowy, indistinct. Ari frowned. He didn't look like Josh or the chief, and the hat was wrong for a state trooper. Then who . . . ?

"Winston," Beth whispered as the man walked farther into the barn, a trooper not far behind.

"Winston!" Debbie exclaimed at the same time, and launched herself from her chair. She flew across the barn and threw herself into the man's arms. "Oh, Winston!" It was a wail. "What am I going to do without her? Oh, what am I going to do?"

"It's all right, Debbie girl." The man patted Debbie's back awkwardly. Now that he was inside Ari recognized him: Winston Barr, Felicia's husband. He was older than Felicia, and was nattily attired in a camel's hair coat and a beret. He looked extremely uncomfortable with Debbie clinging to him, and yet his arms were around her.

"No, it's not. It'll never be all right again. I miss her. I miss her, Winston. She was better to me than my own mother was."

"I know, Debbie. She thought of you as a daughter." He cleared his throat. "We both did."

"I was so lucky. What am I going to do?"

"Winston?" Diane whispered into Ari's ear.

"Felicia's husband." Ari was unable to take her eyes off the pair. "I met him once. He's a charming man."

Debbie's voice rose again. "I'm so sorry."

"It was going to happen sooner or later," Winston said.

"But in such a way!"

"I know. I had a lot of time to think about this on the way here, Debbie love. It's terrible, I won't deny that, but now at least she won't suffer."

"Winston." Debbie pulled away, staring at him. "You can't really feel that way."

"Come, my dear, and sit down. We need to talk." Winston took her arm and steered her toward the judges' table. Once they were sitting, with their heads together, only the murmur of their voices reached the others.

"Wow," Diane muttered. "What is that all about?"

Ari shook her head, equally mystified. "I never expected Debbie to act like that."

"Yeah. She was bouncing off the walls before."

"Maybe she was feeling this way all along."

"Maybe she's nuts."

Ari gave her a sharp look. "What are you saying?"

"Ari, you know she could have done it. And if she's a little off . . ."

Ari frowned. Debbie's grief seemed genuine, so much so that she couldn't watch anymore. "I don't think so. I — hm."

"What?"

"Look at Annie. Be casual about it!"

Diane turned in her chair. Annie, still obstinately separate from the group, was nonetheless glaring at them. "What?"

"Way to go," Ari muttered, glaring at Diane herself. "Real subtle."

"I don't think she even saw us. She's looking at Debbie. What's her problem, anyway?"

"Who knows? She looks mad enough to . . ."

"Kill?" Diane whispered, when Ari didn't finish.

"Yes, but . . ."

"Could she have?"

"Maybe."

"I'm surprised you're not grilling her."

"I told you I'm not investigating," Ari said, exasperated. "I'd know about the *Knit It Up!* article if I was, wouldn't I?"

"I don't know, Ari." Diane was looking at her. "Maybe you did know."

"Diane!" Ari exclaimed. "That's so not fair —"

"But, Winston, what are you doing here?" Debbie's voice cut across the barn. She had stopped crying, but her face was red and swollen, and her voice was hoarse. "Shouldn't you be with the police?"

"I'm here for you, my dear." Winston had pulled back from her. "I knew you'd be upset."

"I'm a suspect."

"Ha. As if you would have hurt her, Debbie girl." He looked around for the first time. "And are all these fine-looking people

153

suspects, too?"

"None of us can prove where we were when Felicia died. Come on." She got up, and, grabbing his hand, pulled him from his chair. He winced, but then seemed to recover. "Let me introduce you to everyone." Arm in arm, they approached the small group. "Folks, this is Winston Barr, Felicia's husband. I don't think you know anyone here, Winston, except for Beth Marley."

Winston's face hardened. "Ah, yes. Hello, Beth."

Beth nodded. "Winston," she said, equally coolly.

Winston turned away, and his gaze settled on Ari. "You look familiar, young lady."

"Yes, we've met," Ari said. "I'm surprised you remember, Mr. Barr."

Winston peered at her for a moment longer, and then smiled. "Ariadne Jorgensen, isn't it?"

"Evans, now."

"Let's see. It was the fifth anniversary party of *Knit It Up!* at our apartment, I believe."

"Why, yes. You have a good memory."

"Felicia thought well of your work."

Ari blinked. "She did?"

"Oh yes. Believe me, it wasn't something

she did often. She — ah. I believe I'm about to be summoned."

Ari saw Josh at the same moment as Winston, walking toward them with his mouth set in a grim line. "Mr. Barr?" he said.

"Yes."

"Detective Pierce. Would you come with me, please?"

"Certainly. Don't worry, Debbie love." He turned and gave her a quick hug before putting his beret back on. "It will all work itself out." He turned and walked out with Josh, and with him went some of the strange lightheartedness that had so briefly filled the barn.

Josh was not feeling kindly toward Winston Barr as they trudged back toward Barn A. When news had come from the gate of the fairgrounds that Felicia's husband had arrived, Josh and the others had perked up. Unlikely though it seemed, since Barr had been in New York at the time, he could be involved in his wife's death. It was axiomatic in an investigation: one's nearest and dearest was often the culprit and always a suspect. To everyone's surprise, though, the maroon Bentley, with a chauffeur at the wheel, had swept by them and stopped in front of Barn B. Josh had been dispatched

155

to fetch Winston Barr for questioning.

Felicia's husband was not a big man. Though he wore an obviously expensive coat, he was shivering when they entered Barn A, and his skin was gray. Still, he paused just inside the door, observing everything warily. This was not a man to be underestimated.

"Gentlemen," Barr said, unbuttoning his coat but leaving his hat on. "I assume you are the ones looking into my wife's death?"

Charlie and Briggs had risen at his entrance and now introduced themselves, first offering their hands to shake. Winston gave them a swift and assessing glance, and then sat in the chair Briggs indicated. He was alone, facing the other three, and yet he exuded confidence and an air of control.

"My condolences for your loss," Briggs said, when they were all settled.

"Thank you. Might I trouble you for some tea?"

"I'll get it." Josh walked to the snack bar. No one talked during the time it took him to pour hot water over a tea bag and return with the cardboard cup.

Winston murmured his thanks, took a sip, and then asked, "Well, gentlemen? Will you tell me about my wife's death, and what you have discovered?"

Josh gave the others a quick look and then launched into a recital of events. Winston listened with his head bowed, looking up only when Josh finished. "Thank you," he said. "Do you believe she suffered?"

That caught them all a little off guard. "If she did, it was brief," Briggs said.

Winston closed his eyes. His color had improved only slightly. "Poor Felicia."

"Were you married long?"

"Ten years. The first marriage for both of us."

"The first?"

"Yes. We both waited a long time for the right person." He paused. "Felicia was a lonely soul."

"We understand that she was a difficult person."

Winston's eyes hardened. "At times. As a businesswoman she had to be. It amazes me, gentlemen, that behavior that would be commendable in a man is less so in a woman."

"Er, yes. Would you say that your relationship was good?"

"Yes."

"No recent quarrels or disagreements?"

Winston frowned. "I find this line of questioning offensive. Is it necessary?"

"Murder is offensive, Mr. Barr. We have

to question everyone, including you. We want to find the murderer as much as you do."

He stared hard at them. "Do you think I hired someone to do it?"

Josh shifted uneasily in his chair. The thought had been in the back of his mind. It wouldn't be the first time a spouse had done such a thing, while staying far away to set up an alibi. Yet, now that he'd actually met Winston, he doubted it.

"It's a possibility," Briggs said, though Josh thought he heard the same doubt in his voice. "However it happened, sir, your wife was murdered."

"Oh." Winston's breath went out of him on a sigh, and he slumped back, his eyes closed and his face gray.

"Mr. Barr." Josh jumped up before the other two could quite react. Kneeling beside Winston, he took his wrist. "His pulse is fast. I think we should call an ambulance."

"No." Winston's voice was sharp, making Briggs pause as he lifted his walkie-talkie. "I'm all right."

"Sir, you could be having a heart attack," Josh said.

"I'm not. Would someone please get me some water?"

"We really need to call the paramedics,

Mr. Barr."

"No!" Winston was still pale, but he straightened in his seat. "I tell you, I'm all right." He took the cup of water Charlie handed him. "Thank you. Oh, sit down, sir. I'm not going to die yet."

"Yet?" Josh said. He had risen, but still stood beside Winston's chair. "What do you mean?"

"I have cancer, young man." Winston looked up at him. "I had chemotherapy yesterday and I'm tired. I'm taking something that's supposed to give me more energy, but it doesn't seem to be working."

"I'm sorry." Josh sat down.

Winston nodded. "Pancreatic cancer. I'm told I have four months at most. I'll be with Felicia soon," he added softly.

The silence was awkward. "Can we assume, then, that you don't benefit from your wife's death?" Briggs asked.

"Financially? No, nor do I need to, especially now. I was quite well off when we met. The apartment is mine, and I made a tidy sum in banking. Felicia spent her money elsewhere."

"Where?"

Briggs hesitated a moment. "There's no reason you shouldn't know. She gave generously to a charitable foundation that helps

Chinese orphanages."

That startled everyone. "Interesting," Briggs said. "Any particular reason?"

"Because of her own experience."

Josh frowned. "Did she adopt from China?"

"No, though I believe she would have liked to. It was because of her daughter."

"Excuse me?" By all accounts, Felicia was childless.

"Yes," Winston said, nodding. "Felicia had a daughter."

CHAPTER 8

The policemen stared at Winston. "You said she'd been married before," Briggs said finally, with admirable calmness.

"She wasn't." Winston's tone was equally calm. "She was young, gentlemen. She had the baby out of wedlock. She considered keeping it, but her parents convinced her otherwise. Nice Catholic girls from Connecticut who were going to Yale simply didn't do such things."

"How old was she?"

"Eighteen."

"So she gave the baby up for adoption?"

"Yes."

"Where?"

"I don't know. She rarely talked about that period in her life, and I didn't like to ask."

"She was your wife."

"Some things were off-limits, gentlemen." He glanced away. "Poor Felicia. She was far more sensitive than people believed."

That tallied with what Ari had said, Josh thought. "Then you knew about this?" he asked.

"No, not until the girl showed up."

"When?" Briggs said sharply.

"Some weeks ago."

"Did you meet her?"

"No. All I know is that she contacted Felicia in some way. Felicia was upset about it."

"And you, too, I imagine," Briggs said shrewdly.

"Yes."

"Did you argue about it?"

"We had words, yes. Frankly, gentlemen, I don't care what she did in her youth. But for her to have kept such a secret from me hurt."

"Any idea why she did?"

"She said it was in the past. It was something she didn't like to think about." He paused. "I think it hurt her."

"In what way?"

"I don't think she ever stopped regretting giving up her daughter."

"Then was she happy to see the girl again?" Josh said.

"Not completely. Gentlemen, would you like it if something from your past, something you'd thought was over, suddenly

162

came back to confront you?"

"No sir, I wouldn't," Josh said through stiff lips. "Still, this changes things."

Winston shook his head. "If you're thinking it gives me some kind of motive, it doesn't. We managed to work things out. In fact, I would have liked to meet the girl."

"Would you?" Briggs's voice was flat.

"Yes. She was part of Felicia's life. I loved my wife, gentlemen." His face twisted. "Poor Felicia. I'm glad she went quickly."

"Why is that?"

He gave them an odd look. "Don't you know yet? She had cancer, too."

Josh, looking at the others, saw that they were as startled by this information as he was. "No," Detective Briggs said. "We haven't received the autopsy report yet."

"I see. Yes, she was diagnosed a month ago, just after I was. She would have hated it. Hated the indignity." He looked off into the distance. "This hat." He tapped his beret. "I wear it to keep my head warm, gentlemen."

He'd lost his hair already, Josh thought, feeling a sudden surge of sympathy for both the Barrs. "Was this widely known?"

"No sir. Felicia wanted to keep it quiet as long as she could."

So the killer had not known that her

quarry would soon be dead, Josh thought.

Briggs leaned forward. "Sir, do you have any idea who might have wished your wife dead, or why?" he asked, adopting Winston's more formal language.

"None, gentlemen."

"We understand that she had enemies," Charlie said.

"I'm afraid so. Felicia often rubbed people the wrong way."

"We've heard that she ruined several people's careers."

"Are you talking about Beth Marley?"

"Among others, yes."

Winston sat back. "Beth still blames Felicia for her downfall."

"Shouldn't she?" Josh said.

"No. Beth brought it all upon herself. She should consider herself lucky."

"In what way?"

"That she's not in jail."

"Jail." Briggs leaned forward, sounding as surprised as Josh, and no doubt Charlie, felt. "What do you mean?"

"Felicia had a reputation for giving good reviews if someone advertised in the magazine."

"Is it true?"

"No. Beth was the one behind that."

"In what way?"

"She knew when someone impressed Felicia and was going to be mentioned favorably. When that happened, she'd call that person about advertising."

"Did the people she called know they were getting good press?"

"She persuaded many to advertise. The magazine grew more prosperous because of that. What we didn't know is that she hinted that she could ensure a good review if they *did* advertise. And we didn't know that she charged extra for that service."

"Extra?"

"Above and beyond the magazine's rates."

"Ah." Briggs sat back. "She pocketed the difference."

"Exactly. She was smart about it. She didn't make that offer to everyone, and she accepted advertising from people whose work Felicia didn't like, so there was just enough uncertainty. Still, Felicia got the reputation of accepting payment for good reviews. It was most unfair."

"How did you find out about it?" Josh asked.

"Beth got too greedy. She began to ask for too much money. Finally someone wrote to Felicia complaining about the practice, not knowing that Beth was the one behind it. When Felicia started looking into the matter, she discovered that it had been going on for a long time. It didn't help that Beth bragged that she was the real power at the magazine."

Josh nodded. They'd heard that already, but this financial motive was important news. It was fraud. "Why didn't you prosecute her?"

"I wanted to. It was Felicia who held back. Not from any love of Beth, you understand. They'd had their problems before that, and of course these shenanigans were too much. No, she felt it wasn't worth it. It would have cost more money to sue Beth than she actually took."

"But she damaged your wife's reputation."

"True, but even apart from this there were people who disliked Felicia."

Now they were getting somewhere, Josh thought. "Can you name anyone?"

"Oh, many people, but I doubt they're here."

"Let me give you some names," Briggs said. "Lauren Dubrowski."

"Lauren." Winston appeared to think about that. "Yes, I seem to remember something about her. I believe she lost a chance at a job because of Felicia, or she thought she did. Which of course amounts to the same thing."

"Annie Walker."

"Who?"

"She's one of the vendors here. She told us there's supposed to be an article about her in the magazine."

"Ah, yes, her. I don't know much about it. You'll have to ask Debbie."

"Will you still keep the magazine going?" Josh asked.

"Oh yes. Felicia would want it that way."

"Who will be in charge?"

"Oh, Debbie, of course, at least for now. She knows the ins and outs of it, and she's quite intelligent."

"How did she and Felicia get along?" Briggs asked.

"Quite well." His gaze became hard. "You surely aren't implying that Debbie would hurt Felicia, are you?"

"Would she?"

"Good heavens, no. Debbie idolized Felicia."

"Mm-hm." Briggs sounded skeptical. "Does Debbie know that she'll be running the magazine?"

"Oh, I imagine so. Felicia relied on her quite a bit."

"Was she actually told, though?"

"Felicia was still getting her affairs in order."

"What about money, Mr. Barr?" Briggs asked. "Did your wife have any?"

"Yes, but not from the magazine. Running a magazine is expensive. She began turning a profit several years ago, but it was not an enormous producer. Most of Felicia's money came from her parents."

"And you think that Debbie knows none of this?" Josh said.

"Not explicitly, no, but she may suspect. Felicia treated her like a daughter. So did I, for that matter. She certainly needed it."

"Why?"

"She left home when she was seventeen. I gather it wasn't entirely voluntary."

"Oh?"

"I don't know all the reasons, but I heard she had a bad relationship with her parents from the beginning. Among other things, Debbie's mother is an alcoholic. I doubt Debbie has contacted her in years."

"Did Debbie know about Felicia's daughter?"

"Not that I know of. So far as I know, I'm the only one Felicia told."

"How did her daughter get in touch with Felicia?" Charlie asked. "A letter? A phone call?"

"I don't know."

"She could have called the magazine,"

Josh said.

"Why would she have done that?"

Briggs shot Josh a swift, approving glance. "Let's say that the daughter discovered that Felicia was her mother. What would be the easiest way for her to make contact?"

"I'm not sure what you mean, sir."

"Through the magazine. She could very well have called the office."

"I've no idea."

"If she did, others could have known."

"I doubt it," Winston repeated.

"Could she have come to the office?"

"No, I don't believe so."

"Then how could she prove who she was?"

"They met," Winston said, reluctantly.

"They did?" Briggs rapped out.

"Against my wishes, yes."

"Why is that?"

"We didn't know the girl. We didn't know what she wanted."

"But Felicia didn't feel the same way?"

"No. At least, she didn't feel as strongly as I did. I think she had mixed feelings about the girl."

"You keep calling her the girl," Charlie said. "You don't know who she is?"

"No, gentlemen, Felicia never told me. But when she mentioned changing her will, I feared the worst."

"What do you mean?"

"I believe she was going to leave her estate to her."

Again, Josh was rattled. He could see, looking in the eyes of both Charlie and Briggs, that they were, too. "Who knew about this?" Briggs demanded.

"So far as I know, just the lawyers and myself," Winston said.

"Not the girl?"

"I couldn't say. I don't believe so, but Felicia didn't confide in me."

"Ever?" Josh put in.

"Not in this case. May I trouble you for some water?"

"Sure." Josh got up to go to the counter, while behind him the questioning continued. No doubt about it. What Winston had just told them changed everything.

"Why not this time?" Charlie asked.

"She knew I disapproved. Thank you." Everything was suspended while Winston pulled out a pillbox and swallowed a good deal of its contents with the water Josh gave him. "I have to stick to a schedule," he commented, putting the pillbox away. "Now. Where were we?"

"Why did you disapprove of your wife's plans?" Briggs said.

"We didn't know anything about this girl,

Captain. She could have been nobody, someone off the street playing on Felicia's sympathies. Felicia could be a soft touch. Oh yes, that's true," he went on, at the others' skeptical looks. "She worked for charities that helped give disadvantaged young women a break. For instance, she donated to one charity that helped girls get funding for an education, and she started a program where women who were going to job interviews could use someone's gently used clothes. That one got a lot of response. Some of those young ladies went to work wearing designer suits. But she was behind the scenes. She didn't do any of that for credit."

"So you're saying this girl, whoever she is, could be one of the girls Felicia helped?"

"It's possible."

"How would she know that Felicia had a child?" Josh asked.

"I couldn't tell you that, gentlemen. As I've told you, Felicia kept that part of her life private."

Josh had been doing some math, based on Felicia's age. "She's in her late twenties," he said. "The girl, that is."

"About that, yes."

There were several people in Barn B who were around that age. "How did she find

Felicia?"

"I'm not quite sure. Adoption records back then were sealed, but I understand there are ways around that. She may have used a private detective. And she must have been thrilled when she found out about Felicia," he said, his voice bitter. "She must have thought she'd landed in clover."

"All right, so let's go over this," Briggs said. "Felicia was thinking of changing her will in favor of the daughter she gave up for adoption. However, no one knows who this girl is. No one knows if she knew about Felicia's will. In fact, almost no one knew Felicia was going to change her will. Does that about sum it up?"

Winston inclined his head. "It does."

"Did Debbie know?" Charlie asked with studied casualness.

"I don't believe so, no."

"But you're not sure."

"No, but I doubt it."

"How do you think she'd react if she knew she was going to lose everything?"

"She didn't even know for sure she was going to get anything! Gentlemen, are we through? I'm rather tired."

Briggs hesitated. "For the moment," he said. "Where will you be staying?"

"I don't yet know."

"There are some decent bed-and-breakfasts around here," Josh said. Somehow, he couldn't imagine Winston staying in the chain motel where most of the festival participants were registered. Among other reasons, he wasn't a suspect.

"Thank you. I will look into that." He rose and then simply stood, holding on to the table's edge. He did look tired; his face was gray and there were circles under his eyes.

"I'll see you out, sir," Josh said, taking the other man's arm.

"Thank you," Winston said and, after putting on his coat, he went out with Josh as an escort.

The silence in Barn B was deafening after Winston left. Even Debbie's sobs had ceased, leaving everyone uneasy and at a loss as to what to say. From Debbie's actions this morning, no one could have suspected that she was so grief stricken. Certainly Ari hadn't.

"Did she really treat you like a daughter?" Lauren said finally.

"Yes." Debbie nodded without looking up. "She was good to me."

"Some mother she'd've been," Beth muttered.

"Oh, stow it, Marley!" Debbie snapped.

"You don't know anything about it."

"Felicia wasn't noted for her kindness."

"Oh yes she was, and you of all people should know it."

Beth opened her mouth to say something, and then apparently thought better of it. Debbie, watching her, gave a short nod and turned away. For the moment, Beth was silent.

"Debbie, Felicia had a rough reputation," Ari said, but gently. She was still stunned by Debbie's outburst. The last thing she wanted was for that to happen again, though she was puzzled by Debbie's cryptic remark to Beth.

"She said what she thought," Debbie said. "It was just her way."

" 'Her way' didn't help me," Lauren said coldly.

Debbie looked at her. "You ended up all right, Lauren. Your designs weren't quite there yet. Anyway, Felicia never criticized someone who didn't deserve it."

"She praised people who didn't deserve it, if they bought ads."

"That's a myth."

"But I've heard that, too, Debbie, and there are times it seemed true," Ari said.

"Felicia didn't do that. Did she, *Beth?*"

Beth muttered something that no one

caught. From the look on her face, Ari thought that was just as well. "It did make things hard on people," Ari continued. "Sometimes she seemed to criticize everything. Like this morning."

Debbie frowned. "I know. I don't know what got into her. I know that there were things here she would have liked ordinarily. You stood up to her."

"I had nothing to lose. I don't — didn't need her approval."

"No. She did like your designs, though. She probably wasn't feeling well. Maybe Winston was right." Debbie gazed unseeingly across the barn. "Maybe this was for the best."

"Debbie!"

"She didn't suffer. Poor Winston."

Ari had been watching Debbie closely and had seen something that might have been relief flicker briefly in her eyes. "Debbie, was Felicia sick?"

Debbie turned to her. "What makes you say that?"

"Was she?"

Debbie didn't answer right away. "Yes. Cancer."

"Melanoma?"

"How in hell do you know that?"

"I don't, but I saw a mole on the back of

175

her neck."

"Another one? Oh, poor Felicia."

"Couldn't they treat it?" Nancy said.

Debbie shook her head. "It had spread. She didn't have much longer, she and Winston. Oh, poor Winston. This will kill him." She closed her eyes. "And maybe that's just as well, too."

"You're doing it again," Diane said.

"What?" Debbie asked, straightening.

"Saying these damned strange things that don't do you any good."

"Is Winston sick, too?" Ari asked.

Once again, Debbie hesitated. "Yes," she said finally. "Pancreatic cancer."

"Oh, no."

"They always said they did everything together," Debbie said, and sank her head to her knees.

"Is he going to be all right?"

"No." Debbie's voice was muffled. "It was strange." She straightened, and though she was pale, her eyes were dry. "Felicia started having tests, and then out of the blue Winston's doctor gave him this death sentence. And then she was diagnosed the next week. It was horrible."

"How many people know about this?" Ari asked, after a few moments of silence.

"Not many. Why?"

"Because whoever killed Felicia must not have known."

"That kind of lets me off the hook, doesn't it?" Debbie pressed her fingers to her eyes. "I loved that woman. I love Winston. I don't know what I'm going to do."

Unexpectedly Lauren got up and slipped past Ari, to sit beside Debbie. "I'm sorry," she said. "I lost my mother last year. It's hard."

"Awfully hard. But at least she won't suffer now."

That much was true, Ari thought, though it was a strange way of looking at things. It also, in a strange way, gave Debbie a motive. Had she loved Felicia enough to spare her pain? It was a twisted motive, true, but in Ari's experience people could kill for the strangest of reasons.

She looked covertly at the people around her, and at Annie, still sitting across from them, furiously knitting. The Suspects Club, Ari thought. Because she still couldn't rule out anyone. Not even Debbie.

CHAPTER 9

Winston Barr had left, with police permission, to find a place to stay overnight. Apart from the fact that he was too tired to make the long drive back to New York tonight, he faced the formality of identifying Felicia's body in the morning. The medical examiner's office in Boston was busy and sometimes got backed up, but Briggs had requested the autopsy to be done as soon as possible to confirm the official cause of death.

By now everyone had been questioned, and most of the festival participants had left. The first phase of the investigation was over, but Winston Barr had thrown them a curveball.

"Everything's twisted," Briggs said.

"Ari's involved," Charlie said, stretching. The three of them were slumped in their seats at a table in Barn A, tired and just a little discouraged.

"That's not fair," Josh protested. "She just stumbled into it."

"Literally."

"If those search warrants would come back, we could find that blue yarn and we'd have our killer," Briggs said.

"Not likely today." Following Ari's description of the blue yarn, the police had applied for search warrants for the possessions and cars of everyone remaining in the barn, but the process was slow. It was hard to find a judge on a Saturday. "Even if they do, what does that prove?" Mason went on. "Without the yarn that Ari saw, we can't link it to anyone in particular. Hell, you could argue that in a place like this, it's easy to pick up yarn. Even if we found it, how'd we know it was the right one?"

"Ari would recognize it," Josh said.

"And are we supposed to take that to court?" Briggs said. "She might know yarn, but any competent lawyer would be able to knock her testimony out."

"We can't even trace the knitting needle to anyone."

The three of them gloomily studied the object on the table. A few moments earlier, a trooper had brought in a knitting needle, found in a garbage can that had already been searched that morning, near Barn B.

It was a size nine, orchid in color, and made of aluminum. It was also a perfect match for the murder weapon.

"Damn," Charlie said, but without heat. "How did the killer get rid of it with everyone watching?"

"She could have wrapped it in her sandwich paper," Josh said.

"And no one noticed," Briggs barked. "I want to know why the hell not."

"I want to know how the killer got away without anyone noticing anything," Charlie retorted. "No one saw her with Felicia. No one saw the attack."

"And no fingerprints on the needle." Briggs's voice was matter-of-fact, calming them all a little. Tempers were starting to run high. It would be bad if they started fighting with each other.

"Do you think Felicia's daughter is here?" Josh asked finally.

"No way to know. We don't have her name." Charlie stretched and rose. "If I drink any more of this coffee I think I'll spit."

"I'll make some more." Josh was glad to have something to do for the moment.

"Do you think Debbie knows about Felicia's daughter?" Josh said.

"No way of knowing without asking her."

"Assuming she tells us the truth." Briggs put down his walkie-talkie. "I've just sent for her."

"Good." Charlie sat down, a fresh cup before him. "Be interesting to hear what she has to say."

"Yeah." Josh sprawled in his chair. He didn't need to say what they all were thinking. If Debbie knew of Felicia's plans, she wouldn't want to see any of that money, not to mention the magazine, go to a stranger.

"I wonder what Ari knows," Josh said softly.

Briggs's look was sharp. "What do you mean?"

"She's stuck in the barn with the others. She's in a better position to learn about them than we are."

"We can't get a civilian involved in this investigation," Briggs pointed out.

Josh was quiet a moment, and then nodded. Things were different this time around than they had been the last time Ari was involved in a murder investigation. Briggs was a very by-the-book cop. "I suppose not."

Charlie leaned forward. "Ari does know more about this world than we do."

"Nothing she could tell us would be admissible in court," Briggs said. "It would be hearsay."

"It might point us in the right direction."

"It might point the killer in her direction. No. We aren't using her."

Not officially, Josh thought, but there were ways for him to find out what she knew without Briggs finding out. He'd just have to be careful.

The door opened at that moment and Debbie came in, with Trooper Lopes just behind her. She was pale and subdued, a far cry from the young woman who had acted so strangely that morning.

"Is Winston okay?" she asked, not making a move toward the table.

"He was a little tired, but otherwise he seemed fine," Josh said, rising and pulling out a chair for her. "Sit down, Ms. Patrino."

"Why?" She didn't move. "I thought you were done with me."

"Some things have come up we'd like your help with," Briggs said.

Debbie moved at last, sitting at the table, again facing the three of them. "I can't imagine what."

"You said before you thought you'd be getting the magazine. Did you know that for sure?" Briggs asked.

"No."

"Mrs. Barr never said anything?"

"Well, she hinted, but that's all."

"How?"

"At first she'd say things like I was really too young to run a magazine. I thought she was criticizing me. That's when I didn't know her well."

"Yes. How well did you know her?"

Debbie looked surprised. "About as well as anyone, I guess."

"Do you know if she helped any charities?"

"No. Did she?"

"You don't know of any young girls she might have helped?"

"No." She frowned. "What is all this?"

"Just trying to get more of a picture of her," Charlie said. "Winston hinted that she'd willed her money to charity."

Something flickered in Debbie's eyes. "I know she donated to the Salvation Army, things like that. Oh, and she'd go to parties put on to benefit charities, but that's all I know about."

"Mm-hm." Briggs sat back. "Would it surprise you to know that she was actively involved in several organizations helping disadvantaged women?"

"Was she?"

"Yes."

"Yes, it would surprise me — no." Again she frowned. "No, maybe it doesn't. She

183

was awfully good to me, and she did say she liked seeing women getting ahead in business."

"Such as you."

"I don't know. Maybe."

"With her magazine."

"I told you, I don't know! I don't know what she planned."

"Hm."

"It's the truth."

"You didn't know for sure," Josh said quietly.

"No," she admitted after a moment. "But if you're thinking I did anything to her to get the magazine, you're wrong. I loved that woman."

"Hm," Briggs murmured again.

"I did! I know I acted weird this morning, but I was in shock." She looked away. "She was like a mother to me."

No one said anything for a few minutes. "But you wouldn't mind getting the magazine," Briggs said.

"Not like this. Not when I knew she was dying anyway." Her eyes squeezed shut. "Why would I?"

"When you say she was like a mother, what do you mean?" Charlie asked.

"She was good to me. She helped me with things."

"Such as?"

"Well, I didn't know how to dress, for one thing, so she took me shopping. She invited me to dinner, a lot." She smiled. "She even tried to fix me up with people."

"She did?"

"I know, that's hard to believe, isn't it? Mostly they were her friends' sons, and we didn't have much to say to each other."

"Why not?"

She shrugged. "They were from places like Danbury and they went to Yale or Princeton or something like that. Out of my league."

"Why is that?"

She looked at them for a moment. Her gaze was shrewd, measuring, and for the first time Josh could guess what Felicia had seen in her. "I was trailer trash," she said flatly. "My father took off when I was young, and my mother — well, let's just say she wasn't motherly. She was bitter. She worked hard as an aide at a nursing home, but there was never enough money. She'd have boyfriends, too, but none of them would last. She used to say that if she didn't have a kid she could have gone places."

"Could she have?"

"I doubt it. She drank a lot, and when I got to be a teenager we fought all the time. She wanted me to quit school when I was sixteen and go to work, but I knew if I did I'd end up like her. Finally I went to live with an aunt, and things got a little better. At least my aunt thought I should finish high school."

"Did you?"

"Of course," she said scornfully. "And college, too. I got a scholarship to a state school. It wasn't much and I had to work my tail off to stay in school, but I graduated."

"Is that when you came to New York?"

She shook her head. "No, I never planned on that. I was going to be a teacher, but I couldn't get a job. So instead I subbed, and I freelanced as a writer. I didn't know much about a lot of things, but I did know how to research. So I wrote articles about all sorts of things, and one of them was crafts."

"Knitting articles?" Josh said.

"A few, but not in *Knit It Up!* if that's what you're thinking."

"How did you get the job, then?"

"By chance, really. One of my roommates moved to New York and she'd really gotten into knitting. I went to a knit lit group meeting with her one time when I was visiting, and Felicia was there."

"Knit lit?" Briggs interrupted. "What's that?"

"It's a group where people get together to knit while someone else reads aloud. Sort of a knitting book club. Anyway, Felicia terrified everyone. She terrified me."

"Why?"

"The knitters, because she could be so critical, but for me it was just her. You saw how she looked — no, you didn't, did you? Well, she looked classy, all in black, like everyone else in Manhattan, and with her hair up and understated jewelry. She was everything I wasn't."

"How did you get the job, then?" Josh asked.

"About a month after I went home, my friend called to tell me she'd heard of a job opening at *Knit It Up!*"

"So that's when you became Felicia's assistant?"

"Oh, gosh, no, I wasn't experienced enough for that. The job was for a general office assistant. To tell you the truth, I didn't really want it. It didn't pay enough for me to live in the city, but my friend convinced me to try. So when I interviewed with Felicia, I really didn't care what she did. I told her that I would still write for other magazines if I was hired, because I had to make a living. She didn't like it, so I thought that was it. I was really surprised when Beth called and offered me the job."

"Beth Marley?"

"Yes, she was still Felicia's assistant. The only condition was that I couldn't write for any competing magazines. So, I thought, what the heck — I'm young and I thought living in New York might be fun."

"But how did you end up becoming Felicia's assistant?"

"Oh, that didn't happen for a long time. My job wasn't much, you know, not at first. I ran errands and made coffee and generally did whatever anyone wanted me to do. But one day Felicia called me into her office. She'd read one of my early articles. She criticized it, of course, because she wouldn't have been Felicia if she didn't, but she also promoted me. I became a staff writer. And things went from there."

Josh leaned forward. All this was interesting, but it didn't answer the central question. Did Debbie know that her chances of benefiting from Felicia's death had been jeopardized? "Ms. Patrino, did anyone ever visit Felicia for something that didn't have to do with the magazine?"

"Not when I was there. Why do you ask?"

"A young woman, about your age or older."

"Or maybe she got a letter," Charlie put in.

"Well, I didn't read her mail. Who would you be talking about?"

"Someone you didn't know."

Debbie's brow furrowed. "There was something. Someone called a few weeks ago for Felicia and wouldn't give her name. I didn't think anything of it because Felicia gets odd calls all the time. She kept calling back, and finally she told me to tell Felicia, 'Hartford CSS.' "

"What?"

" 'Hartford CSS.' I don't know what it means, either. It sounds like some sort of crime show, doesn't it?"

Briggs grunted in reply. "Go on."

"When I told Felicia, she told me to let the woman through when she called."

"Did she call again?"

"Yes, the next day."

"And you put the call through?"

"Actually Felicia was standing at my desk when the call came."

"How did she react?"

Debbie shrugged. "She looked pale, but she was looking pale all the time anyway. Anyway, I transferred the call to her office, and that was that."

"Didn't you think it was strange?" Briggs asked.

"A little, but I was busy, so after a while I forgot about it. It didn't seem that important."

"How did Felicia act afterward?"

"Look, what is this?" Debbie asked. "What does it have to do with anything?"

Josh shook his head. "Maybe nothing. Did you ever find out what this woman's name was?"

"No. I told you, I forgot about it until you asked me just now." She sat back, arms crossed on her chest, looking seriously disgruntled. "Why is she important, anyway?"

"We have to look into everything." Briggs rose. "Thank you for helping us, Ms. Patrino."

"I wasn't aware I had a choice."

"You've been helpful. We're done for now."

"Then can I leave?"

Charlie shook his head. "Only to go to the other barn."

"Why didn't I guess that?" she said, and turned to the door. Trooper Lopes was there to escort her. They were not about to let a possible suspect wander around on her own.

"Well," Charlie said into the silence left after her departure.

"Well?" Briggs echoed.

"Didn't get much out of her, did we?"

"Oh, I don't know." He stretched. "We confirmed that someone *did* contact Felicia."

"What does 'CSS' mean?" Josh said, more to himself than to the others.

"You think Ms. Patrino was telling the truth?" Charlie asked. "I'm not sure I do."

Briggs shrugged. "Hard to tell. If Felicia's husband didn't know the woman's name, it's possible Ms. Patrino didn't, either."

"That's not the point," Josh said. "What matters is if she knew the woman was Felicia's daughter."

"Looks like Felicia played this one close to the vest," Charlie said. "I wouldn't be surprised if no one knows about her."

Briggs reached for his cell phone as it rang. "Briggs," he said, and then looked up at the others. "Good. Yes, I have a pen and paper. Go ahead." He scribbled something down as he listened. "You're sure about that?" he said, his voice suddenly sharp. "OK. Yeah, I see what you mean. When will we get the full report?"

"The autopsy report?" Charlie muttered.

"Monday? That's not good enough. Yeah, well look. Most of our suspects are from out of town. We can't keep them here beyond tomorrow." Briggs paused. "Yeah, true, I do know the important facts. Okay. If that's the way it has to be, then that's it." Briggs snapped his phone shut. "Preliminary autopsy report."

"And?" Charlie said.

"Nothing we didn't already know." He pulled reading glasses from his pocket and studied the paper. "Damn. Can't read my own writing. Cause of death was a stab wound consistent with the knitting needle. The angle of entry is steep, as if the killer was shorter than the victim. It penetrated between her ribs and went through her heart." He looked up. "This is the troubling part," he said. "To be that exact requires either luck or knowledge. It's not easy to find the exact place where something could penetrate past the ribs to the heart, especially not at that angle."

"Then how did Felicia survive as long as she did?"

"The wound wasn't deep enough to kill right away. The needle was bent," he went on, reading from his notes again. "The killer had to use force, and it wasn't strong enough to hold up."

"Just strong enough to do the job."

"Yeah." He put down the paper. "We could be looking for someone with medical knowledge."

"That means checking backgrounds again," Josh said.

"There's no time for it," Briggs said. "You said it yourself just now. After tomorrow, they're gone."

"Not Ms. Evans."

Josh gazed fixedly down at his linked hands. They weren't using Ari enough, he thought. She had more insight into the people involved than they did, even if she didn't know them well. The killer's world was hers, or had been. How well had Ari really known Felicia?

"Considering the time factor, Ari couldn't have done it," Josh said, letting his annoyance show at last.

"I meant that she'll be around if we have more questions about the victim and the people here," Briggs said mildly.

"Yeah."

Briggs leaned back in his chair. "She might have more to tell us than we realize — hold on." He opened his cell phone, spoke into it, and then closed it again. "Well."

"What is it?" Charlie asked.

"That was Winston Barr. He thinks he might have seen Felicia's daughter."

CHAPTER 10

Josh stood beside his car, not opening the door in spite of the rain. Winston's news had galvanized them all; it could mean a break in the case. After much discussion, he, Briggs, and Charlie had decided not to bring Winston back for questioning in light of his worsening health. Instead Josh was being dispatched to talk to him at the bed-and-breakfast where he was staying.

Josh was glad to be leaving the fairgrounds, at least for a while. The atmosphere had become claustrophobic, and he'd been there all day. A change of scenery might give him a fresh view on this whole thing. Bouncing ideas off someone else would help, too.

With sudden decisiveness, Josh turned and strode toward Barn B. Inside, the air was closer and the light dimmer than ever, but he was aware of the small group of women seated to the right of the door. They watched him, all wary, as he approached them. He couldn't blame them, he thought as he walked in. They'd all been through a lot today, innocent or not.

"Josh?" Ari said as he neared them. "When can we leave?"

He shook his head. "Not yet. But, Ari, we need to speak with you."

"Again? I've told you everything I know."

Josh shrugged. "There are a few things we want to go over."

"Darn it," she grumbled, and reached for her parka. "All right. But I hope this won't take long."

"It won't. But the quicker we can clear this up, the better."

"I don't know what I can tell you that I haven't already," she grumbled as they went out. "Seriously, when is this going to end? It's getting late."

"Soon enough. We're just about done questioning everyone."

"And?"

"Most people didn't have anything to do with it, as far as we know."

"Then who does?"

"Just you and the others in the barn."

"The Suspects Club," she murmured.

"What?"

"Oh, that's just what we're calling ourselves. What is this?" she asked. They had stopped beside Josh's car. "I thought we were going to Barn A?"

"No. I need to talk with you." He opened the passenger door of his Volkswagen and glanced around to make sure nobody saw them. "Here, get in."

She didn't move. "Josh, what is this?"

"I'll tell you on the way."

"To where?"

"Ari, would you just get in?" he said, exasperated. "Before someone notices."

"Oh, all right," she said, and climbed into the car.

"Finally," he muttered, and went around to his side. Ari was looking at him as warily as any of the suspects in the barn had. "What?"

"What do you mean, 'before someone notices'?"

He put the car in gear and drove toward the gate. "That you're with me."

"What?" She stared at him. "Josh, what is going on?"

"I need to ask Winston Barr some questions. And I think you can tell me things we wouldn't find out otherwise."

"I've told you everything I know." She was frowning at him. "The state police don't know about this, do they? Chief Mason and

Detective Briggs. They don't know I'm with you."

"No, they don't."

"Josh, for goodness' sake!" She shifted in her seat to stare at him. "You're going to get in trouble."

He shrugged. "I don't think so. Ari, can you tell me about the others in the barn?"

Ari glanced out the window. They had passed a farm or two, and now they were passing developed land with houses too big for their lots. "You know, I don't think the Wool Festival will be around for much longer."

"After this, you mean?"

"The murder? No. It's not rural enough around here anymore. I can remember when the festival was twice the size it is now." She paused. "It is a strange place for a murder."

"Mm. So, what about the others?"

"I don't know, Josh. I only know them from today. Oh, except for Nancy and Rosalia, of course, who regularly frequent my shop. But I don't know Rosalia that well."

"Is she from around here?"

"She's from Acushnet. She was a year behind me in high school."

There were houses on both sides of the

road now, and traffic grew heavier. It felt strange being in a busy area after the isolation of the wool festival. "So she's about your age? Almost thirty?"

"Yes. Why?"

"No reason." It was odd that so many of the people now left were around the same age, but then, a lot about this case was odd. "Which way do we go?" he asked, as they stopped at a traffic light.

"I don't know. Where are we going?"

"Sorry. I've got to ask Winston Barr something. He's staying at the Edgewater."

"Oh. Turn right, then."

Josh swung the car onto a more heavily traveled road. "What's your take on him?"

"On Winston? I told you. He's very gentlemanly."

"Mm." He'd struck Josh that way, too. "And you only saw him that once, at the party at his apartment?"

"Yes."

Again he wondered how well Ari had really known Felicia, but decided not to bring up that topic yet. "He and Debbie seemed close."

"I know. Like father and daughter. I had no idea."

He took his eyes off the road for a moment to look at her. "Then you didn't know

Debbie in New York?"

"No. I met Beth, but only once. At that same party."

"What did you think of her? Then, I mean."

Ari sat still for a moment, her lips pursed. "Now that I think about it, I think I decided she couldn't be trusted."

That made Josh look at her in surprise. "Why?"

"I don't know. There was something she said to me about my success. But I remember she didn't sound sincere." Again Ari fell still. "I heard her talking to someone, praising her work, and then later making fun of it to some other person. It made me think she was a backstabber. Oh!"

Josh grinned at her. "Good choice of words."

"Josh, could she have done it?"

"It's possible."

"I think she has it in her, and I think she would do it in a sneaky way."

"Mm." Beth had struck Josh that way, too. He wasn't about to tell Ari, though, that the crime seemed to be one of opportunity. "Is she being very friendly to the others?"

"No. She's saying snarky things whenever she has the chance, particularly to Debbie. There's no love lost between them," she said. "Turn left here."

Josh turned onto a side street that led toward Freeport's waterfront. "What about Debbie?"

"She's pretty much ignoring Beth, although she's said a few things back. Josh, she mostly acted . . . weird."

"Who, Debbie?"

"Yes. Like she was crazy. Manic. It was as if she was happy that Felicia was dead." She was quiet for a moment. "Except that she fell apart when Winston arrived."

"Mm."

"Could it have been an act?"

"Which part? The craziness or the collapse?"

"The collapse. It didn't seem fake, but . . ." She trailed off. "Josh, does she have a motive?"

"How did she strike you apart from that?" he said, not answering her. "Was she upset about Felicia?"

"She seemed mostly excited about running the magazine."

"Yes, that's a possible motive," he conceded. And it was odd that Debbie had been so open about it with the other women. He wondered what she loved more, the magazine or Felicia. "Tell me about these people."

"What people?" Ari asked, sounding surprised.

"These magazine people. What are they doing here?"

"I've been wondering that myself," she said. "They said they came to the festival to write about it, but why? It's not that big or important."

"Is there *anything* about it that makes it stand out?"

"Well, it is one of the oldest in the country, and one of the longest running, too. Continuously, I mean. So I guess that makes it interesting. Still." She frowned. "I can see why Beth would be here. Her magazine sent her to do an article. It even explains why Debbie is here. But Felicia?" She frowned. "Why would the owner of a successful magazine come to our small festival?"

"That's something we're wondering ourselves. What about the other people?"

"I'll find out soon enough. Well, you know Diane, of course. You know she didn't do it. And Rosalia and Nancy didn't have anything to do with Felicia."

"That we know of."

"You can't be serious."

"It's early yet. Is that the Edgewater?"

Ari glanced where he pointed, at a stone and shingled house. It was old and sprawling, set back from the street with a broad lawn in front. Rhododendron bushes stood to either side of the front steps like sentinels, and sodden daffodils drooped in the narrow flower beds that edged the house. Across the street from it was a seawall, and beyond that the harbor, which gave the house its name. "Yes. It's supposed to be very nice."

Josh nodded, and turned the car into the small parking area across from it, facing toward the rough gray water. "Let's sit here a minute."

Ari sighed. "Let me guess. You're not going to let me go in with you, are you?"

"No." He unbuckled his seat belt and turned toward her. "Ari, what I really need is any information you can give me about the people in that barn."

"I really don't know anything about them, Josh." She spread her hands. "They all seem nice. When I was wet this morning, Lauren — Lauren Dubrowski — put one of her afghans around me. She didn't have to do that."

"And?" he said, when she didn't go on.

"Well. Do you know that she lost a job because of Felicia? Or at least she thinks she did."

"Yeah, we know. How did she react to that?"

"I think she's still mad about it, Josh, though she seems to have a better job now."

"So she was mad at Felicia," he said thoughtfully. "Just about the job?"

"Yes. What else is there?" She studied him. "What is it you're not telling me?"

"Nothing. So." He held up his fingers and began counting off. "Diane, Rosalia, Nancy, Beth Marley, Debbie Patrino — who am I missing?"

"Me."

He shook his head. "Not you. Oh, yeah. Annie Walker."

Ari frowned. "I don't know anything about her, Josh."

"Didn't you talk to her?"

"Yes, a little, but she's pretty much kept to herself."

"Why?"

She shook her head. "I don't know. She was pleasant enough this morning, but this afternoon she's not talking to anyone. I did notice her do something strange, though."

"What?"

"When Winston came in, she was glaring at Debbie, like she was really angry."

"Did she know Debbie before?"

"She could have. She says she remembers me from New York."

Josh stopped in the act of reaching for the

door handle. There was something he had to ask, and he didn't want to. "Ari, how well did you know Felicia?"

She looked at him in surprise. "Not well. Why?"

"How long did you live in New York?"

"I don't think I like where this is going," she said, her eyes narrowed.

"You were there . . . a year? two years?"

"Not quite a year. And, yes, I did know her. You know that already."

"Mm-hm. Did she give you a hard time, too?"

"She gave everybody a hard time, Josh."

"Hard enough to chase you away?"

"What?" She stared at him. "What do you mean?"

"Is she why you left New York?"

"Felicia? No, of course not. She never did anything to me."

"No?"

"What is this, Josh? You know I didn't kill her. What reason would I have?"

He stared forward, through the rain streaming down the windshield at the storm-tossed water. He had to ask these questions. Of course he knew Ari hadn't killed Felicia. She didn't have a reason — at least not one that he knew of. But he did wonder why she'd left New York, and if Felicia had anything to do with it. "Did you ever have any of your designs reviewed in her magazine?"

"No, I knew her only through Knitting Guild meetings. I didn't like her — oh, all right, I was scared of her just like everyone else."

"Yet you weren't afraid of her today," he pointed out.

"No, because I've changed a lot since then. I've been through more, and she has — had — no power over me." She huffed out her breath. "Josh, I was not about to let some la-di-da New Yorker come into my town and look down on me."

He nodded. "Why did you leave, though?" he asked, more for himself now than for the investigation. "I thought you were successful."

"Not very." She was looking out her window. "I had that one piece in *Vogue Knitting* and I did sell a few designs freelance, but companies weren't exactly knocking down my door. It's expensive to live in New York, Josh, even with roommates."

"Did Felicia have anything to do with it?"

"What, with my failure? Not that I know of. It's just a very hard business to succeed in. I gave it a shot, and then I came home. Felicia was right about that," she added.

"This morning she said I ran away, and I did."

He was quiet for a moment. "What haven't you told me?"

"Nothing," Ari insisted.

"I don't mean about Felicia."

Ari crossed her arms over her chest. "Nothing that has anything to do with Felicia." Her gaze bored into him. "Why do you care, anyway?"

God knows, he thought, and reached for the door handle. He believed Ari. She had no reason to lie about her experiences in New York. Yet he felt she was holding something back. "I've got to go talk to Barr," he said.

"Is it really that important that you had to come here rather than talk on the phone?"

"Yes," he said, and got out, shutting the door quickly behind him. He battled the storm, worse here with the wind whipping across the water, and climbed the steps to the Edgewater's porch. A few moments later he was shown into the sunroom. Large windows curtained by sheer lace draperies looked over the same scene he'd studied earlier. He could see his car, with Ari an indistinct figure inside it. He hadn't really learned anything concrete from her, and yet she had given him a bit more insight into the suspects. Beth was surly, Debbie a little strange, the locals seemed uninvolved, Lauren Dubrowski had reason to dislike Felicia, and Annie Walker didn't want to get involved. He didn't blame her for that.

Winston was seated in a white wicker chair facing the windows. He still wore his beret, though he'd shed his overcoat to reveal a well-cut suit of navy worsted. He looked shrunken somehow, and paler, but his face was resolute.

"Mr. Barr," Josh said, pulling another chair closer. It had a brightly colored cushion that was probably cheerful in the right weather. "How are you?"

Winston nodded. "This is a comfortable place."

"Good." Josh was a bit surprised at his own attitude. Usually he wasn't so gentle with witnesses, even those who had recently suffered a bereavement. "You said you had something to tell us," he said, getting right to the point.

"Yes. I think I may have seen Felicia's daughter."

"When?"

"One day when I was returning from work. My driver had pulled up in front of our building. Felicia was just under the canopy, talking with a young woman."

"Could you see her face?"

"No, she had her back turned to me," he said regretfully. "I had the impression she was angry. Certainly Felicia looked upset."

"Why would you think she was Felicia's daughter? Didn't anyone from the magazine ever come to your apartment?"

"Rarely, though sometimes we got calls from unhappy designers or vendors. We're very careful to screen our calls. It's difficult when someone is in the position Felicia was."

Josh nodded. "Could you describe the girl?"

Winston spread his hands. "I didn't see her well. I'd say she was of average height."

"Meaning?"

"Five six or thereabouts. She was a bit taller than Felicia."

"Mm-hm. Thin or heavy?"

"It was hard to tell. She was wearing a bulky coat, but she didn't seem overweight. It was winter."

"And her hair?"

Winston shook his head. "She had a hat pulled down, so I couldn't see it. A knitted hat, of course," he added.

"Did she see you?"

"No, but Felicia did, when I got out of the car. She said something, and she looked angry. The girl pulled back, and then she turned."

Josh leaned forward. "Could you see her face?"

Winston shook his head regretfully. "No. She was to my side when I got out of the car, and that's the way she turned. Her back was still to me. But I'd remember her walk," he went on. "Very strong, very determined. Of course, she might just have been trying to get away from me."

"Why?"

He shook his head. "I assume because she didn't think I knew about her."

"What did Felicia have to say?"

Winston shook his head. "That it was something to do with the magazine. But she was upset all evening. I didn't believe her. No," he added softly, "I didn't believe her."

Josh bent forward, forearms resting on his thighs. "Mr. Barr, how certain are you that this was Felicia's daughter?"

"Nearly positive, Detective. You see, she walked the way Felicia does, and there was something about the set of her shoulders."

"I see." Josh leaned back. "Would you recognize this girl if you saw her again?"

"I don't know. Perhaps if I saw her walk." He rested his head on the back of the chair, his color worse than ever. "I'm sorry, but you'll have to excuse me. I'm rather tired."

Josh looked at him closely, and then nodded. "I won't take any more of your time, sir," he said, getting up. He'd get no more from Winston Barr today. "But I'd like to set something up for you to look at some people."

Winston's look was keen. "The remaining suspects?"

"Yes sir.

He nodded. "I'll do whatever I have to. Now, if you'll excuse me."

Josh reached out a hand to help the other man to his feet, and then withdrew it in the face of Winston's innate dignity. He was handling a difficult situation with a great deal of grace. "I'll be talking to you," Josh said, and went out.

Ari was sitting with her arms still crossed when Josh got back into the car. "Anything?" she asked.

He shook his head. "Not that I can talk about," he said, starting the engine.

She looked at him curiously. "Now you're holding out on me."

"I have to. Damn, I hate going back to that place."

"So do I." She sighed and brushed back a strand of her hair. "Josh, when are you going to let us go?"

"Soon, I hope," he said, and lapsed into silence as he considered what he'd learned from Winston. He was relieved that Ari was quiet as well. He was tired. They were all tired. Unfortunately his work wasn't done. Not by a long shot.

Back at the Yarn Festival, Josh escorted Ari to Barn B and then returned to sit with Charlie and Detective Briggs. He told them in as much detail as he could what he'd learned from Winston. When he was done there was silence. "He knows something," Briggs finally said. "You should have brought him back."

Josh shook his head. "He wouldn't have been able to tell us anything tonight. He was practically asleep on his feet."

"We still have tomorrow," Charlie said. "We'll set something up for the morning, while everyone's still here."

"Where'd we find for the out-of-towners to stay tonight?" Briggs asked.

"The Welcome Inn. They already had reservations."

"The motel near the highway?"

"Yeah. We'll have people there watching them, of course, and patrol cars driving by the local people's houses at regular intervals."

Briggs rubbed at his chin. "All right," he said finally. "I guess I see your point. We'll let them go for tonight, as long as the out-of-towners go straight to the motel and not to New York."

"I'll station a car at the motel to make sure everyone gets there."

Briggs nodded. "We'll give backup. All right. Let's go tell them they can go."

Ari was tired. It had been a long and traumatic day, and being stuck in this barn didn't help. Nor had that brief, strange trip with Josh, which she kept to herself. As far as anyone else was concerned, she'd simply had to answer more questions. Now she sat slumped on her metal chair with the other suspects. She was cold, hungry, a bit wet about the edges, and very bored. "I wonder if they're ever going to let us go."

"Nah." Diane stopped spinning and stretched out, her arms folded across her chest. "They're going to keep us here until one of us breaks."

"They can't hold us that long, can they?" Nancy asked.

"No, I don't think more than twenty-four hours. That means tomorrow morning." Ari looked around at the group. Debbie was sitting a little apart, arms crossed on her chest and staring ahead. She hadn't said a word since her return to Barn B. "Was anyone planning on going home tonight?"

"No, I was going to stay anyway," Lauren said. "It's too long a ride back to New York for me."

"Me too," Annie put in.

"I just want to go home, get something to eat, and get dry," Nancy said.

"Did you get any good pictures?" Diane asked.

Nancy looked down at the bench beside her, where her digital camera sat. With its large lens and sturdy body, it was a cut above the average digital camera. "Yes, I think so. I think they're okay."

"I'm sure they're better than that," Ari said. "The pictures you took for my patterns are terrific."

"Thank you." Nancy picked up the camera and flicked a switch. "Today's pictures are mostly of the Sheep to Shawl competition. My sister's team would have won."

"Are you going to sell them to the *Clarion*?" she asked, referring to the small local newspaper.

"Probably. Let me see what I've got."

"Is that you shearing the sheep?" Lauren asked. She was looking over Nancy's shoulder at the camera's screen.

"No, that's my sister. She was in Barn D all day, lucky thing," she said, flicking the switch again. "These are the ones I took in here. Here's one of you, Ari."

Ari twisted to look at the screen, and then turned back toward the door as someone spoke. "Folks, can I have your attention please?" Charlie said. Josh was at his side, with Briggs slightly in back.

"We're calling it a day, for now. Now, wait." He held up his hand as several people started talking at once. "That doesn't mean you can all go home. Those of you from out of town have to stay here."

"I think we all have rooms, anyway," Lauren said. "Right?"

Several of the others nodded. "At the Welcome Inn," Beth said. "God-awful place."

"Figured that. And the locals — Ari, Diane, Nancy, Rosalia — you can go on home, but we'll have troopers driving by to check up on you throughout the night."

"Can't we even get some dinner?" Lauren asked.

"You can get something delivered to the motel."

Debbie was looking at him through narrowed eyes. "You want to know where we all are."

"Yes."

"You still think one of us did it."

Charlie paused. "Let's say we can't rule anyone out yet."

"Why? I never had contact with Felicia," Nancy said.

"I did, but it was positive. This isn't fair," Annie said.

"What happens next?" Ari asked.

"We need to do more questioning and investigating," Briggs said, coming forward.

"You can't keep us beyond tomorrow," Beth said defiantly. "My lawyer told me that."

He nodded. "That's true. But we'll be talking with you all again before you go."

"We don't have anything more to tell you," Lauren said.

"Mm. You might have seen something without realizing its importance," said Briggs.

"I doubt it," she muttered.

"We'll see you all again tomorrow morning," Charlie said.

"Where?" Ari asked. "At the police station?"

Charlie shook his head. "Not enough room for all of you," he said. "The motel's going to let us use their conference rooms."

Nancy glanced across the barn. "Will it be

okay if I leave my fleeces here?" she asked.

"Are you sure you want to do that, Nancy?" Charlie asked.

"I just don't want to lug them home. I'm tired."

"They're a big investment for you."

"I know. That's why I want to know if they'll be safe here for tonight."

Charlie and Briggs looked at each other. "I can't guarantee it, but we'll have police stationed here. They should be safe," Charlie said.

"Good." She yawned. "I really didn't have anything to do with this. Do I really have to go tomorrow?"

"You're a suspect," Briggs said crisply. "Anyone who is missing will be in serious trouble." He waited, but no one said anything. "Good. Nine o'clock sharp tomorrow morning." With that he turned and walked out of the barn, Charlie behind him. Only Josh paused, his eyes locked with Ari's. Then he, too, left.

"Joe is going to be ticked," Diane said, getting up.

"Like we're not?" Beth shot back.

"I hope Winston's okay," Debbie said. She hadn't moved, though nearly everyone had gone to their original tables to pack up.

"I'm sure he's all right," Ari said. "There

are some good bed-and-breakfasts in the area."

"He'll need me to stay with him."

Ari touched her hand. "I'm sorry."

Debbie nodded. "Thank you," she said, and pulled back. "I'll call him at the bed-and-breakfast once we're at the motel."

"I'm sure he'll be happy to hear from you," Ari said, and at last walked over to her table to pack up her belongings.

"Joe will be ticked," Diane repeated in a low voice. "That cop of yours . . ."

"It was the chief and the state cop, and you know it." Ari tiredly brushed at a strand of hair. "I just want to go home and get warm."

"I do, too," Diane said after a minute. "I'm going to bring my car over to the door."

"I'll come with you." Together they walked to the door. This wasn't over, Ari thought. Not by a long shot.

CHAPTER 11

The light lasted longer now at the end of April, but the late afternoon was unrelentingly gloomy when Ariadne reached her shop. The light shining through the large plate-glass window beckoned to her as, holding her hood to keep it from being blown off by the wind, she dashed inside the building. Ariadne's Web was an oasis of calm and light and color, and for the first time that day Ari felt herself relaxing.

"Ari! I didn't think we'd see you here today."

"Yes, they finally let us go, Laura," she said to her aunt standing behind the counter. "How has it been?"

"Busier than I expected. Take a look."

Ari gazed around the shop and smiled. Nubby or smooth, thick or thin, pastel hued or jewel toned, yarn was everywhere. It was stacked in diamond-shaped bins and piled on low shelves beneath the windows; it spilled over from large wicker baskets on the floor. Knitted goods of all kinds, sweaters and shawls and hats, were displayed in the front window and on the tops of the counters running down the middle of the shop. Near the sales counter were racks of knitting needles and other notions. A rocking chair with another basket of yarn beside it was nestled in a corner. The shop was homey and bright and comfortable, a balm to Ari's soul.

"You sold a lot," she commented as she walked through the shop. "Hi, Summer." Ari smiled at the young woman who knelt on the floor, straightening the bins on the side wall.

"A lot of the lighter wool went today," Laura said. "No one wanted cottons yet. Ruth Taylor was in, too, for baby yarn."

Ari looked out from the back room, where she had gone to hang her coat. "Don't tell me. Another grandchild?"

"Yes. She wants to make an afghan. I convinced her to buy Peruvian wool for it."

"However did you do that?" Ari asked. Though an avid knitter, Ruth was stingy, and the yarn she'd chosen was not cheap.

"It's her daughter Carol's first one. I told her a first baby deserves something special. And how was the festival, dear?"

Ari, standing with her elbows on the sales counter, gave her aunt a look. "You know quite well how it was."

Laura laid a hand on her arm. "I know. How are you?"

"Hanging in, I guess. It wasn't a lot of fun." She shuddered at the memory of Felicia sagging against her. "Have people been talking about it?"

"Of course they have, dear. We heard that you stumbled over the body."

"Not quite," Ari said, and went on to relate what had happened. In a town of this size, rumor, accurate or not, spread faster than light. Too many local people, participant or customers, had been at the festival for the story to be contained. That meant she'd be the center of attention again.

"How did Ted take it?" Laura asked when she finished.

"About how you'd expect."

"Oh dear. That bad?"

"He was ready to ride to my rescue and tear every cop apart if he had to."

Laura smiled. "He still cares about you, Ari."

"I know," she said gloomily. That fact had made their divorce that much harder. If he did care about her, why hadn't he shown it when they were married? "Thank God he has Megan this weekend. At least she's away from it."

"I hope he didn't tell her anything."

"He has more sense than that." Ari stretched, and turned to look at the clock at the back wall. Usually on a Saturday she stayed late, doing miscellaneous paperwork, making notes on orders for the next week, and tidying up. Today all she wanted was to get home, pour herself a glass of wine, and sink into a hot bath.

"I'm heading home," she said. "Can you handle closing?"

"Of course I can, dear. You need rest."

"That's for certain." Ari walked to the back room for her coat and then came back out. "Thanks. I'll talk to you tomorrow."

"Call me if the police come after you."

"I will," Ari said, and went out.

To her surprise the rain had let up into a drizzle. A patch of sky glowed in the west with an orange sunset underneath lowering clouds. The storm was passing over at last. What would have happened if there'd been no rain today? Would Felicia have been killed? It was something to ponder, and yet, as Ari headed home, she pushed it from her mind. She'd had enough of murder for one day.

■ ■ ■ ■

The long spring twilight was fading into darkness. At the Welcome Inn, where the participants of the festival were staying, state and local police were stationed in the corridors and in the parking lot outside. The suspects were in their rooms, recovering from the rigors of the day. At least, most of them were.

Quietly, Beth Marley, toting behind her a small wheeled suitcase, slipped out of her room. Earlier she'd been annoyed at being given a room at the end of the corridor, making her walk farther than the others, but now she was glad of it. The state trooper standing at the intersection of the motel's two wings, near the elevators, was at the moment looking the other way. Someone on the other corridor had opened a door and put an empty tray outside, catching his attention. Taking advantage of his distraction, Beth opened the fire door near her, closed it softly, and made her escape.

Chief Mason, sitting in his unmarked car in the parking lot below, stretched and then reached for the cardboard cup of coffee from his cup holder. It had gone cold, and the doughnut he'd bought to go with it was long since eaten.

Damn, this wasn't how he'd planned to spend his Saturday night. He'd made reservations at the Harrison House for a date with Eileen, hoping that the romantic setting would finally make an impact on her. Though he'd been seeing Ari's mother for a few months, he'd yet to make any headway with her. She remembered him too well as the class clown from their days at Freeport High, and as a result she sometimes treated him as an erring student rather than a grown man. Charlie could be patient when he needed to be, and he knew that the death of Eileen's husband at sea while fishing had hit her hard. They'd married relatively late in life, and by all accounts their marriage had been good. But that was years ago. It was time for her to start living again, he thought, and maybe a class clown was just what she needed.

A movement at the far end of the parking lot caught his attention. He squinted, trying to make out who it was. Age was catching up with him. Lately he'd started wearing bifocals. He didn't recognize the car, but that wasn't surprising. Other people were staying at the motel, after all, including some who made it a temporary residence. It wasn't until the car passed him that he noticed the out-of-state plates and the telltale pink beret. What the hell was Beth Marley doing out, and how the hell had the trooper stationed on her floor missed her escape?

Putting his car in gear, he reached for his radio and called for backup. Beth was heading for the connector to Route 195, which hooked up with Route 95 in Providence. From there she could head to New York, or anywhere else she wanted. "Suspect on the move," he said tersely into his radio, and took off.

For someone unfamiliar with the area, Beth drove surprisingly fast, and was nearly at the ramp to the highway when a Freeport cruiser caught up with her, lights flashing and siren blaring. At first it seemed she might make a run for it, but the long, curving ramp defeated her. With a jerk, she pulled her car to the side of the road and opened her door, making a car behind her swerve, its driver honking his horn angrily. Charlie pulled up alongside the cruiser and stepped out of his vehicle. Other cars abruptly slowed at the sight of the police cars.

Beth stood by the side of her car, fists

balled on her hips and her chin stuck out. "What?" she demanded. "Why are you chasing me?"

Charlie ambled over to her. "Going somewhere, Mrs. Marley?"

"I need some things," she said, glaring up at him.

"Such as?"

"Things. You wouldn't understand."

By now the state trooper had left his car, too, and was standing at Beth's rear bumper. "I thought you already had a reservation at the motel," said Charlie. "Didn't you bring a suitcase?"

"I wasn't prepared."

"Oh? I thought the motel sent up any toiletries people needed."

"Women's things, okay?" she snapped.

"Ah. I'm sure they have those, too."

"I use a certain brand."

"But the stores are that way," Charlie said, pointing back to where they'd come from. "You're going in the wrong direction."

"Oh. Am I?" she said, suddenly flustered. "I didn't realize. Thank you for telling me."

Charlie didn't trust her meekness any more than he had her belligerence. "You have to go back to the motel. We'll give you an escort."

"I can find the way, thank you," she

snapped as she opened her car door.

"Regardless, we're gong to be accompanying you. Carney, would you lead the way?"

"Yes sir," the trooper said, and got back into his car.

"I'll be behind you," Charlie said, as the trooper pulled up in front of Beth's car.

"This is so unnecessary," she muttered as she started her engine.

"Wouldn't want you to get lost, now would we? We'll see you back at the motel." He waited until the trooper had started off, with Beth behind him, before returning to his car. Slowly the small procession returned to the motel. Charlie took Beth's arm as she got out, personally escorting her inside. For once, she didn't protest, but he could feel her anger and tension as he led her back to her room.

He took out his phone and paged Josh. "I'll have a word with you later, Mackie," he said to the trooper who still stood guard on Beth's floor, and walked out. It was high time they found out more about Beth Marley.

Home was a haven. Freshly showered, wearing her old fleece robe and suede moccasins, Ari settled in front of the television in her living room with her dinner on the coffee table before her. It wasn't much, just frozen lasagna tossed into the microwave, but the wine she'd chosen was good and there was a figure-skating competition on later. For the moment, life was fine.

She had just finished her meal and was using the remote to flick through the channels when the phone rang. It was an unpleasant jolt. "Go away," she muttered, and reached for the receiver. "Hello?"

"Good, you're home."

Ari blinked. It was Ted's voice, but without his usual belligerence. Of course. Megan was with him. "Yes, I just got in. Everything's all right," she added quickly, before he could start up.

"You're saying it's all settled?"

"No. Is Megan there?"

"Yes."

"Let me talk to her."

"In a minute. What happened?"

Ari sighed. "They don't know who the murderer is. They sent the out-of-town people to a motel, and the rest of us home."

"That was stupid. Someone will take off. You wait."

"Maybe." She rested her forehead against the wall. "I'm okay, Ted. They don't think I did it." At least she didn't think so.

"They'd better not. They —"

"Is Megan there?" she interrupted, before he could go into another tirade.

"Yeah. You're sure you're okay?"

"Yes, Ted. Please put Megan on."

He said something she didn't catch, and then she heard Megan's excited voice. "Mommy?"

"Hi, honey," Ari said, smiling as she always did when she talked with her daughter. "How was your day?"

"Oh, super, Mommy. Daddy took me to Providence Place and we went to the Omni. It was cool."

"I'll bet," Ari said, amused and touched at the image that conjured up. It wasn't just the thought of Ted at an upscale shopping mall, but the idea that he'd taken Megan to see a movie on an enormous screen in spite of his occasional vertigo. "What else did you do?"

Megan chattered on happily, talking about all the shopping they'd done. For some reason she adored home goods stores, and had apparently dragged Ted through Restoration Hardware and Crate & Barrel. Fortunately Megan was still young enough that it didn't occur to her that her mother had a life. Ari was grateful not to have to field any awkward questions.

Eventually Megan wound down. Ted was

going to make popcorn and had promised to play a board game with her. Ari hung up at last, wishing she could be there with Megan, and yet relieved to be alone after the events of the day. After bringing out some crackers and cheese, she poured herself another glass of wine and sat back. She was watching figure skating when the doorbell rang, startling her. Annoyed at the second interruption, she went to the door. "Who is it?"

"It's me, Josh."

"Josh?" She undid the locks and opened the door, wondering why he so often showed up when she looked her worst. "What are you doing here?"

"Can I come in?"

"Of course, but what about them?" She gestured toward the patrol car driving by slowly past her house.

"Oh, don't worry about them," Josh said.

"Okay." She stepped back from the door, but not before seeing a curtain twitch in the window of the house across the street. Mrs. Dean was keeping vigil, as usual. By tomorrow everyone would know about Josh's visit. "Come in, sit down."

"Thanks. I'm not interrupting anything, am I?"

"No, why?"

"You don't have any company?"

"Oh, you mean the wine and cheese? When Megan's not here I treat myself. Would you like a glass, or are you working?"

"No, I'm on a break. If you have any beer I'll take it."

"Of course." A few minutes later she came back from the kitchen with a bottle of Sam Adams Pale Ale and a glass. To her surprise, Josh was staring intently at the screen. "Here you are."

"Thanks." Josh took a long pull from the bottle. "Are these the World Championships?"

"No, Worlds are in March. Do you like figure skating?"

"My mother does. Sometimes I watch it with her. You can keep it on," he added as she reached for the remote.

"No, it's okay. I'm taping it." How many men would do that with their mothers, let alone admit to it? Josh, she thought, was a nice man.

The silence that fell between them was companionable, and yet filled with unspoken words. Ari put her feet up on the coffee table, crossing her legs at the ankle. "Go ahead," she said to Josh. "It's an old table. I really should get something new."

"Are you ever going to do anything with this place?" he asked as he put his feet up. The living room was a symphony of beige and tan, in stark contrast to the colorful yarn shop.

"Someday. I never seem to get around to it. Anyway, right now it's good to have furniture that Megan can knock around and not be worried about it. Although she's getting into decorating," she said, and told him about Ted's ordeal of the afternoon.

"He's a good father," Josh said when she'd finished.

"Yes, he is."

He turned to look at her. "How did you two ever get together anyway? You seem so different."

"Yes, I know, but he made me laugh when I needed it."

"What do you mean, when you needed it?" Josh asked.

She looked away. Earlier today, when he'd been about to interview Winston Barr at the bed-and-breakfast, she'd been aware that he wanted to know more about her time in New York. "It doesn't have a thing to do with Felicia," she said firmly.

"I didn't think it did."

"Then why do you want to know?" she asked.

"I care about you."

The words hung silently in the air for a moment.

"I was seeing this guy," Ari finally admitted.

"Mm-hm."

"It's the old story, Josh. He had someone else."

"And?"

"And what? That's it."

"Is it?"

"Oh, all right. But I don't like talking about it." She leaned forward, her face in her hands. "God, I was such a fool."

"Why?"

"Because he was married." She looked up at him. "I didn't know. He didn't wear a wedding ring. I was waitressing at a small restaurant near Wall Street — I had to make some money — and that's how I met him. He was young, well dressed, always polite. We got to know each other and, well, things went on from there."

"Weren't there signs? Didn't you notice things about him that were off?"

"Oh, looking back, of course. We never went to his place. He always had some sort of business on the weekends. My roommates didn't like him, either, though they never said anything. I didn't want to notice, I guess." She took a deep breath. "On top of that, my career wasn't going well. Every design I submitted was rejected, and I didn't have the money to start a company on my own. I needed something positive in my life. He seemed to be it. Until I found out about his wife."

"How?"

Ari shook her head. She wasn't sure why she was pouring all this out to him, except that his quiet sympathy was comforting. She'd gotten over it, of course, but sometimes she felt a faint residual pain, of humiliation and rejection. "It was awful. He and his wife attended a charity event together and their picture was in one of the papers. One of the girls I worked with made sure I saw it."

"Aw, hell."

"I was devastated, Josh. I really loved him, or I thought I did. The next time I saw him was at the restaurant. I managed to get a break, and I told him what I knew. And do you know what he did?"

"No."

"He told me that it didn't matter that he was married, that his wife didn't understand him, that he was waiting for his kids to grow up so he could leave her. Josh, I almost believed him, but he had this look on his face."

"What look?"

"Smug. He looked smug, like a little kid getting away with something. That's when I broke it off." She looked away. "That did it for me. I'd made a fool of myself, and I was failing at my work. I hated the city. Too big, too noisy, too impersonal. So I left New York, got some work here at home at a yarn shop, and started figuring out what I wanted to do with my life. Then I met Ted."

"Rebound," he said.

"No." She frowned. "Of course not. Actually, I knew him already. He was a few years ahead of me in school. Someone fixed us up on a date, and I had a good time." She looked up at him. "Most people don't believe it, but Ted can be very funny when he wants to be."

"I've never seen that side of him."

"No." She sighed. "Lately all he is is angry, especially since things started going wrong in our marriage. I understand his anger," she went on before he could say anything. "It's how he learned to express his emotions. But it's very hard to live with."

"Then he must be very emotional," Josh said dryly.

Ari smiled. "You must admit that things

have been stressful."

"A little," he said.

But I can't complain too much." She smiled. "I have Megan because of Ted."

"Yes," he said, and their gazes held for a long moment.

Ari, a little startled, a little uncomfortable, was the first to look away. "What's happening in the investigation, or can you tell me?"

He blew out his breath. "I shouldn't. Briggs would have my hide if he knew."

"What about Chief Mason?"

"Him, too."

"Is Briggs in charge of the investigation, Josh?"

"Yes. Once the staties come in, they take over."

"Did you ever find Felicia's coat?"

He paused. "Yeah, but I probably shouldn't say anything."

"Then why are you here?" she said, exasperated. It certainly wasn't for personal reasons.

"I need to get away from it for a while." He looked at her. "You can understand that, can't you?"

Ari looked at the TV and then at her wine. Yes, she understood quite well.

"I'm not used to dealing with things like this," he went on. "These damned complicated investigations that get all tangled up and take days to unravel."

Ari turned her head to hide her smile at his unintended knitting puns. "You'll get it, Josh."

"Maybe. The first twenty-four hours are critical. Once we let the out-of-towners go, who knows what will happen?"

"Drink your beer," she said gently. "You do need a break."

Josh rested his head on the back of the couch and stared up at the ceiling. "Maybe we should have gone out tonight."

She looked at him, startled. "What?"

"It would have taken my mind off things."

"Oh," she said, looking down at her glass, unreasonably disappointed. For a little while this afternoon there had seemed to be a rapport between them. Now, buried in Josh's obsession with the investigation, it was gone. "So I'll put the skating back on. Michelle Kwan can take your mind off anything."

He gave her a quick, distracted smile. "No, never mind. I'll try to be better company."

She shifted on the couch, tucking one leg underneath her. "Okay," she said with a sigh. "You're not going to relax until you get it off your chest."

"Too much to think about for that. Damn, I'd almost rather have a drive-by shooting."

"Josh," she protested.

"At least we usually have a good idea of who the bad guys are, even if we can't prove it."

"I thought you left Boston because of things like that."

"Yeah, and stepped into Murderville instead."

"That's not fair, and you know it." They were quiet for a while. "Why did you leave, then? Because of the drive-bys?"

"That was part of it."

"But not all?"

"No." He was quiet for so long, Ari thought he wasn't going to continue. "You know, Ari, all my years on the force in Boston, I only had to draw my service revolver three times. Never had to fire a round . . . until a few months before I came here." He looked at her, and the pain in his eyes was so deep she wanted to flinch. "Have you ever heard of suicide by cop?"

"No."

"Well, I came up against someone who wanted to kill himself, and he chose me as his method."

"What do you mean?" Ari asked, dread pooling in her stomach.

"I mean I shot him, Ari." He looked at her. "I killed him."

The fairgrounds were quiet after the suspects left. The police had packed it in long ago; the detectives were gone, as well as the crime-scene van. That left only some state troopers to guard the entrance and the grounds themselves, which were dark and somehow menacing tonight. Trooper Allen, new to the job and eager to prove himself, conscientiously inspected the buildings, one by one. Barn A was deserted. So was Barn D, except for the sheep, who stirred at his entrance. The doors to Barn C had police seals on them, and were further surrounded by crime-scene tape. No one would disturb that building tonight. That left only Barn B.

Barn B was darker, and chillier, than ever. Allen didn't like dark, open spaces, but he ignored his feelings as he flashed his light around, illuminating corners and leaving wide swathes of gloom. It was empty, with most of the belongings of the various suspects removed. All that were left were the looms inside the Sheep to Shawl enclosure and the fleece bins, one of which was still full. Allen shone his light on the bin, turned, and then looked back. What had he just seen?

He was crossing the barn to the bins to take a closer look when he heard a bell ringing. It wasn't coming from outside, he thought, stopping to listen, or from one of the other buildings. It drew him, though, to that one full bin. Someone had lost a phone in there, he thought, as it chirped one last time. It would be easy enough to do. Bend over too far, and it would probably fall to the bottom.

Leaning over the bin, still wondering what he'd seen, Allen began shifting the fleeces. They were heavier than he'd expected, and far denser. He began to revise his thoughts about the phone. It couldn't be too far from the top. If that were so, why hadn't the owner found it?

He pulled back another fleece and stopped dead still, realizing he'd found his answer. What he saw, instead of a cell phone, was a foot. Someone was buried under the fleece.

CHAPTER 12

What Josh had just told Ari shook her to the core. "Oh my God," she exclaimed, before she could stop herself.

"Yeah." He stared ahead, and she wondered if he was reliving the event. "Yeah, it kind of changed my life."

She drew her legs up tighter beneath her. "How did it happen? If you don't mind my asking."

He looked at her intensely. "I don't know why I'm telling you this."

She had told him about her life, but this wasn't exactly the same. "Maybe you need to," she said gently.

"I don't know." He blew out his breath. "God, I'm tired."

And vulnerable. She shouldn't take advantage of that, and yet she sensed he needed to talk. She doubted he'd told many people about this. "What happened?"

"Oh hell. All right. It came out of nowhere. My partner and I were returning to the station after responding to an assault call. There was a blue-and-white with a car pulled over to the curb on Bowdoin Street — this was Area A, by the way, Government Center area — nothing that seemed unusual. But just before we passed them the car took off at high speed. Luckily it was early morning, 'cause that part of the city's pretty busy during the day. The uniform called for help and we took off after the vehicle."

"Uh-huh," Ari murmured, not wanting to disturb his train of thought. She had been to Boston and was familiar with the area near City Hall, and several federal buildings nearby. Massachusetts General Hospital was located there also. "What happened?"

"Well. He sped down Cambridge Street and took off onto Storrow Drive at Charles Circle. How he ever took that exit, I don't know. He just missed taking out another car. You familiar with Storrow Drive?" he asked, looking at her.

"Yes."

"You know how narrow and curvy it is."

"Someone painted 'The Curse' over 'Curve' on the Reverse Curve sign," she murmured.

That made him smile. "Yeah, and the Sox

241

finally won. Anyway, it was a tough chase. We got up to eighty at one point. He was weaving back and forth, and finally he lost it at the Mass. Ave. bridge. Went right into the abutment. Well, we thought he'd had it and we jumped out, but then he came out of his car, bleeding from the forehead and ready to shoot."

"He had a gun?"

"Yeah. We drew our weapons and yelled at him to drop the gun. But he just kept coming closer, screaming that he was going to shoot."

"And?" she prompted when he didn't go on.

"We fired," he said flatly. "He got off a round and I fired."

"But not just you."

"No. No. Three of us. There were other cop cars there by then, but no one else in position. Five rounds, and he went down. We're trained to shoot for the middle of the body, and I did."

"And?"

He shrugged. "DOA at Mass General."

"Oh, Josh."

"Whenever you fire your weapon there's an investigation. The autopsy showed it was a bullet in the heart that killed him. And guess whose gun fired that round?"

"Yours."

"Mine," he agreed. "We were all on administrative leave until they figured out what happened. The investigation found that we acted the only way we could, considering the circumstances, so we were reinstated. Life goes on."

"But there's more to it than that, isn't there?" Ari asked after a moment.

"Yeah. Turns out the guy had been depressed for a while and had been talking about death."

"Suicide by cop," Ari said, understanding now.

"Yeah. God damn it. He wanted to kill himself, and he chose me."

"Josh, not you," she said gently. "Any cop would have done."

"Yeah, but it *was* me, Ari, and I have to live with it. I had counseling afterward. It helped some. I realize that I had to act the way I did, considering the way the guy behaved. I believed I was in danger."

"But still . . ."

"But, still," he agreed.

"So that's why you came to Freeport?" Ari said after a while.

"That's part of the reason. I've told you I was getting sick of it all. The random assaults, kids getting caught in crossfire from the drive-bys, all the scum and the crap we see. It's endless, day after day, the same thing, and you don't feel you're making a dent. At least, I didn't feel that way. It wasn't why I became a cop."

"Why did you become one?"

"To help people." He smiled briefly. "I was idealistic. I really thought I could make a difference."

"Don't you think you did, though? Don't you think you might have touched someone's life?"

"I don't know, Ari. Maybe. It just didn't seem like enough. I took a couple of weeks off, and I knew pretty quickly I didn't want to go back. So I quit."

"And came here."

"Not right away. I had the rest of my vacation time coming, and I had a hell of a time." This time his smile was wider. "I did all the things I never had time to do. I went to the beach, watched cooking shows, caught up with all the books I'd been meaning to read. I spent time with my mother, too. I think you'd like her."

"Mm-hm."

"I thought a long time about what I wanted before I started job hunting. I figured that in a small town I could accomplish things. I know there's crime everywhere and problems no one can solve, but here I can interact with people on a more personal basis, and the crime's not as serious. Usually," he added. "I didn't sign on for knitting murders."

"Well, neither did I," Ari said wryly.

Josh leaned his head on the back of the sofa, far more relaxed than he'd been just a few minutes ago.

"So are you happy here?" she asked, not yet wanting to return to the subject of murder, or anything concerning it.

"Happy enough, I guess. It's a nice town, the people are friendly, and there's enough to keep me busy without being overwhelming."

"Josh," she began, and then stopped.

"What?"

"Last fall, I know I trapped you into going out with me because I wanted to be in on the investigation."

"Oh yeah. I felt *real* trapped," he said with a smile.

She frowned. "What do you mean?"

"Ari, do you think that if I had wanted to find a way out of dating you I couldn't have?"

"But — but I told you I could help you, I could tell you things, but we had to make it look natural —"

"I had plenty of people ready to tell me things."

"But I had information you couldn't get otherwise."

"Not easily, no. That's true."

Her frown deepened. "Are you saying you could have figured things out without me?"

"No, Ari. I'm saying that I went out with you because I wanted to."

"You mean — you really did want to?"

"Just said so, didn't I?"

She straightened and pushed her hair back over her shoulder. "So if we've been going out since last fall, why hasn't anything happened?"

"Such as?"

"You know damned well what I'm talking about."

"Come on, Ari." He had rested his head on the back of the couch and was regarding her steadily. "I wanted to see you, but how did I know you felt the same?"

"Because I asked you out. I can't believe I'm saying this." She looked away. "I'm never this aggressive."

"Don't stop. I like it."

"Oh, do you? Then why haven't you taken me up on it?"

"Ari, for God's sake. You asked me out because you wanted to be involved in the investigation."

"Yes, that was part of it, but —"

"The idea was for other people to think we were dating while we were actually working together. Right?"

"Yes, but —"

"A man doesn't like to think he's being used."

"That wasn't it at all!" she exclaimed, sitting bolt upright. "All right, yes, I did want to be involved in the investigation. But, Josh, can you imagine me asking the chief to go out with me?"

That made him look at her oddly. "What?"

"Maybe I wanted to . . . see you, too."

He gazed at her a moment longer, and then a smile spread slowly on his face. "Oh. So that's how it is?"

Her face was flushed; her chin was raised. "Yes."

"Then that's a different story, isn't it? Us both wanting to see each other outside of the investigation," he said, and leaned toward her. Ari closed her eyes and let him press his lips against hers.

It seemed like a very long time before the kiss ended. Josh brushed back a strand of Ari's hair and smiled. "Better?"

"Much." Ari was smiling, too, as she

rested her head on his shoulder. "It's about time."

"Mm-hm."

"So now what?"

"What do you mean?"

"Where do we go from here?" she asked.

"Wherever it is, we take it slow."

"Why?" She sat up, pushing her hair out of her face. "We both just admitted there's something between us."

"Something that maybe shouldn't be rushed."

"I don't think that's what we're doing."

He drew back. "Ari, how long have you been divorced?"

"A year and a half. Why?"

"Because you do your share of backing off."

"I do not."

"After being married to Ted I don't blame you, but . . ."

"That has nothing to do with it."

"Ari, there were times when I asked you places and you wouldn't go."

"I had Megan," she said defensively.

"Your mother would be happy to babysit."

"One of the times you asked she was out to dinner with Chief Mason."

That stopped them both, and they exchanged smiles. "What do you think's happening there?"

"I have no idea. She doesn't talk about it to me. I do know that she's furious with him right now."

"Yeah. I was there when she brought your clothes today. The chief's a bulldog, though. He won't give up."

"We'll see. My mother's a stubborn Irish girl."

"Whatever. It's their problem, not ours." He gazed at her seriously. "I *do* like you, Ari."

She leaned into his hand, which was now cupping her cheek. "I like you, too."

"I think what we have is too important to be rushed."

She took a deep breath. He was right. Maybe it was too soon. Maybe they should take this slowly. "Yes," she agreed.

"Well, then," he said, and lowered his head again. Just as he was about to kiss her, his pager went off. He glanced at it and sighed. Swearing, Josh got up, running a hand through his tousled hair. "Can I use your phone?"

"Of course," said Ari whose own hair was tousled. She sat and waited as he took her phone into the kitchen. All she could hear was the murmur of his voice. When he returned, he looked resigned.

"What is it?" she asked, remembering another time when he'd been here and his pager had summoned him to attend to a brutal murder.

He shook his head. "Nothing, just the chief wanting to know where I am."

She sighed and handed him his jacket. "This always seems to happen to us, doesn't it?"

"It's my job." He shrugged into his jacket. "It's not usually so crazy. Anyway, I should get going. I have reports to write."

Ari got up and walked with him to the door. "We always seem to get close during a murder investigation."

"We'll change that this time." He took his jacket from her and put it on. "When this is over, I'll take you to Roseland."

"Where?" Ari said, thinking confusedly of a nursery in Acushnet.

"Roseland. The ballroom in Taunton."

"Is that still open?"

"Last I checked."

"You're not seriously going to tell me you ballroom dance?"

"Hey, I do a mean rumba," he said, holding out his arms as if he were partnering a woman and taking a step, making her laugh. "What can I say? I decided to give it a try. So?" He smiled down at her, his head cocked to the side. "What do you say?"

"Will I have to wear a slinky dress and stilettos?"

"No. At least not the shoes," he said, waggling his eyebrows.

"Ha. All right. It sounds like fun."

"Good. Let's get the investigation behind us, and we'll make it a date." He bent to give her a quick kiss that turned out to last a lot longer than either of them expected. "Gotta go," he said finally, his voice hoarse, and then was gone.

Sighing, Ari closed the door behind him and walked back to the sofa, where she automatically clicked on the television again. On the screen the United States figure-skating champion was just finishing a program that, by the reaction of the audience, had been fantastic.

Ballroom dancing, of all things! What a man, she thought. He cooked, danced, and solved murders. Maybe she could even teach him to knit. Once the investigation was over, that is.

Josh stared with loathing at the report forms on his desk. There were forms to fill out about the initial call to the fairgrounds. There were forms detailing what he had found and what he had done and in what order. There were even forms about Beth Marley and her attempted escape, though he'd had nothing to do with it. Beth, Charlie had told him, was still hanging tough. She had clammed up, just as she had that afternoon. Even worse, her lawyer had finally arrived and was advising her not to talk. Josh glared at the forms. Damn Beth Marley. Damn everything that had happened today.

The phone rang and Paul Bouchard, at his desk across from Josh, picked it up. Immersed in his typing, Josh paid little attention until a certain urgency in Paul's voice made him look up. "She hasn't?" Paul said. "Could she have gone out on an errand?" He listened for a moment and then reached for a pad. "Okay, we'll get on it," he said, and hung up. "That was Rosalia Sylvia's husband. He says she never came home."

"Is he certain?"

"He says he is."

"How come he's just figuring this out now?"

"He works the three-to-eleven at the hospital."

"So he just got home. I wonder —" Josh began, and at that moment his pager went off again. He reached for his phone, his face going rigid as he listened. "I'll be right there," he said, and banged the receiver down, rising and reaching for his jacket. "We've got another one."

"Another murder?" Paul asked, getting up as well.

"Yeah. At the fairgrounds."

"Oh God. Don't tell me —"

"Yeah. Rosalia Sylvia."

The fairgrounds were dark as Josh drove in, much too fast, so that his car skidded on the still muddy ground. Bright light spilled out of Barn B, and he approached it grimly. The death of an outsider was a tragedy, but the death of a local resident felt personal. Dimly Josh noted the change in his attitude. Now that he belonged to this town, he wanted to protect the people living there. He strode into the barn.

The floodlights that had been placed in one corner of the barn illuminated a surrealistic scene, but they didn't penetrate everywhere, leaving ominous-looking patches of shadow at the corners of the barn. The strobe lights of police cameras, and the flash of blue and red lights from cruisers parked outside only added to the unreality of the scene.

"Josh." Charlie turned as Josh came near. "Over here."

"What've we got?" he asked as he joined Charlie, though he already knew.

"The victim's in there," Charlie said, indicating the farthest bin from the door.

"In the fleece bin?"

"Yeah, of all places."

"Her husband called the station looking for her just before you paged me."

"We're pretty certain it's her. There's a tote bag on the floor, on the other side of the bin, with everything spilled out. I took a look at the wallet, but we're not touching anything else until Briggs gets here. Where were you before, by the way?"

"I was at Ari's."

Charlie's eyes widened, but if he knew more than Josh was saying, he didn't let on. "Good, because you won't be getting another break for a while."

"How'd it happen?"

"Can't say for certain yet, but it looks like she was smothered."

"In the fleece?" Josh looked at the bins in disbelief. Of all the screwy ways to kill someone. "Are we thinking it's the same person?"

"Has to be. How many murderers could be running around this place?"

"Plus the only people left besides police were the suspects. Christ." Josh rubbed his hands tiredly over his face, feeling nostalgic again for Boston. At least there he'd known where he stood. "How could this have happened?" he said, more to himself than to Charlie. At the very end of the afternoon, people had been bustling about, packing up tables and spinning wheels and their wares, and bringing them to their cars. The confusion wouldn't have been enough to cover this, though. "Didn't anyone here realize Rosalia hadn't gone home?"

"Not right away." Charlie gestured toward the door. "Take a look outside. Her car's not there."

"Any idea where it is?"

"Around back."

"So someone drove it there?"

"Yeah."

Josh blew out his breath in a silent whistle. Someone's head was going to roll for this. "And *no one* noticed Rosalia didn't make it home?" he asked.

Charlie shook his head. "The patrol car driving by her home thought she'd parked in the garage and there were lights on inside the house."

"She might have had them on a timer," Josh pointed out. "We'll have to ask her husband about that."

Josh moved a little closer to the bin,

though with the crime-scene technicians there, vacuuming the floor and dusting for prints, he had to keep a distance. The vacuuming probably wouldn't do much good. In a place like this fibers were everywhere, both loose and embedded in the dirt floor. He didn't envy the lab its job. "Who found her?"

"One of the state troopers," Charlie said. "He was checking up in here and he heard a cell phone ringing. He traced it to the source and found the body."

Josh added carelessness to their killer's profile, or perhaps haste. There probably hadn't been time to search the body for a phone. "Where's everyone now?"

"Still at the Welcome Inn, and Winston Barr's at the Edgewater B and B."

Josh studied the bins. They were low enough for people to examine the fleeces, but also high enough to make putting something heavy into them difficult. "She might not have been alive when she went in. Or conscious."

"I thought of that. She would have struggled otherwise."

"Yeah, and screamed. Jeez." Again he rubbed his hand over his face. "You know, we might just have caught a break."

"How so?"

"Now we can hold the out-of-towners for another twenty-four hours."

A smile spread over Charlie's face. "Yeah. We can. Chances are good at least one of them's involved in this. We should be able to get fiber evidence, too, if we narrow it down to one person. She's bound to have wool on her."

"Huh. Everyone here will have wool fibers."

"True, but we may be able to link them to those fleeces in particular."

Charlie nodded. "It's a thought. But we'd better get a suspect first, so we can get a search warrant. As it is, we don't have probable cause."

Josh nodded, his mind returning to the problem of how the killer had managed to kill Rosalia and still get away. Apart from the participants, the fairgrounds had been filled with police at the end of the day. "Chief, do you know if there was a list —"

"That's probably Briggs," Charlie said at the same time, at the sound of an engine stopping just outside the door. "Got the DA coming back, too. What was that you were going to say?"

"It'll keep," Josh said as Captain Briggs walked in. He looked a little more disheveled than he had this morning; his hair was a little tousled, and his coat, a Burberry this time, was unbuttoned. Still, he radiated the same air of cool efficiency and command.

"Different method this time," Briggs said without preamble.

Charlie nodded. "Yeah. Still knitting related, though."

"Our killer uses whatever's at hand," Josh said.

"The question is, why?" Briggs's hand was on his chin.

Charlie shook his head. "Don't know. We don't know the connection yet. Rosalia Sylvia's a local girl. She didn't have anything to do with the out-of-towners."

"But did they have something to do with her?" Josh asked.

"What do you mean?" Briggs said, looking at him.

"Maybe Rosalia saw something she shouldn't have."

"Such as?"

Josh shrugged. "A certain knitting needle, say. Or maybe she saw the killer coming into the barn at the wrong time, and mentioned it. We should go over the notes from her interview, just in case."

Briggs moved toward the bins. "Have you touched the body?"

"Not yet," said Charlie. "The only thing

we looked at was her wallet. Crime-scene techs should be done any minute."

"Medical examiner coming?"

"Yeah, but he won't be here for a while, since he's coming down from Boston."

Briggs nodded. The technicians were finishing up. One of them signaled to Briggs. He went to talk to the technician, and then came back. "They're done, but they need the fleeces taken out and put on that tarp," he said. "We'll need them for fiber evidence."

"Okay, so let's see what we've got," Charlie said, gesturing toward the fleece. "Josh?"

Josh sighed inwardly. Since he had the lowest rank here, he was bound to get the more unpleasant jobs. Face set, he reached down and began pulling out fleeces. "These are heavy," he noted, carefully placing each fleece on the plastic sheets. "How the hell did the killer manage to move all this?"

"Any thoughts?" Briggs asked.

"Yeah. Find out when each suspect left the barn, for a start. Jeez." He had lifted out the last fleece, and was now looking at the body. Rosalia's face had a waxy look to it, and blood was pooled in the cheek that had rested on the fleece. Death had left its mark, yet she looked oddly peaceful. Whatever had happened, she hadn't known she was dying.

"No way to know if she struggled," Briggs said, leaning in to look. "Fingernails aren't broken, though."

"We'll know more after the autopsy."

"Where are all the wool nuts?" Briggs asked.

"Who?" Josh exclaimed involuntarily.

"The people from the festival."

"All in their rooms," said Josh.

"Even Beth Marley," Charlie put in with a grin.

"Hm." Briggs rubbed his chin again. He didn't have to say what they were all thinking — that Beth was in for more intense questioning, if her lawyer would ever let her talk. "We need to know who was here, and when. Where's the record of when people left this afternoon?"

"Did someone keep one?" Josh asked. It was the very thing he had been thinking.

"Yeah. I had one of my troopers keep a list," Briggs said. He spoke briefly into his walkie-talkie, and a few moments later a trooper handed him a clipboard. "Let's see." Briggs's blunt-tipped finger traced down the paper. "Annie Walker left first, followed by Diane Camacho, and then" — he squinted at the paper, trying to make the writing out — "Marley. Your friend Ariadne was after her. Hm."

"What is it?" Charlie asked, as Briggs abruptly went still.

"Take a look." Briggs handed him the clipboard. "The last one to leave, at five twenty-three."

Josh looked over Charlie's shoulder, and then made a silent whistle. According to the log, the last person who'd left the fairgrounds was Rosalia.

CHAPTER 13

"She left?" Josh exclaimed. "How could she have?"

"Unless she came back," Briggs said.

"How? We secured the entrances, front and back," Charlie said.

"We'll have to look into that." Briggs stared into space. "Is there another entrance to this place?"

"Not that I know of," Josh said, just as Charlie swore.

"Not an entrance exactly," Charlie said. "There's an old dirt road around the curve on King's Road in Acushnet. There's a connector from here to there. It comes in at the back of the barns."

"Why?"

"To bring animals in, back in the days when there were big agricultural fairs here."

"Who knows about that?"

"Locals."

"That narrows it down."

"I don't know," Josh said. "Does it?"

"How could someone from out of town have known about it?" Briggs demanded. "Are those fleeces in that bin Rosalia's, by the way?"

"No, she was here as a customer. Those are Nancy's, remember? She asked if she could leave them here."

"Is this back road marked?" Briggs asked.

Charlie shook his head. "It's just a local lane, Pine Lane. The connector to the fairgrounds isn't used anymore. It's probably overgrown."

"It might not be too bad this time of year," Josh pointed out. "Nothing's had a chance to grow yet, but the ground is soft. We should find tire prints."

"There might be fingerprints in Rosalia's car, too," Charlie said.

Briggs nodded. "All right. We'll get forensics on it. We need to talk to Nancy — what is her last name?"

"Moniz, and I don't think she had anything to do with this."

Briggs looked up. "She's the one who was in her van using her phone."

"Yes."

"Which she can't prove."

"Bill, what reason would she have?"

"We have to at least rule her out," Briggs

said, though they'd found no real reason to suspect her.

"Chief," Josh said quietly. "Do we know if there are any brochures for the fair around?"

"Maybe. The manager probably has some. Why?"

Josh reached for the paper on the bottom of the pile. "This is an application from a vendor," he said, handing it to Charlie. "Look. It's been cut off from something."

Charlie examined the ragged edge and then looked up, his face quizzical. "So?"

"So isn't it possible that the brochure had a map?"

"Damn, I bet it did." He turned toward one of the troopers, but Briggs was already on his walkie-talkie.

"We'll have one in a minute," he said. "How long has this Nancy Moniz lived here?"

"All her life." Charlie didn't sound happy. It was easier to take the murders with the belief that an outsider committed them.

"Then she'd know about the road?"

"Her parents were dairy farmers before they decided to sell the farm. They probably exhibited here."

"When was the last agricultural fair held?"

"I don't know. A good ten, fifteen years ago. But yeah, she'd probably know about the road. Acushnet police have had trouble with it."

"Why? Teenagers having parties?"

"Yeah, among other things. It's a dark road where young couples like to go . . ."

"Why would Nancy kill Felicia?" Josh asked, changing the subject. "There's no connection between them."

"That we know of," Briggs said. "Is she adopted?"

"No," Charlie said, frowning. "I know her father."

"Then you knew her as a baby?"

"Well, no."

"She doesn't look like Felicia," Josh said.

"She could look like her biological father. It's something to check."

"Yeah," Charlie said, his tone skeptical. For Josh, too, it was a reach, and yet he knew that they had to investigate every possibility if they were to solve the murders.

"Charlie, go call her — What is it?" Josh turned to the trooper who was holding out a sheet of tan paper folded in thirds.

"We found these in the office, sir," the trooper said.

"The brochure?" Charlie asked.

Briggs nodded, and unfolded the paper. The name of the festival, along with a picture of a flock of sheep, was on the front third of the brochure. The middle third was blank except for a space for an address, and there was a return address in the upper-left corner. The application form was printed inside the back third. The remaining area of the paper was dedicated to information about the festival, including directions and a small map. In the harsh light, Josh looked closely at the map and gasped. There, printed faintly but recognizably, was the forgotten back entrance to the fairgrounds. It didn't matter if the suspects were local or from out of town. Anyone could have figured out how to get back onto the grounds. The investigation was still wide open.

It was now seven on Sunday morning, and Josh was back at his desk. He and the others had all gone home to catch a few hours of sleep. There were more reports waiting for him. As first detective on the scene, his report on the crime scene was crucial. So were the reports on the interviews he'd conducted. Even though they could hold the out-of-towners a little longer, they had little time to spare. It would help if they could find out who Felicia's daughter was.

He looked across the room. Paul Bouchard, their computer expert, was at his desk, frowning at his screen. "Any luck on the adoption agencies?"

Paul looked up from the computer. "Do you have any idea how many there are in Connecticut?" he demanded. "Not to mention she could have gone through New York or Massachusetts."

"She lived in Simsbury. That's the middle of the state." Something echoed in Josh's head as he said this, but he couldn't quite catch it.

"Yeah? Well, what if Felicia went away to have the baby?"

"What, to some sort of home?"

"Why not? She came from a middle-class Catholic family. They were probably embarrassed."

"Maybe." It still seemed like an old-fashioned concept to Josh, but then, it had happened more than twenty years earlier. Things had changed since then. "Give me the names of some agencies close to Simsbury. We'll start there."

Paul pressed a button and then crossed the room to the printer. "Here." He shoved a piece of paper at Josh. "Sunday morning. Good luck to you."

"At the worst we'll get answering machines, and at the best answering services," Josh said, picking up the phone.

Half an hour later, Josh had lost whatever

optimism he'd started with. He'd left count-less messages on countless machines, and pressed countless buttons in response to voice mail instructions. Only one agency had an answering service. Its operator sounded dubious but promised to pass on the message anyway. Josh finally hung up and then sat back, frustrated. On his desk, his fifth cup of coffee had gone cold. He got another one and set to work on his reports. Pretty soon he and Charlie, along with other police, would be heading to the Welcome Inn, where two conference rooms had been reserved for them. All of the suspects, including the local ones, would be there for questioning.

He was just finishing his report on the interview with Winston Barr when his phone rang. "Freeport Police," he said absently, and was met with total silence. "Hello?"

"I was told to call this number," a voice said briskly on the other end of the line. "May I ask whom I'm talking to?"

Josh sat up straighter. "Yes, ma'am," he said, "This is Joshua Pierce of the Freeport Police Department."

"Freeport?"

"Massachusetts. Who is this, please?"

"Jennifer Newcomb from Wide World

Adoptions. Did you call us?"

"Yes." Josh sat back in his chair. "We're trying to trace someone who gave up a child for adoption about twenty years ago."

"Adoption records were sealed then."

"Yes, we know. We'd appreciate any help you could give us."

"Why?" she demanded.

"Police business, Miss Newcomb. We need to know —"

"I'm afraid you'll have to do better than that, Officer."

"Detective," Josh said, put off by her abrupt manner. "It's a matter of homicide."

"Murder?"

"Yes."

"Who?"

Josh wanted to retort that they couldn't reveal that information, but of course that wasn't true. They needed all the help they could get. "As I said, we're trying to trace a woman who needed adoption services some years back."

Jennifer sighed. "I'm afraid I can't help you, Detective."

"Look, we're going to have a hard time getting court orders. If we could have some help, even if off the record —"

"It's not that," she interrupted him. "We only do international adoptions, and we weren't in business that long ago."

"Oh," Josh said, and any hopes that he'd had fled. "I see."

"But, I wonder." She was quiet a moment, and Josh didn't interrupt. "Could you give me some of her background?"

"Sure." Josh filled her in without giving Felicia's name. When he was done, Jennifer was quiet again.

"Simsbury," she said finally.

"Yes."

"I wonder if she went to the diocese."

"The diocese?"

"Yes. The Hartford archdiocese. Considering she was Catholic, she may have gone to Catholic Social Services."

Hartford CSS. That was the little nudge he'd felt in his brain a while ago. Hartford was in central Connecticut. "Do you have a number for them, Miss Newcomb?"

"Hold on and let me look." She returned to the phone a few minutes later and rattled off a string of digits. "No one will be there today."

"I know. Thank you for your help," Josh said. He disconnected the call and immediately dialed the number Jennifer had given him. To his surprise, it was picked up almost immediately.

"Maxie, I told you, I need to get some

work done," a female voice said impatiently.

"I'm sorry," Josh said. "I must have the wrong number."

"No, no. Who were you trying to reach?"

"Catholic Social Services."

"That's me. I'm sorry, I thought you were my daughter. She's been calling all morning. I'm Elaine Albright. Can I help you?" she said, belatedly turning more professional.

"Yes." Josh quickly explained who he was. "I didn't expect to find someone in the office on Sunday."

"Paperwork."

"I understand that."

"I imagine you do. What can I help you with?"

"I'm looking for information on a woman named Felicia Barr, from about twenty or so years ago. Her name then would have been" — he glanced at the paper on which Felicia's background information was typed, "O'Neill."

There was dead silence on the other end of the line. "What about her?" Elaine said cautiously.

"I need to know if she had a child at that time."

"Most adoptions from then were closed."

Bingo, Josh thought. "Why would you

think this is about an adoption, Mrs. Albright?"

"Why else would you be calling us?"

"Did she give up a child for adoption?"

"I can't give you that information."

Hot damn, he thought this time. "Do you know who can?"

"You'd need a court order to unseal the records."

"Which jurisdiction?" Josh asked, scribbling notes.

"Hartford County. I don't think you'll have any success."

There was such a thing as interagency cooperation, Josh thought, especially where murder was concerned. Maybe the Simsbury Police could run interference for them. "Mrs. Albright, this concerns a murder case," he said, deciding to come clean in hopes of shocking her. "We need information."

"I can't tell you anything."

"Mrs. Albright, there may be other lives at stake. We think this person has already killed twice."

"My God! You don't think it's —"

"Felicia Barr's child?" Josh said, when Elaine stopped abruptly. "It could be."

There was a long sigh. "Detective, I wish I could help you. I really do. But without a court order, my hands are tied."

"If I can get the court order . . ."

"Call me back. I do want to help, Detective."

"Thank you," he said, and hung up, staring into space. They couldn't spare anyone to go to Connecticut for a court order, assuming they could find someone to issue one. He needed help.

Josh dialed the Simsbury Police Department and soon was talking to a Detective Buehle. He explained the situation, including what he needed, and then listened to a silence not unlike Mrs. Albright's.

"You don't ask for much, do you?" Detective Buehle said after a moment. "We've got our own problems."

How much crime could there be in a small Connecticut town? Josh wondered, and then chastised himself. After all, he worked in a small town with its share of problems. "This involves homicide," he reminded the other detective.

Buehle sighed heavily. "You won't get a judge to sign a court order today. It's Sunday."

"Anything you could do we'd appreciate."

"Who got killed, anyway?"

There was no harm in giving out that information. "A local woman, plus a New

Yorker named Felicia Barr. She came from your area —"

"You don't mean Felicia O'Neill, do you?"

Josh's heartbeat quickened. "Do you know her?"

"Hell, I went to school with her. So she finally went and got herself killed?"

Josh wondered why people kept saying that about her. "Was she really that bad?"

"Around here? Nah. I dated her once or twice. But after she left we heard stories."

"When did she leave?"

"When she was in college, twenty, twenty-five years ago. She did come back for a while a few years later, but no one saw much of her."

"Are her parents still alive?"

"No, they both died some years back. She's got no family around here now. Jeez, Felicia O'Neill."

"Did you see her when she came back?"

"Nah, I never did run into her."

"I just thought, since you dated —"

"In high school. You know, a few people did see her back here after she'd gone to Yale. She'd let herself go, I guess. Gotten fat."

"Fat."

"Yeah. Kind of surprising. She was always ahead of the styles. Even I knew that."

"Could she have been pregnant?"

"I don't know," Buehle said, startled. "I don't remember hearing she had a kid."

"Is there anyone you can ask?"

"I don't know. That was a long time ago, you know." He paused. "You're asking a lot of us, you know."

"I know, but it could break this thing for us."

"If we get the court order, you'll have to come down for it."

"Yeah. Listen, any time we can help you, let me know."

"Yeah," Buehle said skeptically, and hung up.

Felicia had returned to her hometown, Josh thought. If Winston Barr was right about the age of her daughter, that would have been around the time she'd been pregnant. It was funny that she'd left Yale, where she likely didn't want anyone to know what had happened to her, for a small town where everyone knew her, but she must have had her reasons. Maybe she didn't want anyone there to know about the baby, either.

Maybe she didn't want the father to know. Josh sat up straighter. He was losing his edge. The father's identity probably had little bearing on the investigation, but in homicide all bets were off. Finding his name would be difficult, if not impossible, now that Felicia was dead. There wasn't even a guarantee that he'd been identified on any of the adoption papers. Damn weekends, anyway, and damn judges who likely wouldn't issue court orders on a Sunday.

"Any luck?" Charlie asked from behind him.

Josh turned and quickly outlined what he'd found out. "We'll have to wait for the court order before we know anything," he concluded.

"Can't hang around here until that happens." Charlie was pulling on his jacket. "Come on. We've got some suspects waiting for us."

Ari pulled her comforter tighter around her and groaned as her alarm went off. Usually on a Sunday she could sleep in, especially if Megan was with Ted. Today, though, she had to appear at the Welcome Inn with the other suspects. She had just enough time to shower and have breakfast before she headed out.

It was a brilliant morning, as befitted the first day of May; sunny and warm, with a cloudless blue sky. If it had been like this yesterday, would things have happened the same way? The rain had provided a convenient screen for the murderer, and had destroyed alibis for other people. Whoever had killed Felicia had taken advantage of the weather. That made her resourceful as well as quick to action. It also made her dangerous. Last fall Ari had nearly been killed trying to catch a murderer. She had no intention of letting that happen again.

She was just putting her cup and cereal bowl in the dishwasher when the phone rang. "Oh, shut up," she muttered as she crossed to it. "Yes, Josh. I'll be there," she said into the receiver.

There was a brief silence. "I'm sorry, Ari. I didn't realize you were expecting a phone call."

Ari was glad that she didn't have a video phone because she was certain her mother would see her blushing. "No, no. It's just that I've got to get over to the Welcome Inn in a little while, and I thought . . ." She let her voice trail off. Why had she expected Josh to call her, anyway? Just because things looked promising between them, and just because she'd dreamed about him last night, didn't mean that he was thinking about her as much as she was about him. After all, he had a murder to solve. Honestly, Ari, she chastised herself. This was so high school. The next thing she knew she'd be doodling "Mrs. Joshua Pierce" on everything.

"And of course you'll be careful," Eileen said.

"Yes, Mom," Ari said, realizing two things at once. Her mother had apparently been talking for some time, and Ari had indeed scribbled Josh's name several times on the notepad she kept by the phone. Quickly she tore off the top sheet and crumpled it. "I don't think much will happen in a conference room."

"Thank heavens. I'd dread the thought of your returning to the fairgrounds. It's such a dangerous place."

"Well, I wouldn't say that. I don't know why Felicia was killed there, but I'm sure it had nothing to do with the festival."

"What about poor Rosalia, then?"

"Rosalia? What about her?"

"Oh, Ari. Haven't you heard? She fell into a bin filled with fleece and was smothered."

Ari's first reaction was to laugh, it sounded so improbable. "You're kidding."

"Do you mean to tell me you haven't heard yet?"

"No," Ari said, realizing all at once that her mother was serious. She also knew, deep in her heart, that there was nothing accidental about Rosalia's death. "When did it happen?"

"Last night sometime. You didn't see anything while you were there yesterday, did you?"

"No, of course not." If she had, she probably would still be at the fairgrounds. "How could it have happened?" she said, more to herself than to her mother. "We all left around the same time."

"Josh would know."

Ari's memory flashed back to the page Josh had received. Had he found out then? No, there'd been no hint on his face to indicate that something serious had happened. And if there had, would he have mentioned going ballroom dancing, of all things?

Eileen was still speaking, bringing Ari back from her reverie.

"I have to go, Mom," she said, interrupting Eileen midspurt. "I'll find out more about what happened when I get to the motel."

"You will call me, won't you? I do worry about you."

"Yes, Mom, I know." After accepting Eileen's offer to look after Megan if Ari didn't get home in time, Ari hung up and headed for the shower, her mind buzzing. How in the world could Rosalia have been killed at the festival?

When Ari reached the Welcome Inn, she found a group of people as confused and distressed as she was. "Did you hear?" Diane demanded as soon as Ari walked into the main conference room. "About Rosalia."

"Yes, my mother called me this morning."

"She was smothered in a bin of fleeces, Ari! How could that have happened?"

"With everyone there? I don't know. Will you let me hang up my sweater and get some coffee before you start interrogating me, though?"

"I just thought that your policeman told you something last night."

Ari gave her a sharp look as she hung her sweater on a large clothes rack. "What do you mean?"

"Wasn't he at your house last night?"

Ari let out a sigh and headed toward the table where a continental breakfast had been set out. Her neighbor must have spread the word. "I see the Suspects Club is no longer in order," she said, avoiding the subject.

Diane glanced over her shoulder. "No,

everyone's been sitting apart since we came in."

"I thought there'd be a lot of talk about Rosalia."

She shook her head. "No, I think everyone's in shock. You know that no one much cared about Felicia, but this is a different story."

"Yes." Ari gave the Danish pastry and the donuts a long look, and then placed some fruit on her plate instead. "Have you talked with anyone?"

"No, I got here just before you did."

"Hm." She glanced across the room. "Debbie looks lonely," she said and, giving Diane a look, crossed the room.

Debbie did look lost, sitting as she did on one of the small, uncomfortable padded chairs that all hotels seemed to use in their conference rooms. There seemed to be a zone of space around her, as if people feared she was contagious. "Hi," Ari said, sitting next to her.

Debbie started. "Oh. Ari. Hi. It's awful, isn't it?"

Ari sipped her coffee and nodded. "I still don't quite believe it. Rosalia, of all people."

"I know. I can't get over the shock."

Ari sat back to look at her. Debbie looked terrible. There were dark circles under her eyes, and her cheeks were puffy. She was wearing yesterday's clothes, which didn't help. "I would have brought you a change of clothes if I'd thought of it," Ari said. "We're pretty much the same size."

Debbie shot her a quick, distracted smile. "That's not the most important thing today."

"I suppose not."

"They'll keep us longer now, won't they?"

"I don't know." Ari hadn't thought about it, but now that she did it made sense. The police were now investigating another murder. She didn't for one moment believe it was an accident. "Probably."

"Good." Debbie's voice was grim. "I want them to find Felicia's killer."

"They will. It might take time."

"Then they'd better hurry up. I don't know how much Winston can take."

"How is he?"

"About as well as he can be. Thank God he's not a suspect, so he doesn't have to be here today." She twisted around in her seat. "Is there anyplace I could get a cigarette? I'm dying for one."

"I don't know. Maybe the police will let you go outside."

"I doubt it, after Beth's little trick last night."

"What was that?"

"Didn't you hear? She took off."

"She did?"

"Yes. She claimed she needed some things, but I heard she was halfway to New Jersey by the time the cops caught up with her."

"Did she really think she'd get away with it?"

"She probably didn't think at all." Debbie's voice was scornful. "She's not too bright."

"You'd better not say that in the magazine. I know you're going to go after everyone, but you don't want to open yourself to a lawsuit."

"If I get the magazine."

"What do you mean?"

"I talked with Winston last night. He doesn't know what was in Felicia's will."

"But why wouldn't you get it, Debbie? Felicia trusted you."

Debbie shrugged. "It might go to her daughter."

CHAPTER 14

"Her daughter?" Ari said carefully.

"Yes. I thought you knew."

"Yes," Ari said, feeling her way now. "But I didn't think you did."

Debbie nodded. "For some time now."

"She told you?"

"Yes."

"Then you know who it is?"

"No. All I know is that all of a sudden this woman shows up, claiming to be Felicia's long-lost daughter. I didn't even know Felicia had a kid."

"Do the police know about this?"

"Not that I know of." She frowned. "Come to think of it, though, they did ask a lot of questions about someone calling the magazine. I didn't know why. Now I wonder . . ."

"What did you tell them?"

She shrugged. "We're always getting calls from people who want to talk to Felicia

284

personally. We don't let the ones we don't know through."

"And yet this daughter got to her somehow."

Debbie was frowning again. "I wonder."

"What?"

"There was one woman. She never identified herself, but she did say something that made Felicia react."

"What was it?"

" 'Hartford CSS.' And no, I don't know what it means, either."

Ari thought for a moment. "SS. Social Services?"

"Maybe. Yeah. It could be." She stared into space. "Felicia grew up in Connecticut."

"So how did you find out?"

"Felicia told me."

"She did?"

"Yes, but not right away. I remember now, she looked upset for a few days. Then she had a luncheon appointment and she wouldn't tell me who with. That was unusual. I kept track of her calendar."

Which raised another question in Ari's mind, but she pushed it aside for a minute. "You think it was the daughter?"

"Yes. In fact, I know it was. It was a few days later that Felicia called me into her office and told me about her."

"You must have been surprised."

"Ha. That's putting it mildly."

"Did she say anything about the magazine?"

"No. If you're asking did she tell me she planned on giving it to this woman, I don't know. I don't know."

"It would hurt, wouldn't it, if you didn't get the magazine?" she said gently.

Debbie glared at her. "What do you think? Anyway, I don't know what's going to happen. No one does. God, I want that cigarette."

Did Josh know about this? Ari wondered. Did he know that Debbie knew about Felicia's daughter, who might inherit the magazine? She looked around the room for Josh, but saw only state troopers that she didn't know. She'd have to tell him about this conversation, even if she didn't want to. She liked Debbie. Unfortunately she'd just made herself into a stronger suspect. "What are those?" Ari asked

"Hm? Oh, these." Debbie looked at the pictures she held loosely in her hands. "Nancy took them. I wanted to look them over in case we did do an article on the festival. You can look at them."

Ari took them, giving them only a perfunctory glance. She'd look at them later, when she could concentrate on them. Right now she wanted to keep Debbie talking. "Debbie, you said you kept Felicia's schedule?"

Debbie looked up from pulling a pack of cigarettes from her pocketbook. "Yes. So?"

"When did you know you were coming here?"

"Monday. She had to cancel a dinner for it." She frowned. "I thought at the time it was strange. No offense, Ari, but this wasn't the kind of thing she went to."

"None taken. It was a surprise to me, too. Do you think she could have come here to see someone?"

Debbie's head whipped around. "What do you mean?"

"Her daughter?"

"Jesus. Maybe."

"Would you recognize her daughter's voice?"

"I doubt it. I only spoke to her twice, and that was on the phone."

"Did she give you any idea how old her daughter is?"

Debbie shook her head. "No. She didn't tell me anything else. I'm not sure she was happy about it, though."

"Why not?"

"The way she looked most of the time. Of

course, she and Winston had both just found out they were sick, so that could have been it. But I don't think so. I asked her once about the daughter, and she changed the subject fast. And then she decided to come here." Again she shook her head. "I don't understand any of it."

Neither do I, Ari thought as she handed the pictures back. All she knew was that Debbie's motive for killing Felicia was stronger than she'd realized. Why she'd kill Rosalia, too, was another story. Unless . . .

"Good morning," a voice said at the back of the room, and she turned to see Chief Mason. Josh was behind him, looking tired and grim. "I'm sure you've all heard the news by now. Before we begin, does anyone have any questions?"

"Yes. How long are you going to keep us here?" Beth Marley asked.

Charlie gave her a long look, but she didn't flinch. "It'll be a while. We need to ask everyone some more questions."

"Chief, was Rosalia murdered?" Ari asked.

"That's one of the things we're investigating. We'll be using another conference room for questioning. We'll call you in one by one. Depending on what you tell us, you might get to go home." He paused. "Or not."

"Humph. So you're going to keep us

prisoner?" Beth said.

"A little strong, Mrs. Marley, but if that's the word you want to use . . ." He shrugged. "Nancy, why don't you come with me first."

"All right." Nancy, her shoulders squared, rose and followed Charlie from the room.

The room was almost unnaturally quiet in the wake of Nancy leaving. Covertly Ari glanced around. Most people had brought something to keep them busy. Lauren and Annie were both knitting, while Debbie was staring at a copy of the *New York Times*. Even Beth had opened a shiny leather portfolio and, with much ado, was using a blue pencil to make broad, sweeping marks across some papers. Someone's article was getting savaged, Ari thought, and was glad she didn't have any association with Beth beyond the events of the past days. She was especially glad she wasn't in Nancy's shoes. She'd had enough of police questioning for a while. Someone could go first.

Josh was tired of interrogating people he strongly suspected were innocent. He watched Nancy as Charlie ushered her into the small conference room, noting her pallor and the circles under her eyes. This had been tough on everyone.

"Good morning," he said, rising from the

table and coming around to pull out a chair for her.

"Will this take long?"

"No."

Nancy's eyes filled with tears. "I couldn't have killed Rosalia. She was a good friend."

"I'm sorry." Josh leaned forward. "I know this is difficult for you. What we need to know — and we'll be asking this of everyone — is if you saw anything out of the ordinary yesterday afternoon."

"Everything was out of the ordinary yesterday."

"Did you see Rosalia, Nancy?" Charlie asked gently.

"Yes, I suppose so, but only in the way I saw everyone else. We all had a lot to pack up and load into our cars. I was busy." She fumbled in her bag for a Kleenex. "If only I didn't leave those damned fleeces behind."

"I think, Nancy, that whoever killed Rosalia would have used whatever she found."

"She used my fleeces." Nancy wiped her eyes. It was obvious that she was holding on to her composure by sheer willpower. "Why?"

There was no answer. Josh knew about living with the guilt of being the unwitting instrument of someone's death. There wasn't anything he could say to comfort her.

"Just a few more questions, Nancy, and then you can go."

"Home?"

Charlie shook his head, reluctantly. "I'm afraid not. We still have other things to figure out."

"I didn't kill that other woman. I didn't even know her. I told you that. And I told you I didn't see anything."

"We know. But think back. Was there anything different about yesterday afternoon? Did you see Rosalia talking to anyone in particular?"

Nancy's brow wrinkled. "No. I know she helped some people bring things to their cars —"

"Who?"

"Diane, because she had her spinning wheel. But I think she also helped the out-of-towners. I know I saw her with Debbie. She was comforting her. But she also helped Lauren and Annie."

"Did you see her after that?"

"No, now that I think of it, I didn't. I assumed she went home."

Josh and Charlie exchanged looks again. "Can you think of anything else, Nancy?"

Nancy's head was lowered. "No."

"All right. If you do, let us know." Charlie rose and escorted her to the door, his hand under her elbow. "Patrolman Ross will bring you back to the main conference room."

Nancy nodded, and let herself be led away. Charlie watched her for a moment, and then turned back into the room, eyebrows raised. "What do you think?"

"She saw Rosalia with her killer."

"My thoughts exactly." Charlie sat down and stretched out, arms behind his head. "I think she just told us how the killer did it, too. At least, part of it."

"You're thinking she dragged Rosalia into her car?"

"Yeah."

Josh nodded. "I think so, too. Then she headed out to King Street — no. The staties would have noticed anyone who didn't go toward the motel."

"So she turned around someplace."

"She has nerve, whoever she is."

"We guessed that already." Charlie sighed and reached for the legal pad on which he'd scribbled notes from the interview. "Well, let's get Ari in here and get her interview over with."

Ari paused at the doorway to the motel's smaller conference room, and then walked in. Josh rose at her entrance and walked to meet her, his hand extended. "Good morning," he said coolly, as if last night had never happened.

"Good morning." Her voice was equally cool. To be fair, she knew that their talk of last night was personal, but it was a bit of a jolt to see Josh so distant. "Why would someone kill Rosalia?"

Charlie shook his head. "We don't know. Ari, we need to know if you saw anything yesterday afternoon. It looks like you left before Rosalia."

"I don't know. I wasn't paying much attention. I just wanted to get out of there."

"I understand. Most people felt that way. But someone had other ideas."

"Do you think it was the person who killed Felicia?"

"Ari, we can't discuss the case with you," Charlie said, giving Josh a quick look.

Ari wondered how much Charlie knew about her talk with Josh yesterday. Probably more than he would let on. "Yes, but I can think about it."

Charlie groaned. "Ari, please, don't tell him any of your crackpot theories."

"I'm not a crackpot," she protested, hurt.

He shook his head. "Sorry. It's been a tough couple of days, but I didn't mean to take it out on you. I just meant that Briggs won't listen if you do come up with something."

"Because I'm not a cop?"

"Yeah."

"I don't have to be one to know that there's something fishy about two murders in one place within a few hours of each other. Do you know if Rosalia was adopted?"

"Her husband says not, but we're getting her birth certificate from him to be sure. Why do you ask?"

"Well." She took a deep breath. She felt as if she were about to betray someone, and yet if she could help, she had to. "I was talking to Debbie earlier," she said, and went on to relate the conversation. When she was done, the room was quiet.

"I like Debbie. I think she loved Felicia. But . . ."

"But what?"

"She said Felicia was like a mother to her. Wouldn't it have felt like a betrayal if Felicia suddenly left everything to some unknown daughter?"

"Meaning that Debbie has a motive beyond the financial one?" Charlie looked at Josh. "What do you think?"

"I think it's possible," he said. "Especially

since she seems to be a bit unbalanced."

"I'm not sure she is," Ari protested. "I think it was just the way she reacted to the shock."

"She sure has a lot of ideas for that magazine, though, doesn't she?"

Ari looked away, and as she did so something ghosted through her mind; something she'd seen, something connected with the magazine. Try though she might, she couldn't bring the memory back. "She's ambitious. But I do believe she loved Felicia."

"What about the daughter?" Charlie asked.

"Maybe," she said reluctantly, and then frowned. "How could she have killed Rosalia?"

Charlie and Josh looked at each other again. "Oh, hell," Charlie said. "You might as well tell her."

"Tell me what?"

"Are you familiar with the back entrance to the fairgrounds?"

"Of course. A lot of people used it yesterday."

Josh leaned forward. "We don't mean the official back entrance, but the road that branches off King's Road in Acushnet."

To Ari's horror, she could feel herself

coloring. "Uh, yes. I do know about that road."

"Well, Ari," Charlie said, a smile in his voice.

"That was back in high school, Chief! Everyone who was dating went there," she explained to Josh. "It was just something we did, and —"

"I think you'd better quit while you're ahead." Charlie was grinning now.

"It was a long time ago. But is that how the killer got in?" she said, trying to change the subject.

"We think so. There's a team out there now looking for evidence."

"Could you tell me how it happened? Please?"

"We don't know. Rosalia had left the fairgrounds."

"She did?"

"We believe she came back in on that road."

"But why? She had nothing to do with Felicia. It was just bad luck that she was there."

"Unless, as you said, someone thought she was Felicia's daughter," Josh said.

"Are you saying she went back to meet with the killer?"

"It's possible. We found her SUV behind Barn B."

"But that doesn't make sense."

"Murder doesn't always make sense, Ari. You know that."

"I just can't figure this out. I don't know why she'd go back."

"But we know, unfortunately, that she did."

Unfortunately. Ari sat back, and the three were quiet. She was about to speak when the door opened and Captain Briggs walked in. Today he'd left off his leather trench coat in favor of a well-cut tweed sport jacket and gray flannel pants. A blue shirt and a conservatively patterned tie completed his outfit. The shirt brought out the color of his eyes, she noted, just as a sweater would. He could be an attractive man, if he would just smile.

Briggs nodded at them and then, setting his coffee cup on the table, sat beside Charlie. "Ms. Evans," he said.

"Captain," she said equally formally, and braced herself for dismissal.

It came a moment later. "We have things to talk about," he said to the two officers. At that, Josh got up and crossed to Ari. Together they walked out of the room.

"Josh," she whispered once they were out in the hall linking the two conference rooms. "Could you keep me up to date on things?"

"I don't know. There might not be time. Anyway, Briggs will be here."

"Yes."

"I have to get back in there, Ari —"

"Josh, what about the baby's father?"

"Felicia's baby? We don't know. Winston couldn't tell us anything, and unless we get a court order to unseal the adoption documents, there's no way we can find out."

"Unless she told her daughter."

"Are you thinking you could find out?"

"Josh, how many people here knew about her daughter?"

"From what I can tell, just us and Debbie."

"Do you mind if I tell people?"

"Ari, you know we don't like to release everything we know. That's an important fact. We can't waste it on some harebrained idea of yours."

First she'd been called a crackpot, and now harebrained. "I see," she said coldly, and walked away.

"Ari, I'm sorry, I'm tired. I was only thinking of what Briggs would say —"

She smiled at the trooper who held the large conference room door open for her, not looking at Josh. "Never mind," she said, and went in.

Damn it, Josh thought, combing his hair

with his fingers, and then turned away. Making amends would have to wait for later.

Briggs was on his cell phone when Josh walked back into the smaller room. He looked up, gesturing Josh to a chair, and went on taking notes on a paper on the table. Josh raised his eyebrows at Charlie, who only shrugged. After all, Briggs was in charge.

"That was the forensics team out on the lane behind the fairgrounds," Briggs said, closing his cell phone. "They found some brush broken at the drive into the fairgrounds."

"So someone did go in through Pine Lane," Josh said.

"Yeah, and it could have been anyone." Charlie reached for the sheet of paper that detailed who had left the fairgrounds yesterday and when. "Did they find tire prints?"

"Quite a few. A number of vehicles have been down that road, considering the weather."

"Well, last night was Saturday. Date night. What about the branches? Were they freshly broken?"

"Yes. It's possible one of the local teens saw our murderer going onto the fairgrounds that way."

"It is," Charlie agreed. "We'd have to put

out a request for information to find out. It'll take time."

"Kids might not want to admit they were there," Josh said.

"True. In any event, there were several tire tracks at the beginning of the entrance, but only one that went farther in. The same tracks, incidentally, that we found near Rosalia's SUV. Just so you remember," he added, "the left rear wheel shows more wear."

"Mm." Both Charlie and Josh were quiet for a moment, digesting this. They already knew there had been a set of tracks near Rosalia's car. This was only confirmation of their theory. The problem was finding the car with the tires that had made the tracks.

The search warrants they'd requested yesterday, to hunt for the blue yarn, had, as they'd expected, been refused, for lack of probable cause. They had more of a chance of getting a warrant to take casts of everyone's tires, but that would take time. From that end, they were stuck. They would have to find out what they could through interviews alone.

"All right," Briggs said after a minute. "We don't necessarily know that the tracks have anything to do with the crime. Let's start seeing everyone. Ms. Evans have anything to tell you?"

Josh shook his head. "I talked with her last night. There are people who can vouch for her."

"I wasn't thinking of her for this," Briggs said impatiently. "The techs say the tire prints are from another SUV, like most of the suspects drive, or a large car. Ari drives a Toyota. That lets her out for Rosalia's death."

"What about Debbie?"

"She was driving Felicia's car. A Cadillac SUV. Beth's car is an old Oldsmobile."

"Ari did find out something," Charlie said, relenting. They would have to talk more with Debbie Patrino.

"All right, let's bring her in next," Briggs said finally. "If she held out on us about Felicia's daughter, who knows what else she knows?"

"All right," Josh said, and went out, though he wondered what more they could get from Debbie. He didn't think she'd come back to the fairgrounds to kill Rosalia. Gut instinct told him she was innocent. Instinct wasn't evidence, however. The only reason Debbie could have had was if Rosalia had seen something. Come to think of it, that was a good motive for any of the suspects. The problem was, what did Rosa-

301

lia see?

Ari headed for the coffee urn as soon as she returned to the larger conference room, though she was already buzzing from the caffeine she'd had earlier that morning. "Anything?" Diane asked as Ari joined her.

Ari shrugged. "Just that Captain Briggs doesn't need to go on that show where straight guys learn how to dress."

"Ari."

"Well, it's true," she said, and as she did, that errant memory went through her mind again. *Damn it!* She had a feeling it was important, and yet she couldn't grasp it. What was it she'd seen or heard?

"There goes Debbie." The two of them watched as a trooper escorted Debbie from the room. The bounce that had been in her step yesterday was gone, but she held her head high. Ari felt a reluctant stab of pity for her, in spite of all that she had kept hidden. She hated to think of Debbie as a murderer. But then, she hated to think of anyone here as a murderer.

Ari took a covert look around. No one had moved from their positions since she'd left. Lauren and Annie continued to knit in muted colors of beige and rose that were remarkably similar, Nancy rattled her newspaper ostentatiously, and Beth was still glaring at everyone. It would be convenient, and satisfactory, if Beth were guilty, Ari thought with a small spurt of malice.

"The question is, who knew about that back entrance?" she said, more to herself than to Diane.

"What back entrance?"

"The one from King's Road in Acushnet."

"Oh-ho."

"I was so embarrassed, admitting that I knew about it."

"Hell, Ari, everyone around here knows about it. Everyone's been there at one time or another."

"My wild past catches up with me."

"Hah."

"You're right, though. Anyone from around here would know about that road, and that it leads to the fairgrounds."

"Is that how they think the killer got in?"

"I think so, from the way they asked me about it."

"Hm." Diane frowned. "Ari, there was a map of the fairgrounds printed on the entry form."

"Was there? Oh. So anyone here could have known about it."

"How do you think she did it? We'd all left. She'd have had to lure Rosalia back here somehow."

"Mm. Poor Rosalia."

"I know. She never did anything bad to anyone."

"No. You know, Diane."

"What?" Diane asked, when Ari didn't go on.

"Felicia's daughter would be about our age."

"So?"

"Look at the people here. Beth is the only one who's older than we are."

"Are you saying that Felicia's daughter is here?"

"She could be." Without turning, Ari listed the other people in her head. Nancy had gone to Freeport High School a year after they had, but Ari didn't know anything of her background. Nancy could be adopted. So, for that matter, could Lauren or Annie.

"I've met Rosalia's family," Diane said, breaking into her thoughts. "She looks just like her mother."

"No, she wasn't adopted."

"Ari, what about Debbie?"

Ari shook her head. "I don't know. If she thought Felicia was going to change her will, she had a motive. But she really seemed to love Felicia."

"Sure, if she was her daughter."

"Oh, come on. What gives you that idea?"

"I don't know. It's a thought."

"Debbie already told us about her mother, and she said that Felicia treated her better." She gnawed at a fingernail, and then quickly pulled her hand away. In moments of stress, she tended to resort to that old habit. "But if the daughter found out she was going to be in the will . . ."

"Why kill Felicia before she had a chance to change it? I think you're reaching, Ari."

"I know." She blew out her breath. "But someone here did it. You know as well as I do."

"You can't figure this one out, Ari. You don't know enough about anyone, or about their background. Let the police handle it."

"I suppose I'll have to, she said gloomily, and reached for the packet of photographs Debbie had left behind on a nearby chair. "Did you see these?"

"No, what are they?"

"Nancy took pictures yesterday. Debbie was thinking of using them for *Knit It Up!,* but I don't think there'll be an article now."

"Hm." Diane flipped through the pictures. "They're not very good."

"No," Ari agreed. The light in the barn yesterday had been so murky that most of the pictures were dark, except for close-ups of someone's work. Those tended to be washed out. "That one of you is priceless."

Diane scowled at the picture of herself at her spinning wheel. Her face was screwed up in concentration, with her tongue sticking out a little. "Ugh. Felicia would have used this."

"Debbie probably will, too." Ari grinned at her. "Want to guess what the caption would be?"

"No."

" 'A baa-d spinner.' "

"Ha. Here. You can have these."

Ari took the pictures back and shuffled through them idly. She was about to return them to the envelope when that stray memory, stronger this time, nudged her again. She'd seen something.

This time she paid more attention to the pictures, studying each one for a moment before putting it aside. No, there was nothing in the picture of the Sheep to Shawl contest, or in the one of the vendor with the natural-dyed yarn, or the one of the woman who owned the llamas. "There's one of Rosalia near a table — Holy crap."

"Ari, Ari. If your mother could hear you."

"Never mind," Ari said impatiently, and shoved the photograph at Diane.

Diane stared at it for a moment and then looked up at Ari, her eyes wide. "Holy crap."

CHAPTER 15

"Wait a minute," Diane said, looking up. "It doesn't mean anything that she was using aluminum needles."

"Mm." It wasn't the needles that had caught Ari's eye, however, but the light blue yarn on them.

Diane didn't know about the blue yarn, and Ari herself didn't remember seeing it, but that didn't necessarily mean anything. People often switched projects. She thought this might have been a baby blanket.

Something pinged in Ari's mind at that, something she had seen, but she couldn't quite grasp it. Darn it, she thought. She was getting tired of that happening, whether the memory was important or not.

"It's hard to tell the color of the needles," Diane went on. "These just look light."

"The yarn's covering them. What color were they, anyway?"

"I can't tell you."

"Fine. Be that way." Diane returned to the picture. "I wonder if she really did it."

"Huh. I wonder."

Diane looked at her. "What?"

"Think, Di," Ari said. "Why was Felicia here? Debbie said they were thinking of doing an article on wool festivals, but why this one?"

"Okay, I'll bite. Why?"

"To see her daughter."

"Oh, come on, Ari. That's really reaching."

"I know, but what do we really know about the people here?"

"Are you seriously saying that one of them could be her daughter?"

"Maybe."

"Then why kill Rosalia?"

Ari briefly closed her eyes at that thought. "There's one person here who has a motive to want Felicia's daughter dead."

"Debbie," Diane said after a beat of silence.

"Yes."

"Didn't you tell me she doesn't know who the daughter is?"

"She could be lying. How would we know?"

"You sound like you want her to be the murderer."

Ari shook her head. "No, but someone did it." Ari looked at the pictures again. "We have to find out more about her," she said, tapping the picture.

"We?" Diane pulled back and looked at her. "What do you mean 'we,' kemo sabe?"

"The police, of course."

"Uh-huh. You meant us. Not this time."

"Okay. So I'll tell Josh. There must be things they can do if they have a suspect." Like search for the blue yarn. Ari didn't remember seeing that yarn yesterday afternoon.

"You swear?"

"Yes," Ari said impatiently. Diane was right. Investigating further on her own would be stupid. This was a person who'd killed twice, and who took advantage of whatever methods were at hand. It didn't matter that they were chancy; the important thing was that they had succeeded. Ari didn't want to be victim number three. But on the other hand . . . "Anyway, what kind of danger am I in at the Welcome Inn?" she asked. "We're all here in plain sight."

"They'll have to let us go sometime. If you try anything and you fail, she'll find some way to get at you. It'd be easy for her to find out where you live. Just let the police handle it."

Ari shuddered, not so much for herself as for Megan. She couldn't put her daughter in harm's way. What Diane was saying made perfect sense. She had no way of proving who the murderer was. Something still bothered her, though. "All right. I'll get this to Josh somehow."

"Maybe the camera, too."

"Why?"

"Nancy uses a digital camera."

"That's right. I'd forgotten. She must have printed these out last night." She took a quick glance around. Nancy had picked up the newspaper that Debbie had left behind and was hidden behind it. "I wonder if she has it here today. Should we ask?"

"Ari, for God's sake —"

"Yes, I know, leave it to the police. But, Diane, who knows what else is in that camera?" She looked back at the pictures. "I wonder when she took these. In the morning, I'd think," Ari went on, answering herself. "There are other people around and you can see other tables in the background. It has to be before the murder, because there're still two needles here." Ari frowned. "I don't remember seeing this knitting project. Do you?"

"No, but I wasn't paying attention."

"I was. I always look at what people are

making." And there was that little niggle again, of something more than she had seen. This time she shrugged it off. It would come back of its own accord, or not at all. "Josh really needs to see these." She turned around to look at the door where a trooper she didn't know stood guard. If she got up to give something to the trooper, she'd likely catch the killer's attention. "Stupid," she muttered, and picked up her cell phone.

Josh answered a few moments later. "What is it, Ari? We're busy here."

"I've got something I need you to see," she said in a low voice.

"Give it to the trooper."

"I can't. I don't want the murderer to see me. Josh, call me out for an interview again. Make it look as if you've discovered something that makes me look guilty."

"Okay," he said after a moment. "When we're done here."

"How is it going?"

"I can't talk," he said brusquely, and disconnected.

"Humph." Ari flipped her phone shut and put it back into her pocketbook. "So much for that."

"Did he say what's going on?"

"No, of course not, not with the others right there."

"So what is going on?"

"I just told you."

"I meant with you and him."

Ari looked at her and grinned. "Maybe something. Maybe not."

"It's about time."

"Do you really feel that way?"

"Yeah. No." Diane looked away. "I could wish you'd chosen anyone else, but I'm glad you're finally seeing someone. Ted did a number on you."

"Yes, he did," Ari said after a moment. "I'm glad you're okay with it."

"Hey, what are friends for?"

Ari was about to answer when the door to the room opened and Debbie, looking wan and tired, walked in. "Ms. Evans?" the trooper said. "Come with me, please."

Ari, hoping she looked convincingly surprised, got up. She palmed the picture in her left hand and held it close to her She hoped that no one in the room would notice it. Glancing around casually, she saw that no one was paying particular attention to her. Good, she thought, and let the trooper escort her from the room.

Josh looked up from studying the photograph lying on the conference table. "Are you sure this is the yarn?"

"No," Ari said. "It's hard to tell from the picture. But I'd know it if I saw it in person."

Josh nodded. This picture had galvanized all of them, enough so that they'd called Nancy in again to ask her about her pictures. There was now a patrolman en route to her home to get her camera.

"What do you think?" Josh asked Charlie.

"I don't know." Charlie glanced at Briggs. "Is it enough for a warrant?"

Briggs shrugged. "I'd think so. At least now we have an idea of who to search."

Josh nodded. Search warrants could be tricky to write. Last night, without a sure suspect, they'd been unable to get one. Today looked better. "It'll have to be comprehensive," he said. "We'll need to look at all her belongings."

"Plus we want to get a cast of her tires," Charlie said. "Need to have the mud on them analyzed, too. There should be grass and such mixed up in it." He looked up at Ari. "Thanks, Ari. This was good work."

"I hope so," she said, smiling a little.

"It's a start. You can go back to the other room," Briggs said.

"Okay," Ari said, disappointed to be dismissed. She turned at the door to see Josh watching her. To her surprise, he indicated the chairs at the back of the room with a jerk of his head. She nodded and went to sit down.

Josh turned back to the others. "When did our suspect get back to the hotel?"

"Let's see." Briggs, reading glasses perched at the end of his nose, pulled a piece of paper toward him. On it were listed the people who had stayed at the motel last night and the time they had checked in. "She registered last."

"Of course, that doesn't mean anything if she came in with the others," Charlie said.

"There weren't any stragglers," Josh said. "Still . . ."

"Let's try for that warrant again," Briggs said. "We've got enough evidence this time."

"I'll call Bouchard to get the application together." Charlie pulled out his cell phone and made the call. He had just disconnected when, after a brief knock, the door opened, letting in a Freeport patrolman.

"The camera, sir," he said, handing it to Charlie. "Also the papers you asked for."

"Thanks, Mike." Charlie dismissed him with a nod. "Let's see what's on this baby."

Josh watched as the chief turned the camera on and flicked a switch to display its pictures on a small screen on its back. "We'll be able to prove where the pictures came from," he said, looking over Charlie's shoulder.

"Yeah, and that they haven't been doctored."

"Let's tag it, then," Briggs said, taking the camera from Charlie. He put a manila tag on it, thus making it official evidence.

"It's not proof," Charlie said.

"Everything helps."

Charlie nodded and reached for some large envelopes lying on the table and pulled out some papers. "Nancy Moniz's birth certificate," he said, carefully separating one paper from the pack with the tip of his finger. "There are her parents' names on it, Michael and Sandra Erickson. So that rules her out."

"Birth certificates are amended when someone's adopted," Josh said, making the others look at him. Last night before going to bed, he had done some quick research and had learned some things about the legalities of adoption. "At least they are in Massachusetts."

"Hell, Josh, I know her father," Charlie said. "Anyway, you know we had to rule her out."

"Rosalia wasn't adopted, either," Briggs said. The birth certificate Briggs was studying was written in a foreign language. "According to this, she was born in Portugal."

"Then we're back to these." Charlie looked at the photographs. "With no proof that she's Felicia's daughter."

"And no way to find out without a court order," Josh said gloomily. A call had come in from the Simsbury police a little earlier. Without more evidence, no judge in Hartford County was going to issue a court order to unseal Felicia's records. They might have their suspicions, but they had no way of proving them. At least not yet. Careful not to let the others see, Josh turned and looked at Ari for a long moment.

Ari returned Josh's look and nodded slightly. From the beginning of this case — was it only yesterday? — he had given her subtle hints that he wanted her help. This was more than subtle, though. She shouldn't be here, not with two other investigators in the room. Josh was likely to land himself in serious trouble for letting her stay.

Charlie's cell phone rang. "Charlie Mason," he said, and listened. "What the hell — why?"

"What?" Briggs said, and Charlie motioned him to silence.

"Not enough? What the hell more does he want? Oh. She? So what does she want? Never mind. Call the DA's office and see if they can do anything. Damn it," he said as he flipped the phone closed.

"The warrant?" Briggs asked.

"Yeah. We didn't get it. Insufficient grounds, still."

"We've got a picture of the weapon. What more does the judge want?"

Charlie gave him a look. "Judge Fitzpatrick."

"Oh Christ. She practically likes us to catch the perp in the act."

"Is she the one who's soft on crime?"

"Yeah. We'll have to find better evidence."

The men sat in silence. Ari leaned forward, frowning. If they'd exhausted all the investigative tools at their command, at least for the moment, then they were stuck. Certainly they could hold everyone from the festival for several more hours, but eventually they'd have to release them. She didn't need to be a cop to know what that meant.

Briggs turned, hooking his arm over the back of the seat. "What do you think?"

Ari, startled, looked around, but there was no one else in the room. "Me?"

"Yes."

"I — I don't know."

"Ari." Charlie turned as well. "What the hell are you doing here? No, don't answer." The look he gave Josh told her there'd be

318

hell to pay for this. But Briggs had somehow known she was here, and hadn't said a word.

"I might be able to help," she said.

"How?" Briggs asked, and this time Charlie looked at him in disbelief. Briggs seemed very much a by-the-book man, and yet he was breaking every rule to include her.

"You don't have any solid evidence," Ari said, stating the obvious. "You have physical evidence you can't link to anyone yet. What make was the car?"

"The one that made the prints? Probably a Jeep. An SUV, anyway."

"Ari, are you sure about that yarn?" Charlie asked.

"No, not without seeing it. Not about the needles, either. All I can tell is that they're aluminum, and old. I'm not even sure about the color."

"So what do you think?" Josh asked.

"I think the only way we're going to catch the killer is to get a confession out of her."

Briggs raised an eyebrow at her. "How do you propose to do that?"

"By presenting the evidence to her and making it sound like we have more than we do."

Briggs looked at the other men, and for the first time this morning, exasperation showed on his face. "Is this how she did things last time?"

"Ari, you can't play Nancy Drew again." Charlie's face was both stern and drawn.

"No, not Nancy Drew. I was thinking more along the lines of Nero Wolfe. You know, gather everyone together and lay out the case. It's too bad we don't have the leather chairs, or someone to serve drinks."

Charlie glared at her. "Ari," he growled.

"I don't intend to get myself into any danger," she assured him. "I'm not going to do anything without any of you there."

"And where are you planning this confrontation?" Briggs asked. "In the main conference room?"

"Oh gosh, no. At the fairgrounds, of course."

The day might have been sunny, but the mud at the fairgrounds had yet to dry completely. Barn A, so warm and inviting yesterday, was chilly today. It looked tawdry in the bright sunlight. The chairs from the snack bar were old and uncomfortable, with cracked red vinyl seats and uneven chrome legs.

As if she were still part of the Suspects Club, Ari sat with the others in a semicircle, noticing their postures and wondering if she could spot guilt. What she saw was mostly annoyance and anger.

"Why'd they drag us back to this godforsaken place?" complained Beth, the first to speak. "Why don't they just let us go?"

"They can't," Ari said. Today she had no knitting to keep her busy, but that was by design. After much discussion, the police had reluctantly agreed to let Ari conduct this meeting, while they stayed out of sight and listened. "They can keep us longer because of Rosalia's murder last night."

"This is your cop's doing, isn't it?" Beth accused.

"I don't know. All I can guess is that this is convenient."

"It's uncomfortable," Annie said, her soft voice taking most of them by surprise. Since yesterday Annie had said very little.

"Why *are* we here?" Diane whispered to Ari.

"Because it is uncomfortable and two murders happened here," Ari whispered back. "If anyone's going to confess, it'll be here."

"Ha. There are some tough cookies in this bunch."

"My lawyer's advised me not to say anything to anyone," Beth said, proving Diane's point.

"Ari?" Nancy leaned over. "When will the

police come in? Why can't they get this over with already?"

"Why are you asking me?" Ari said.

"Because of your cop."

"He's not *my* cop," Ari protested, but without much conviction. After last night, that was no longer true.

"Oh, c'mon, Ari." Diane lounged in her chair. "You've got to know more than we all do."

"I don't. If you think about it, you all know the same things I do."

"I don't know anything," Lauren said. "Nancy's right. Why don't they just get this over with?"

"We all know that yesterday someone stabbed Felicia Barr in the back with a knitting needle," Ari said. "She stumbled into me, said a few words, and died."

"She said something?" Debbie said sharply. "What?"

"None of us here can prove where we were when Felicia died," Ari continued, ignoring Debbie, "or we had had some association with her. Beth Marley had a fight with her —"

"I knew you'd try to hang this on me," Beth said.

"You *did* fight with her, in full view of everyone," Ari pointed out. "And you left the fairgrounds, too, so you can't account for your time."

"I rode by your yarn shop. It's quaint," Beth said, sneering.

"And you've got a motive," Ari went on, ignoring her. "Felicia fired you, and you hated her for that, didn't you? Never mind that you'd been embezzling from *Knit It Up!* by accepting extra money from advertisers and promising better reviews and articles."

"This is slander!"

"It's fact, and you know it," Debbie shot back. "You're really lucky Felicia decided not to prosecute."

"I've never been part of something so stupid in my life. You're trying to get me to confess, aren't you? Well, it's not going to happen."

"Actually I don't think you did it, Beth," Ari said.

"What?"

"Why would you? There might have been bad blood between you two, but you stood to lose more by killing Felicia, didn't you? If you did, the news about what you did at the magazine would come out."

"How did *you* know about that?" Debbie asked.

Ari ignored her. If they guessed how much the police had told her, no one would say a word. "Of course, it's not your fault that it has come out."

"So that's how Felicia got that reputation of favoring advertisers," Lauren said. "Beth, that was really rotten."

"What did Felicia say to you, Ari?" Debbie asked.

"She said something about mud. 'I tried to get the mud.' "

Debbie frowned. "That doesn't make sense."

"No, at the time it didn't. But that's because no one knew where she was killed. It was raining hard when I left here with coffee and I had my head down, but I think I would have seen someone stab Felicia if it had happened right in front of me." Ari leaned forward. Unconsciously the others did, too. "That means she was killed someplace else. She didn't have her coat on."

For a moment there was silence. "She left it somewhere," Debbie said, figuring it out first. "Was she trying to get mud off it?"

"Yes. I think she was trying to tell me who killed her."

"What!" Debbie's exclamation was followed by others. "Who?"

"I don't know. No, I really don't," Ari said, raising her hands as if to ward off an attack.

"Where was she killed?" Lauren asked.

Ari leaned forward again. "The police found her coat in Barn C."

"But that was empty," Nancy said.

"Where's Barn C?" Annie asked. She, too, was staring at Ari.

"Between Barn B and Barn D. Nancy's right. It wasn't being used, so it was perfect for the killer's purpose."

"Why would Felicia have gone in there to get the mud off her coat?" Debbie asked, frowning. "I know she hated the weather here yesterday because of her clothes, but that doesn't make sense."

"Then she shouldn't have tried to flaunt them," Beth said.

"Actually I think she would have gone into Barn B, but someone stopped her. Someone wanted to talk to Felicia about something important."

"What?" Debbie demanded.

"Maybe about an article in the magazine. Maybe about something she made. Or, maybe, because she was Felicia's daughter."

That announcement caused another uproar. Ari had expected it, but she hadn't thought it would mask the reaction she'd been hoping to see. Everyone looked surprised, not just one person. "Are you saying her daughter was *here?*" Debbie asked.

"Yes. Debbie, you told us that you and Felicia came here to do a story on the festival."

"Yes, that's what she said."

"That sounded like a pretty thin story to me. I mean, why would Felicia come here for such a small festival? There are others closer to New York. But then I found out about her daughter."

"From your cop," Beth said derisively. "Does he know you're here spilling all this?"

Ari bent her head to hide her expression. If anyone guessed the truth, her plan would fail. "Anyway, I began to wonder if she came here to see her daughter."

"But the daughter got in touch with her in New York," Debbie said. "Why would she need to come here?"

"Because of something that happened lately that changed things for her. Felicia was diagnosed with cancer."

"My God. Really?" Beth asked.

"Yes."

"My God. Poor Felicia. Well, I didn't like her," she said, at the scornful looks the others gave her, "but I wouldn't wish cancer on anyone."

"Commendable," Debbie said dryly.

"Why would Felicia having cancer make a difference?" Annie asked.

"Maybe she wanted to see her daughter one last time."

"If she had a daughter and gave her up for adoption, why would she bother?" Annie replied.

"Ari, are you saying the daughter killed her?" Nancy asked.

"It's possible. As I said, Beth, you were a strong suspect. So were you, Debbie."

"Me?" Debbie looked up. "Why?"

"You get the magazine, don't you? Also, you'd be the most logical person to go into the barn with Felicia, since you were with her all morning."

"I didn't."

"I know. You were aware she was dying. Even if she wasn't, you could have killed her at any time back in New York. However, if she did come here to see her daughter and you knew it, then you had a reason."

"No I didn't."

"What if she told you she was considering changing her will? She was, you know. You might not have gotten the magazine."

"She wouldn't have cut me out," Debbie said, but she sounded uncertain. "She was like a mother to me."

"Until her own child came along," Ari said.

"That's not fair!"

"Of course it isn't. You must have been hurt, at the least. We all heard how much you loved Felicia."

"I just wanted her to be happy."

"But it hurt."

"All right, so it hurt! I've been hurt by plenty of things, but I've never killed anyone because of them. Why would I start now? And don't tell me it was because I'd lose the magazine."

"No," Ari said softly. "You were afraid you'd lose Felicia's love."

"Oh, damn you."

"So you had motive, and you had opportunity. What you didn't have was means. That's a problem. How did you get a knitting needle? I know, there were plenty being sold, but this was an old needle. That makes me think someone was using it, and not just carrying it around. No one saw you with a project yesterday. Besides, if you did want to kill Felicia, it was a pretty chancy way. But a lot of people here had needles."

"Like you," Beth said.

"No." Ari shook her head. "Not the right size, and the needles I was using are newer ones, with the plastic buttons. This needle had a steel button. Beth, you probably have a project with you, don't you?"

"Maybe."

"So you could possibly have had the needle with you yesterday. But I don't think you did it."

"Then who did?" Nancy said. "Everyone had needles with them."

"I didn't," Diane said. "I was just spinning, not knitting."

"So Diane's out of the running, and so am I," Ari said. "But, Nancy, you were knitting, and you were using old needles."

"Yes, so? I had no reason to kill Felicia."

"But you're the right age."

"The right age for what?"

"To be Felicia's daughter."

Nancy laughed. "I wasn't adopted."

"I know. Rosalia was also the right age," Ari went on, "but no one thought that she'd be the next one killed."

That brought silence. "Why was she killed, Ari?" Nancy asked finally. "Do you know?"

"I can guess. I think she saw something she shouldn't have."

"Do you mean she saw the murder?"

"No. But she might have seen something else. Nancy, it shows up in your own pictures, the ones you took yesterday. I think you're lucky to be alive."

"What?"

"You took a picture of the murderer using

the murder weapon, and you didn't even know it."

Again there was an outburst, of people demanding to know the identity of the murderer. Ari let it play out, and then held up the picture of the woman knitting that had so stunned her this morning. "You. Lauren Dubrowski. You killed Felicia."

CHAPTER 16

Everyone in the barn gasped as they turned toward Lauren, sitting still as a stone. "Lauren, you're the right age," Ari went on, shuffling the pictures in her hands. Although she was certain she was right, talking about it in this way was making her nervous. "You had reason to dislike Felicia, though you claim you're better off with your new job. But that's not why you killed her. I think you killed her because you found out you're her daughter."

Lauren's eyes widened as Ari continued. "Now, I don't imagine your reunion was easy. You may have been angry at her for abandoning you all those years ago, so you lured her into Barn C where you could confront her in private. But when Felicia bent over to try to get the mud off her coat, you got angry. You saw your chance to hurt her for all the years she had hurt you. So you stabbed her in the back with the knitting needle.

"But I don't think you were planning to kill her. We've all discussed how chancy a weapon a knitting needle is. I think you probably just meant to hurt Felicia, and you were shocked when you thought you'd actually killed her, so you panicked and fled Barn C. You thought you could talk your way out of it by being up front with the police about how Felicia had criticized your work, but then you realized there was another threat — Rosalia.

"Rosalia saw something that tied you to the murder. Something that could incriminate you and send you to jail for the rest of your life. You knew you had to get rid of her. So when we were all packing up to leave the barn, you asked her to help you carry supplies to your car. You knew about a back way into the fairgrounds because it's printed on the registration brochure, so you had parked your SUV there out of sight. Then you knocked her out and hid her body in your car. You drove her body back here and put her in the fleece bin, where you knew she'd suffocate.

"But you didn't want police to be suspicious, so you took Rosalia's keys and drove her car out the main gate, making sure the police would have her vehicle on record as leaving the fairgrounds. You drove back to your own car, hidden on the back road, and switched vehicles, leaving hers there. It gave you just enough time to get to the motel to check in."

As everyone stared at Lauren with horror, Ari watched as a strange smile appeared on Lauren's face. The reaction unsettled her.

"I admit a lot of this is conjecture," she went on, "but we do have solid evidence that you were seen using the murder weapon earlier in the day. You were knitting something out of light blue yarn, using the knitting needle that killed Felicia. We can prove it!"

With that, Ari shoved the picture of Lauren knitting at her. Lauren looked at the photograph closely and seemed puzzled. The others around the circle stared at Lauren. Their expressions ranged from shock on Debbie's face to anger on Annie's.

"Aluminum needles," Ari went on, "and light blue yarn."

"You've got to be kidding me," Lauren finally said, putting down the picture and laughing softly. "Oh, how could you be so right and so wrong at the same time?"

Lauren's reaction rattled Ari. For the first time, doubt crept into her mind. "What do you mean?"

"The murder weapon? Oh God." Still laughing, Lauren reached into her knitting bag and pulled out the project shown in the picture. It was, indeed, light blue and still attached to two aluminum needles with old-fashioned buttons at the end. "How could one of these be the murder weapon if I'm still using it?" Lauren said.

Ari glanced at the doorway, suddenly disconcerted. "What are you making?" she asked stupidly.

"A baby sweater for a friend. Yes, that's the project in that picture, but I was working on this well after Felicia's death. Someone must have seen me. I can't believe you think I'm the murderer."

"Lauren, could you do something?" Debbie asked. "Say, 'Hartford CSS.' "

Lauren stiffened and her smile disappeared. Ari glanced at the door. Just outside, she could see Josh, his face tense. "Why?" Lauren asked,

"Just say it."

"Hartford CSS," Lauren repeated. Debbie's face fell.

"What does that mean?" Ari said, confused.

Debbie shook her head. "I didn't know what that meant at the time, but it just came to me. 'SS' stands for Social Services. I think it's the agency Felicia used to place her daughter for adoption. Someone called the office and said that." She frowned. "But your voice isn't the one I heard."

"What?" Ari exclaimed.

"Lauren and I talked a few times over the phone when she was having trouble with Felicia. I'd know her voice, and that's not the one I heard. The accent was wrong."

"I told you," Lauren said, relaxing into a smile. "You're so right in some ways and so wrong in others."

Ari glanced back at the door as her case began to collapse beneath her. Briggs was standing beside Josh. His face was impassive, but there was a gleam in his eye as he watched the other suspects. She turned to see what he was looking at, but saw only what she had before: people sitting with varying degrees of incredulity, shock, and anger on their faces. "Are you Felicia's daughter?" Ari asked Lauren, not certain of anything anymore.

"Yes."

"What!" Debbie exclaimed. "You never said that."

"No," Lauren agreed. "I never saw any reason to tell her."

"But she was your mother," Ari sputtered.

"No. Vivian Dubrowski was my mother."

Lauren looked straight at her, serious now. "David Dubrowski is my father. They're the ones who raised me. Felicia only gave birth to me."

Ari frowned. "You're from New York, though, not Connecticut."

"No, actually I grew up in Delaware. My parents were living in Connecticut when they adopted me, and then we moved because of my father's job."

"Weren't you ever curious about Felicia?" Debbie asked, leaning forward.

"Not for a while. You see, I always knew I was adopted. When I was a teenager they sat me down and told me they'd help me find my birth mother if I wanted to. Well, I didn't want to. I loved my parents and didn't want to hurt them."

"What changed your mind?"

"My best friend is pregnant." Lauren held up the baby blanket. "I started to wonder about my medical history and realized I should find out more about my birth parents for that reason. So I hired a private investigator."

"I thought adoptions were sealed."

"Yes, mine was, but there are ways of finding out."

Ari looked down at the picture again. She had been so certain she was right.

"But you did contact her, Lauren," Josh said as he entered the room. "You sent your designs to her."

"For what that was worth," Lauren snorted. "We always wondered if my artistic skills came from my birth mother, but I didn't really care. When I found out Felicia was my birth mother, it knocked me for a loop. I would have told her I was her daughter," she said, turning to Debbie, "but when she turned out to be so mean I decided not to. I didn't call the office and say the name of the adoption agency."

Debbie nodded. She looked shaken. "And yet she was like a mother to me."

"Ha." The sound came from, of all people, Annie Walker. "We all know she was a bitch."

A sudden silence fell across the room as everyone turned to face Annie. "But she praised your work in the magazine," Ari said.

"Yeah, but what did she say in the office? She told you it wasn't really very good." Annie glared at Debbie. "Don't bother to deny it. I heard it from one of the assistants, who's in the Knitting Guild with me."

"Linda Doyle?"

"Yes. She was happy to tell me, too."

"I'm going to fire her when I take over

the magazine. She never could keep her mouth shut." Debbie and Annie glared at each other.

Ari sank down into a chair, looking down at the pictures she still held in her hand. She was about to put them aside, feeling defeated since she'd publicly accused the wrong person of murder, when she glanced at the photograph on top of the pile. She stiffened. That feeling that she was missing something hit her with full force. How could she have been so blind? Someone else had been using blue yarn yesterday, and she'd seen it.

Josh. She had to speak to Josh. She looked up to see that he was watching her, his eyes intent. She gave him a look and inclined her head toward the photographs in her hands. As the women around them argued back and forth, Josh sidled up to Ari and glanced down at the top photo. He then returned her startled gaze. "Well," he said.

"This is ridiculous," Beth said, getting up. "I don't know why you brought us back to this place, but I want to go back to the motel. My lawyer is going to have a field day with this."

"I just want to go home," Nancy said, and got up as well. As if that were a signal, the others rose angrily.

"All right, folks," Charlie said. "Everyone just calm down. I know there's been some confusion here, so for now we'll take you back to the motel."

What were the police thinking of? Ari wondered frantically. In a few minutes they'd lose the advantage they had, of being at the scene of both murders. "We need more evidence," Josh said softly, leaning down to her.

"You need a confession," she whispered back, and stood up as abruptly as Beth had. "Annie," she called.

Annie turned. "What?"

"You were working on a baby blanket yesterday," Ari said.

"No, I was working on a shawl. On bamboo circular needles, remember? You saw it." Annie's voice was scornful. "What would I want with an old pair of orchid aluminum needles anyway?"

"Who said they were orchid-colored?" Ari asked.

Annie's face went wary. "Everyone knows that." She looked around the room.

"I didn't know what color the murder weapon was," Lauren said.

"Neither did I," Nancy chimed in. "The needles Lauren's using are pink, Ari. I can see why you made that mistake."

"Oh my God." Debbie was staring at Annie, as if seeing her for the first time. "If you lighten her hair —"

"I saw it yesterday," Ari interrupted her, pleased to be right about something. "When I saw Annie I thought she looked familiar, but then she said we'd met at a Knitting Guild meeting. But that's not it. She looks like Felicia." She stared up at Josh. "My God. Twins?"

Josh nodded. "Yes."

"Then is Annie —"

"Felicia's daughter? Yes."

"She was never my mother! She deserved to die!" Annie screamed, and dashed for the side door, straight into the arms of a waiting patrolman.

"Twins," Josh said. He and Ari were standing outside the Freeport Police station, the first chance they'd had to speak to each other since leaving the fairgrounds. "Who could have known?"

"They really don't look alike, except for their eyes." Ari frowned. "Is it certain?"

"That they are twins? No." Josh shook his head. "We'll need to get a court order to unseal the adoption records. But with Winston as executor of Felicia's estate, we'll probably get them."

"I'm sorry, Josh. I made a fool out of all of us."

"I'm not so sure," he said. "I think Briggs had an idea all along."

"I was wondering about that. Is that why he let me run with it?"

"Yes. Also, he knew you could connect with everyone on a different level than we could." Josh smiled slightly. "Briggs finally had to admit that knitting murders are a little out of his experience."

"Mm."

"Listen." He tilted her face up. "You weren't totally wrong. We were all misled by that picture of Lauren. It's just a coincidence that she's making something similar to Annie's project."

"Maybe." Ari was silent a minute. If Annie and Lauren were indeed twins, there might be a connection between them that they had never realized. "Did they know they were twins?"

"I don't know." He reached for the door. "Let's go in and find out."

A little while later, Josh, Charlie, and Briggs sat in an interrogation room at the Freeport Police station. Annie was across the table from them, handcuffed, her face angry and defiant. She had been read her rights and was glaring fiercely around the room.

Ari stood in the back of the room. She had strict instructions to stay quiet during this part of the interrogation. It had been a fiasco in the barn, her falsely accusing Lauren of a murder she didn't commit. It had turned out right in the end, though, when she saw the picture of Annie.

With a suspect finally in custody and under arrest, the police had been able to get a search warrant, which was being executed this minute. Preliminary reports were encouraging; there was an uncompleted blanket of light blue yarn in Annie's bag, on a stitch holder. There were no knitting needles to accompany the project. That was suggestive, but not proof of anything.

The police were far more interested in the facts that the tire prints taken from behind the barn matched Annie's tires, and that Rosalia's fingerprints had been found in her SUV. It looked as if they'd be able to tie her to at least one of the murders. What they didn't know yet was why Annie had committed either one.

"Now, Annie," Charlie said. He was leaning back in his chair, his arm slung over the back of the one next to him, by all appearances at ease and comfortable. "Is there anything you'd like? A cup of coffee?"

"No," she said stonily. "Ask your damned questions."

"All right." Annie had waived her right to having a lawyer present during her questioning. She could, of course, change her mind at any moment, but Josh knew they should try to question her as much as possible before she clammed up.

"Why did you do it?" Josh asked, almost gently. "Why did you kill Felicia Barr?"

"Because she didn't want me," Annie spat. "All that crap that Lauren spouted about having good parents who loved her — that's a lot of bullshit. They're not her real parents. Real parents accept you. They don't care where you come from. And real parents don't give you away like you're a dog or cat."

"Annie, your parents would be distressed to hear about this," Charlie said. "Are you sure you don't want to call them?"

"They don't give a damn about me. They never did. My father never wanted to adopt me. It was all my mother's idea, but then she turned, too. When I was a teenager, she told me I was just like my slut of a mother. Oh God. I didn't know what she was talking about."

"You didn't know you were adopted?" Josh said in surprise.

"No. My father didn't want anyone to

know. He's a banker, very concerned about his reputation." Her laugh was bitter. "Just like Winston Barr. How do you think he feels?"

"How did you find out about Felicia?"

"My parents said that if I wanted to act like my mother, I should find out who she was. They hired a private detective. I think he bribed someone to get a copy of my records. That's when I found out about Felicia . . . and Lauren. Twins." Her voice was full of anguish. "She had twins, and she didn't want either of us. How could she give us up so easily?"

"From what we've learned, her parents didn't give her much choice." Josh's voice still held that gentle note. Rough treatment might make Annie clam up. "Did you try to contact Lauren, too?"

"Not at first. You know, one thing she said was true. I always was artistic. That's one thing my parents liked about me, though they kept saying they didn't know where it came from. They're all left-brained, my dear family."

"So she didn't know?"

"No. I decided not to ruin her happy, middle-class suburban life."

Ari, facing Briggs, raised her eyebrows. He looked at her a moment, and then nodded as if to say, *Go ahead.*

"You wanted a family, didn't you?" Ari asked.

Annie twisted to glare at her. "What's it to you?"

"Everyone wants to be accepted, Annie. I'd think it was natural that you'd want to meet Felicia, find out more about your past."

"Well, she didn't want to see me."

"Did she tell you that?"

"No, not right away," Annie said reluctantly.

"It had to be a shock to her."

"I don't care! She didn't have to treat me like that."

"Were you the one who called the magazine's office?" Charlie asked.

"Yes. I'd tried to get my designs into the magazine, you know. I thought I could meet her that way. But she rejected them!"

"Were you really at that Knitting Guild meeting where you said you saw me?" Ari said.

"Yes."

"You had to have seen Felicia then, too."

"I didn't know anything about her yet. I was still a kid. She didn't mean anything to me."

Ari nodded. "It must have hurt that she

rejected your designs."

Annie shrugged. "I expected it. But then I had to find another way to meet her, so I called her office. She didn't want to see me at first. She didn't believe me."

"But you convinced her?"

"No. She thought it was a shakedown. She agreed to meet me for lunch."

"A shakedown?"

"A way to get my designs accepted. But I knew things about her that I shouldn't have known, and she finally had to admit that I wasn't lying about being her daughter. *Then* she said she'd publish my designs." Annie glared at Ari. "She told me that Debbie thought they weren't that good. And Debbie says Felicia was like a mother to her. A *mother!*" she spat. "She sure wasn't a mother to me."

"Annie, she didn't know you," said Ari. "If she'd had time —"

"Oh, she had time. She told me she didn't want to see me ever again. She said that part of her life was over and that I should let it go. My own mother!"

"But you couldn't let it go."

"No. No. So a few weeks later, I sent her the brochure from this festival. I didn't really think she would come. I was stunned when she did. She called and said she wanted to talk to me in person."

"That must have felt good," Ari said.

"Yeah, for about a minute. I saw her when she came in the barn, but she ignored me like she didn't even see me there. Then I went out after her — no one saw me, I was stuck so far back in the barn — and I heard her tell Debbie to go to their car to get warm. She said she had mud on her coat and wanted to get it off, and she was going to go back inside."

"So you followed her."

"Yes. I caught up to her and said we needed to talk. Well, of course she didn't want to go anywhere people could see us. That would mean having to explain who I was, right? So I tried the door to Barn C — it was the closest — and it was open. We went inside. And that's when she told me . . ."

"What?" Ari prompted, when Annie didn't go on.

"She didn't want me." Annie's head was lowered now, and her voice was muffled. "She told me that she didn't like to think of that part of her life — she didn't like to think about me! — and that I'd have to accept it. But she said she'd give me money, if that was what I wanted."

"That must have hurt."

"Hurt? I got so angry. What did she think I was? And I'd brought the sweater I was making to show her, too. She didn't even look at it. And after she'd said that thing about the money, she turned and began cleaning the mud off her coat like I wasn't even there. I was so *angry*," Annie repeated.

The room was hushed. No one wanted to break the spell now, or remind Annie of where she was. "I didn't think about what I was doing," she said. "I just wanted to hurt her, the way she hurt me. So I pulled the needle out of the sweater and I stabbed her with it. Oh God!" It was a wail. "I didn't know it would go in so far. I never meant to kill her. But she fell and she didn't get up. I didn't mean to kill her, I swear."

"She wasn't dead then, Annie. If you'd acted, you might have saved her life," Josh said, though they knew it wasn't true. Annie's aim had been more accurate than she'd realized. "You could have called for help," he pointed out.

"I couldn't. I couldn't. I was so scared, I just ran out. It was raining so hard, there was no one around. And no one paid any attention to me when I got back to my table. No one ever pays any attention to me."

"When did you realize what you'd done?"

"When I heard she was dead. There was a

commotion in the barn. Oh God. But I didn't want to get caught, I didn't want to go to jail. I put the sweater on a stitch holder. Then, after lunch, I wrapped the other needle in the sandwich paper and threw it out."

Charlie nodded. That much, they knew. "But someone did see you, right? Rosalia saw something."

"She didn't see me with Felicia. But she did see the sweater, and she commented on it when I was working on the shawl. That's when I knew she was dangerous. Sooner or later she'd figure out the aluminum needles were mine."

"How did you lure Rosalia to your car?"

"I said I needed help loading things. I could have done it myself, but I would have had to make a few trips. And when we got to my car and she was putting stuff in, I hit her." She shook her head. "I didn't mean to hit her that hard. But when I saw her like that — well, I never learned karate, but you see these moves on TV, and that's what I did." She rubbed the side of her hand. "It hurt."

"What did you do, Annie? Put her into your car?"

"Yes. I covered her with my things and drove out. Well, what else could I do? Oh

God." She covered her face with her hands. "I never meant to do any of it."

"But you did," Briggs said, and in contrast to the earlier gentle tone of the interrogation, his voice was harsh. Looking at him, Ari realized he was very angry, though his face was still. It was in his eyes. "You could have gotten help for Rosalia after you hit her."

"But then she would have told what she knew."

"What did she know? That you were using aluminum needles?"

"How could I explain where they went?"

"So instead of getting help, you — what? Turned your car around?"

"Yes."

"Did you know about the back road?"

"From the map. Yes."

"You were thinking pretty clearly."

"I always do in a crisis." She sounded proud of herself. "I knew I had to get Rosalia back to the fairgrounds because her car was still there. I didn't mean to hurt her, honest."

"How did you get her back in?"

"I don't know. I kinda dragged her, I guess, but I don't know how I did it."

"Why the fleece bin, Annie?" Charlie asked.

"Well, I realized I couldn't just leave her there on the floor because when she woke up she'd tell everyone what I'd done. I thought if I put her in with the fleeces no one would find her for a while, and by then I'd be at the motel and no one would know I'd done anything."

"You didn't realize she'd smother?"

"No, I didn't. I really didn't mean to kill her. I was as surprised as anyone else when I heard she was dead."

She hadn't meant to do anything, Ari thought, shifting in her chair. She wondered if Annie truly realized what she'd done, or if she'd ever admit to it. "What about Rosalia's car?"

"What about it? Oh. I knew I had to get it out of there, or they'd go looking for her earlier. I hid my face in the hood of my jacket and then at the gate I gave the guards Rosalia's name. They didn't even realize what had happened. I drove her car in back of the barn."

Briggs nodded briefly. Ari could imagine just what the troopers responsible for letting her go were facing. "And then drove off in your own car."

"Yes. When I got to the motel I registered right away. And then I went to my room and fell asleep."

Of everything Annie had said, that was the most chilling, Ari realized. Had Annie's parents' rejection done this to her, left her without a conscience — or had she always been so ruthless?

She looked at Josh, who was staring steadily at her. Leaving Charlie and Briggs to clean up the last few questions, Josh escorted her out of the interrogation room.

Lauren rose from a bench as Josh and Ari entered the main hall. "How is she?" she asked.

Josh looked at Ari and shrugged. "All right."

"Did she do it?"

"She confessed to both murders," Ari said gently.

"Oh God!" Lauren spun away, pressing a fist to her mouth in anguish. "My sister."

"Did you know you had a twin, Lauren?"

"No." She turned, wiping her eyes. "How could she give up both of us, Ari? Why didn't Felicia keep one of us?"

Ari shook her head. "I don't know."

"What happens now then?" Lauren asked.

"Annie will be held for arraignment," Josh said.

"Are you going to stay for her trial?" Ari asked Lauren.

"Yes. I've already called my boss and

352

asked for some personal time. Maybe I can help Annie." She fell quiet for a minute. "It's strange."

"What's strange?"

"I went to see Winston after they arrested Annie. I told him everything. Do you know what he said?"

"No, what?"

"He hugged me. He said . . . he said he would have accepted me as his daughter. He would have accepted both of us. Isn't that ironic?"

Ari laid her hand on Lauren's arm. "You have that, Lauren. It's something."

"Yes." Lauren wiped her eyes and tried to smile. "I've got to get back. I told Winston I'd let him know what happened."

"Call me," Ari said. "I'm in the book."

"I will," Lauren said, and walked out.

Ari gazed after her. "All she wanted was a mother."

"Don't start feeling sorry for Annie, Ari. She killed two people."

"I know. I'm not going to forget that." Ari looked away. "All I want to do now is go home and hug Megan."

"When will she be home?"

"Around seven. Why?"

"What do you say to an early dinner?"

"Dinner? I don't know. Doesn't it bother

you? That there's been two murders?"

"Yes," he said after a moment. "But life goes on, and there's no reason for us to stop living."

"I suppose."

"So? How about dinner?" He smiled down at her. "It's a start, isn't it?"

Ari looked at him, startled, and then smiled. It felt as if she hadn't done so in years. "And dancing?"

"Next Saturday sound all right?"

"Yes."

"And then we'll see."

Oh yes, Ari thought, *they would.* Any earlier reluctance she'd had about starting a relationship with him was gone. She was ready for this.

He slung his arm around her shoulders as they walked to her car. "But you have to promise me one thing."

"What's that?" she asked.

"No more murders."

She sighed, exasperated. As if she'd asked to get involved in another murder! But then she remembered what she'd thought after helping to find Edith Perry's murderer last fall. She had vowed then never to be involved in a murder again. This time she wasn't so sure. What was the chance, though, of lightning striking three times?

"Okay," she said, smiling at him. "No more murders."

AUTHOR'S NOTE

I am a lucky person. Writing a series gives me the chance to revisit characters I've come to love rather than say good-bye to them. As much as anyone, I learned about Ari's and Josh's backgrounds, and their feelings for each other, as the story progressed. I can't wait to find out more.

Freeport is a completely fictional town. While Rochester and Acushnet are real towns, Rochester County does not exist. Neither does the Bristol-Rochester County Fairgrounds, or the yarn and wool festival held there. I've had fun including landmarks that residents of southeastern Massachusetts will likely recognize throughout the story. A writer must have some license.

And yes, figure skating fans, I know that as of this writing (fall, 2006), Michelle Kwan isn't competing. Allow this poor fan some hope.

I love to hear from my readers. Please visit

my Web site at www.geocities.com/
marypkruger, or contact me directly at
marykruger@verizon.net.

PATTERNS FROM ARIADNE'S WEB

AUNT MAE'S PADDED COAT HANGERS

My aunt Mae introduced everyone to these coat hangers, giving them to friends and family alike. While they've become a running joke in these knitting books, they're actually quite practical and easy to make.

Size 10 1/2 needles
Rug yarn
Wooden coat hanger, with no bar across bottom

Cast on 9 stitches. Work in garter stitch (knit each row) for approximately 35 rows, or until piece is slightly shorter than hanger. Cast off, leaving a long thread. Fold piece in half lengthwise. Center it over the hook of the hanger and insert the hook through the piece. Using a large tapestry needle, sew all edges together.

THE "NO HAIR DAY" CHEMO CAP

My mother loved this cap. It was light and comfortable, and from a distance looked like real hair. I made it in conventional colors such as a beige blend and a gray blend, but it would be fun in brighter shades, too.

Fake fur yarn, such as Lion Brand Fun Fur
Size 9 double-pointed needles
Size 9 circular needles

Directions given are for size small. Adjustments for sizes medium and large are in parentheses.

On size 9 circular needles, cast on 60 (66, 72) stitches. Join, being careful not to twist the stitches. Place marker on needle to mark beginning of round. Work two rounds in knit one, purl one ribbing, then knit around until hat measures 6 inches (6.5 inches, 7 inches) from beginning.

Decrease rounds as follows:

Round 1: *Knit 8 (9, 10), k2tog*; repeat from * to end of round.

Rounds 2, 4, 6, and 8: Knit.

Round 3: *Knit 7 (8, 9), k2tog*; repeat from * to end of round.

Round 5: *Knit 6 (7, 8), k2tog*; repeat

from * to end of round.

Round 7: *Knit 5 (6, 7), k2tog*; repeat
from * to end of round.

Round 9: *Knit 4 (5, 6), k2tog*; repeat
from * to end of round.

Round 10: *Knit 3 (4, 5), k2tog*; repeat
from * to end of round.

Round 11: *Knit 2 (3, 4), k2tog*; repeat
from * to end of round.

Round 12: *Knit 1 (2, 3), k2tog*; repeat
from * to end of round.

Round 13:
- For small hat: k2tog around.
- For medium-sized hat: knit 1, k2tog around.
- For large hat: knit 2, k2tog around.

(For medium- and large-sized hats, continue decreasing until knitting 2tog around.)

Cut the yarn, leaving a 10-inch tail. Thread yarn through the remaining stitches. Fasten off on the knit side of the hat. Turn hat so that the purl side is on the outside.

A picture of this cap, as well as more patterns, can be found at www.headhuggers .org.

ABOUT THE AUTHOR

Mary Kruger is the author of *Died in the Wool* and the Gilded Age mystery series. She is an avid knitter and lives in New Bedford, Massachusetts. Visit the author's Web site at www.geocities.com/marypkruger.

We hope you have enjoyed this Large Print book. Other Thorndike, Wheeler, and Chivers Press Large Print books are available at your library or directly from the publishers.

For information about current and upcoming titles, please call or write, without obligation, to:

Publisher
Thorndike Press
295 Kennedy Memorial Drive
Waterville, ME 04901
Tel. (800) 223-1244

or visit our Web site at:

www.gale.com/thorndike
www.gale.com/wheeler

OR

Chivers Large Print
published by BBC Audiobooks Ltd
St James House, The Square
Lower Bristol Road
Bath BA2 3SB
England
Tel. +44(0) 800 136919
email: bbcaudiobooks@bbc.co.uk
www.bbcaudiobooks.co.uk

All our Large Print titles are designed for easy reading, and all our books are made to last.